swerve

Also by VICKI PETTERSSON

SIGN OF THE ZODIAC

The Scent of Shadows
The Taste of Night
The Touch of Twilight
City of Souls
Cheat the Grave
The Neon Graveyard

CELESTIAL BLUES

The Taken
The Lost
The Given

swerve

A Thriller

vicki pettersson

Gallery Books

New York   London   Toronto   Sydney   New Delhi

Gallery Books
An Imprint of Simon & Schuster, Inc.
1230 Avenue of the Americas
New York, NY 10020

First Gallery Books hardcover edition July 2015

GALLERY BOOKS and colophon are registered trademarks of Simon & Schuster, Inc.

For information about special discounts for bulk purchases, please contact Simon & Schuster Special Sales at 1-866-506-1949 or business@simonandschuster.com

The Simon & Schuster Speakers Bureau can bring authors to your live event. For more information or to book an event contact the Simon & Schuster Speakers Bureau at 1-866-248-3049 or visit our website at www.simonspeakers.com.

Interior design by Robert E. Ettlin

Manufactured in the United States of America

10 9 8 7 6 5 4 3 2 1

Library of Congress Cataloging-in-Publication Data is available.

ISBN 978-1-4767-9857-8
ISBN 978-1-4767-9858-5 (ebook)

To Kristine Perchetti,
who allowed me to borrow her name,
her likeness, and her strength in equal measure.
You're my hero in so many ways.

If I keep this oath faithfully, may I enjoy my life and practice my art, respected by all humanity and in all times; but if I swerve from it or violate it, may the reverse be my life.

—Hippocratic Oath

swerve

1

Ghosts in front of us, ghosts behind.

It's not exactly an ominous building, not from the highway. As rest stops go, it could even be called a welcome sight. Sturdy and wide, it's squat like a sumo wrestler, with brickface sprayed glossy brown in order to blend with the rest of the arid desert terrain. Its location on Interstate 15 means it should be well kept too. This is the busiest thoroughfare in the West, after all; the unassuming straight shot that links the artificial glitter of the Las Vegas valley to the natural gold of California's rolling hills. So, given all that, how could I know that in a mere ten minutes I'd be fleeing that crouching, dust-blown building?

That I'd be covered in blood, screaming as I run.

It's July 3, so the sun is a heat lamp with no off switch, the blacktop road a cast-iron griddle, and any living thing caught between the two is just meat set to singe on high. I tried to tell Daniel this. I know this swath of high desert as well as I know his profile. The Mojave's cracked surface is as familiar to me as the dark mole tucked to the side of his right eyebrow—his only imperfection, and one I love.

Unfortunately, a 4:00 p.m. race through the desert is the only way to both complete my twelve-hour shift at the hospital and still reach his childhood estate at Lake Arrowhead before dinner. Cocktails and hors d'oeuvres are to be served on the east patio, precisely at seven o'clock.

I know, right?

At least there's still light to see by inside the rest stop's stifling concrete shell. It'll filter in through the open brick doorframe and allow for a mercifully quick change of clothes. I've made a mess of things in the car, though it could be worse.

It *will* be worse.

///////////

"Sorry," I'd told Daniel five minutes earlier. We were speeding past a stranded Toyota emptied of occupants, its windows rolled down like it was panting in the heat. It was the third such vehicle we'd seen since escaping Vegas, and we were already clocking 'em, taking bets on how many we'd encounter before we reached the mountains. Daniel was an eternal optimist, which meant I was winning. One deserted car barely disappeared into the rearview mirror before another surfaced in the heat haze, ever shimmering, just ahead.

Ghosts in front of us, ghosts behind.

In contrast, Daniel's pristine Beemer set the pace for the moving traffic, advancing with smooth and silent precision. He kept it oiled underneath, polished on top, and free of debris inside. Everything he owned and touched received the same consideration, though he wasn't ostentatious like some of the other surgeons. Too young for a midlife crisis, yet too old to fall prey to insecurities that might otherwise drive him to flash his status, he felt no need to prove his worth. In truth, I'd never met anyone more comfortable in his own skin.

No, Daniel simply believed in investing in quality items the first time around, both in terms of performance and aesthetics, and then he took care of those things forever. Since he'd proposed to me at the beginning of the summer, I was now implicitly included in this unspoken personal philosophy. Which made the iced coffee I'd just spilled across the luxury package leather console all the more galling.

"You should be sorry," Daniel finally said, and I jerked my head up fast to search his face. His eyes were on the road, but he was wearing his half-scrawled smile, the one that came out of nowhere to wallop me every time. "You are an incredible distraction."

He should talk, I think, smiling now too. If there was ever a man built for distraction, this was the one. That's why, when he'd reached up to smooth back my hair, I'd removed my coffee from the center tray and held it, allowing me to lean in close. It was why, despite my tension over the long work week, the desert drive, and even what awaited me at the end of it, I'd closed my eyes and rested my head in his palm. It was why, when he'd dropped a soft kiss to my hairline, I'd slid my fingertips up the almost preternaturally soft skin of his inner arm and sighed in absolute contentment.

He gasped right before he'd swerved.

The car bucked, tires screeching in a fight to realign with the road, but Daniel overcorrected and the luxury machine flew into a pendulum whip. Smoke and burning rubber surged through the vents to fill the car's cabin, turning my scream into a defensive cough. The flimsy cup lid popped in my grip, and coffee exploded over the seats, the dash, my scrubs, and I flailed for the door grip as the desert spun. An image of my Abby—lanky and freckled and gap-toothed at nine—flashed.

Who would stroke her limbs during the nighttime growing pains?

Who would put handwritten notes in her lunchbox?

Who, I had just enough time to wonder, would be her mother?

But by then, we'd come to a jolting halt on the roadside gravel bank, conveniently facing the California border. I whimpered, but finally managed to turn to Daniel. His breath rasped from his throat, louder than the air vents, and his eyes were as wide as quarters when they met mine. Still, not one dark hair on his head was out of place.

"Shit." He exhaled the word.

"You all right?" I asked.

"Yeah. You?"

My nod came out in a betraying jerk. "Abby's life just passed before my eyes."

"Not your own?"

I wanted to tell him that it didn't work that way. I was a mother. There *was* no life without Abby. I just blew out a hard breath and shook my head instead.

Daniel reached back and plucked a box of tissues from the backseat. "Sorry. It's all we have."

He tried for a smile as he handed them to me, but didn't

quite manage it. Not unflappable in the face of every emergency, then.

"I'm so sorry," I said, which was an understatement. I was *appalled*. The way he felt about this car, the care he took with his things—he had not grown up the way I had, where nothing was cared for and everything was disposable. I was ever mindful of that . . . and Daniel knew it.

"Hey," he said, eyes going painfully soft. "I'll have it cleaned, all right? No biggie."

"Let me at least change real quick," I said, palms dripping as I reached for the door. "We'll use my scrubs to clean all this up."

"No way. Not on the side of the road." Daniel grabbed my arm. "Too dangerous."

His touch stilled me . . . and allowed me to finally catch my first full breath. I told myself all was well. Abby was safe back in Vegas with Maria, and we were safe again too . . . even if we still had to drive through this chaparral-studded litter box with a dash decorated in ice and an imminent detour in an already tight schedule.

So I wiped my hands on my scrubs while Daniel waited for a break in traffic.

"Don't worry," he said, accelerating and nodding at the feeder road up ahead. "We were going to have to stop before reaching Lake Arrowhead anyway."

Yes. One couldn't simply mingle with the lake's elite on the sloping Old World lawn of the Hawthorne family estate in dirty scrubs, *dahling*.

I kept this thought to myself as I plucked my wet shirt from my body and shivered in the blast of the AC. We overtook one more abandoned car, a white van tilted helplessly on the highway's lilting shoulder, and then we were wheeling off the highway.

"It's closed," I said, when an orange detour sign mushroomed into sight. The rest stop's lot was being repaved, and the only other vehicle in sight was an orange utility truck, dust-coated and half-hidden behind a metal Dumpster bulging with debris.

"I see that." But this time Daniel whipped the steering wheel left and right with practiced ease. "Because I am the one who is so capably dodging these construction cones."

"Stud."

He smiled as he angled the Beemer on the diagonal over the first two parking spots, now stripped of their yellow lines. I gazed across the empty, searing lot at the ugly brown stain erected against the backdrop of struggling scrub and crusty earth. Sighing, I reached for my tote. "I'll be fast."

"Hold up," Daniel reached for his door too. "I'm coming with you."

"There's no one—"

"It's creepy, Kris." He gave me a look—please don't argue—and I didn't . . . but weren't all open-air rest stops inherently creepy?

Just then, a ringtone pealed through the car, pulling Daniel's attention from me. Good. Because the very first gleeful note had my shoulders knotting up so that they almost touched my ears.

"Green Acres."

Daniel thought the old TV theme song was funny, but I was willing to bet his mother would find the comparison to the aristocratic and entitled Eva Gabor less amusing if she heard it. Even if it *was* true.

"Didn't you tell her we'd call when we got close?" My voice was too sharp, and I regretted it instantly, but Daniel was busy frowning at the phone in his lap.

"Weird," he murmured.

I recognized the singular focus of his gaze from our time spent together in the OR, so I gave his cheek a quick buss and pushed open the door. "I'll be right back."

Sorry, he mouthed, but he was already taking the call. I didn't answer, and I never looked back. After all, it wasn't the last time in this long holiday weekend that Imogene Hawthorne would purposefully drag her son's attention away from me.

2

Not again.

The heat lunges for me as soon as I slam the car door, and I fight the urge to retreat by hurrying forward instead. My footsteps scatter a rabble of cawing, inky crows, and I quickstep over the lot's tarred potholes and cracks, black veins sprawling beneath my feet.

However, my pace slows at the entrance to the women's restroom, and even with the full strength of the high desert sun bearing down on my head and shoulders, I pause to peer around the cinderblock wall before entering. The stench of the toilets smears the air in a fetid blur, and my palms begin to sweat, though that has nothing to do with the smell or the heat. Daniel thinks I overreact to dark, enclosed spaces, and he's probably right. Then again, he's never been trapped in one.

I'm rarely this hesitant. A physician assistant can't afford it. In fact, Daniel once commented that all I needed to save a life was a pocketknife and a plastic straw. This was right after we'd met, maybe my second or third assist in his OR, and though exhausted, hands still encased in crimson-hued, crusted gloves, I beamed. It was the best compliment of my life and—I can say this without conceit—it's pretty well true.

However, I also choose to live in a city with an electrical current so strong it can be seen from outer space. I'm twenty-seven years old and still sleep with a night-light. I can intubate a crashed airway in seconds, but can't make it through your average horror movie. All that fumbling around in the dark, stumbling through a moonless forest, bunking down in some dilapidated cabin next to a murky lake. Are you kidding me?

No. I am no fan of the dark.

I hold my breath and enter the dusty tomb. At least there's still enough light to see by, and a battered sink springs into focus when my eyes finally adjust. A single open-air vent has been cut into the wall above the sink, but the majority of light slips into the room through the doorway where I now stand, and the room elongates into a single line of four dull, steel stalls. The only noise comes from behind me; the cars speeding by on the distant highway, and the crows, who've resumed their raucous scuttling outside. Daniel must still be talking to his mother in the car. I am alone.

My body temperature rockets another five degrees as I step fully inside. I move slowly, tapping open each thin door, making sure every stall is empty. Refusing to rush, I ignore the scent of human waste trapped in the air's stifling hand. I do the same with the feeling that the walls are closing rank behind me, though less successfully, and after locking myself behind the final door, I sigh hard and pull open my bag. Then I just stare.

A delicate white shell set sits folded atop belted linen shorts and flimsy ballerina flats. Daniel has surprised me with yet another gift. He's also packed an outfit chosen less for the drive than for the arrival, and I sigh as I rub the creamy cashmere between my fingers. It's beautiful, I'm grateful, but I'll have to sit up straight for the next three hours just to keep the shorts from wrinkling.

Rough drive, dear? I imagine Imogene saying, her face schooled into bland civility. All but her surgically pert nose, that is. That will wrinkle in delicate dismay. She always looks at me like I'm something Daniel found stuck to the bottom of his shoe.

I push the thought of Imogene behind me, same as when Daniel's phone rang, though this time I imagine balling up her image and tossing it into a basket for three points. I shoot and score, and by the time I pull my coffee-soaked scrubs over my head, I'm almost smiling. Then I pick up the cashmere, realize the sweater alone likely cost more than anything I'd ever buy for myself, and that brings *my* mother's voice to life.

Well, well, Miss Fancy-pants. Puttin' on airs, wearing expensive thangs. Betcha think you're too good for the likes of us now, don't cha dear?

"Good enough to know I don't deserve bad," I say aloud, because mere mental three-pointers won't chase that old voice away. I toe off my sneakers and slide down my scrub pants. After another moment, I relax into the responding silence.

That's when a footstep scrapes across the concrete floor.

Wearing only bra and panties, I stare at the closed stall door like I have X-ray vision. I remain deerlike in the lengthening silence for so long that I begin to think I imagined the sound.

"Daniel?" My ears are pricked for noise. I almost forget to breathe.

Nothing. I glance up, but no face leers at me from over the blunt wall that divides my stall from the next. Though mine is double the length of the others, I can see little of the floor leading back to the entrance. So I kick my soiled scrubs aside and reach for my shorts, hands trembling slightly as I work to fasten them. The near-accident on the road has spooked me more than I'd thought.

"Stupid," I mutter, and jam my feet into the silly leopard flats.

The second footstep falls like a hammer.

My gaze rockets back to the locked stall door, and my heels graze the rough wall behind me. Did another car approach? I didn't hear one, but then I hadn't been listening.

I'm listening now.

"Hello?"

Another footfall scrapes against the concrete, this time followed by a steady second, and my mouth goes dry. The heels fracturing the airless room are too heavy to be a woman's, but Daniel always wears soft-soled shoes like me.

The next step punches the room's middle, and my heart thuds with it. I'm still half-exposed, the flimsy sweater set clutched to my chest as if cashmere were chain mail, and I press my back against the wall, my body so erect that my toes carry my weight. They're just footsteps, I tell myself, yet each one is precision sharp, like guns being cocked, and instinct—experience—tells me these are footsteps with a *purpose*.

I slide into the corner, ignoring the way the rough concrete scratches my back. I want to call out for Daniel, but my throat feels suddenly hollow, like the sound's been scooped from it, and besides . . . what if he does come running? My fiancé is a brilliant surgeon, a kind man, and a thoughtful lover—but let's face it, he's no fighter.

The militant march continues, and I jolt with every sharp step. I can't unclench my jaw, though it aches. I can't even move. All I do is cower in that dirty corner and think, *Not again*.

The stall door next to mine opens with a long, slow squeal that saws down my spine and ends in a shudder. A second later a single brown work boot slides in front of *my* stall. It points my way like a compass, and I bend, just slightly, to see that it's attached to navy cotton pants. Then a second boot squares up to face me.

Not Daniel.

My eyes burn from staring, and something rises in my throat, but before it can bloom, a new sound slivers the air. It starts slow, a gliding screech of metal upon metal that rakes from the top edge of my stall door down to the very bottom. I jump when a knife blade arrows through the door's slat, jammed in at least six inches, all the way to the hilt. It clatters back and forth, rattling against the flimsy lock, the door shaking on its hinges, and the thing in my throat finally pushes free.

The scream rises from me with such piercing terror that it seems to push back the encroaching walls with its force. Even the knife hesitates in its wake.

I do not.

Lunging, I shove my fist into one of my empty tennis shoes,

then pivot to swat the blade from the side. The move lacks even an ounce of finesse, but it earns a surprised grunt from the other side of that door. The blade falls with a clatter, exactly halfway between me and those brown boots.

Not again.

I catch the knife beneath one expensive flat and am sliding my foot back under the door when the thick boot hammers my toes. The pain that flies through those tiny bones steals my responding cry, and my eyes water as I stumble back. Gaze blurred, I watch a black-gloved hand appear to pick up the knife.

I launch myself at the door again, slapping at the opening with my shoe, screaming so that Daniel can surely hear me in the car. So that they can hear me all the way out on the damn highway. *"Get away from me! Get the fuck away! Get out!"*

The boots move—a retreat!—and I'm taking a breath to shriek even louder when a single word blooms.

"No."

The steel door ricochets off my nose, the crack jarring my spine. I feel a warm gush over my face, but before I can lift a hand, the door strikes me again, harder, pitching my skull against the wall behind me. A yellow star flashes, my limbs tingle, and the entire room tilts. I don't feel myself falling, though the concrete beneath me is surprisingly cool.

I think, *Abby.*

I hear, *Krist-i-ine.*

OhGodohGod . . . it's the Coal Man, back from the dead . . . this time he'll reach me.

That's right. I'm coming for you, Kristine. I'm following close. I'm right . . .

The yellow star flares as if the desert sun has burned right through the roof, and then it snaps to black while my eyes roll back into my head. I think I hear my mother cackle. Then the whole world disappears.

3

I take a giant step back.

I bolt upright with the stale reek of toilets heavy in my nose. I try to inhale, but gag on phlegm and blood instead, and my pulse drums from the base of my skull. My foot is throbbing too, but I ignore it to pull in my legs, curling tightly into myself as I touch my tender nose. My hand comes away bloody.

Clearing the junk from my mouth in one inelegant gob, I then claw my way up the wall, the concrete scraping at my bare back while a cockroach skitters behind the toilet across from me.

Far off, in another world, cars whoosh by on the I-15.

Where the hell is Daniel?

Where the hell is *he*?

I grab the cashmere shell from the floor and yank it over my head, causing the room to spin. My gut tries to rise into my throat as I finish shoving the rest of my scattered clothes into my tote, all but my soiled scrub top. I use that to staunch my bleeding nose and get a whiff of coffee when I suck in air. Then

I peer around the half-open door, now red-speckled with my blood.

The three other stall doors are all ajar, but that tells me nothing. Each can still hold a full-grown man with a knife. I'm pretty sure I can sprint past the stalls, even with a spinning head, but the exit burns before me in a blocky wedge of light, threatening to blind me as soon as I flee the dim room.

What if he's waiting outside, just beyond that open doorway? What if he isn't alone?

What if I am?

"Daniel," I try to call out, but my voice has been shocked into a whisper. Yet the thought of Daniel, naively texting or listening to jazz radio or still talking to his mother in the car, is what pushes me forward. I don't know how long I've been unconscious, but I think the attack was quick enough that he hasn't had time to worry—not yet.

I cringe when the stall door announces my movement in an elongated squeak, and press my back against the long wall to sidestep past one and then all of the other stalls. Easing toward the skillet of blinding light, every step is a fight against the urge to retreat, to cower . . . to simply sink in a fetal position on the floor. Soon enough, though, I'm standing directly across from the rusty sink, just inches from the open doorway, and I realize I can see outside. The clouded, dented mirror reflects the entry, an unexpected stroke of luck.

I scan the mirror for movement, but all I see are heavy-shouldered cacti drooping atop the buff-colored terrain. I inch forward a half step, blood thrumming in my ears, stuck in my throat. Two dying palms slide into view. They're tall, but thin, and offer no place to hide. I'll have to step outside if I want to see more.

If I want to see Daniel.

My heart kicks as I bolt past the opening, half-expecting a gloved hand to yank me back by my hair, so I'm shrieking as I race into the flat stretch between those two struggling palms, yet my breath is so thin I think I'm going to pass out from fear alone.

How stupid would *that* be after what just happened?

My heels spew dust as I whirl, head pounding in the blinding light. The truck behind the Dumpster remains silt-covered, untouched. The desert beyond that is fenced off, government land with a view for miles, and there are still no other cars in the lot. No brush to hide in. Nothing moves.

Resetting my sights on the bathrooms, I begin limping toward the Beemer. I try to keep that in view too, but the sun glints atop the windshield in a blinding slash, so I can't tell if Daniel sees my wild waving or not. What about my bloody nose? God, what about my fear?

Because it's spiking again, I realize. Because my arms are pinwheeling and pumping and I'm trying to reach that car on legs that suddenly refuse to work.

Because Daniel always, *always*, sees me.

"Daniel!" My throat burns with the cry, but my shallow breath still unfolds in a desperate puff. I am a rubber band being drawn back, panic pulling at me, even as I fight to gain ground. My hearing thins out, the sound of the crows and interstate traffic stretch into nonexistence, and there's not even room anymore to suck in air. There's only one thing left in the world, and that's the white of the BMW's hood glaring at me beneath the sun.

"*Daniel!*" I scream again.

Then—*snap!*—I'm back, wheezing at the driver's side door with an aching foot and head and nose. My tote falls to the black-veined tarmac, and I cup my hands and peer inside.

The car is empty.

////////////

My heart thumps as I yank open the driver's side door. Un-locked. Unguarded. "Daniel . . . ?!"

Braced against the open door and hood, I whirl back to the sturdy brown building. The men's and women's bathrooms op-pose each other, the twin dark interiors set like black, unblinking eyes. "*Daniel!*"

A sound jingles in the arid stillness. It's a ringtone that calls for a laugh track.

"Green Acres."

I spot it on the white leather of the driver's seat, tucked against the seat back. Daniel's phone.

Because the world is still spinning, because this phone has al-ways been my connection to Daniel whenever he's not right next to me, and because it's the only thing I can think to do, I pick it up.

Imogene Hawthorne's voice trills in my ear, as merry as her ringtone. "Darling, is that you?"

"N-no, Mrs. Hawthorne. It's me. Kristine."

Silence slivers the line before her tone pitches higher. "Kris-tine! Darling, how lovely to hear your voice! And I told you, please call me Imogene."

But I can't even answer. I'm staring at one of the battle-scarred crows, the smell of coffee and blood stuffing my swollen nose.

The bird looks like a chunk of feathered charcoal as it waddles around on cracked feet, panting in the midday sun. It watches me back like it's wondering what I'm going to do.

So, what am I going to do?

"Some old friends just popped in for a surprise visit. We're drinking mint juleps on the north veranda, and I thought Daniel might want to say hello."

I search for a reply, but what are the right words after being attacked in a deserted rape trap, and then emerging to find your fiancé missing?

"No, no, they're on their way . . ." Imogene's voice muffles. She's reassuring her old friends with minty-fresh breath. She enunciates every word, like she's an actor in a play. To me, she broadly declares, "It's absolutely lovely at this time of day. Daniel and you really should be here."

I stare at the gaping mouth of the men's room, thinking we should both really be *here*.

He can't be in the women's bathroom. I've just come from there, and I've had a 360-degree view of the surrounding desert ever since. The only movement comes from the cars on the highway ribboning behind me . . . plus I am certain Daniel would have answered my cries if he'd heard them. He'd have come running at my screams. If he could.

"Kristine?"

"Sorry." I wipe sweat from my brow, and shield my eyes with my hand as I stare at the men's room. My nose has stopped bleeding, but the newly paved blacktop burns through the bottom of my flats, and my underarms are already sticky. *My new cashmere,* I find myself thinking, *is getting soiled.*

"You sound distracted." Imogene is annoyed with me, as usual.

I continue staring at the men's room.

"Kristine?"

"We've run into some . . . some . . ."

Something bad.

"Some traffic?"

"Yes." Emboldened by my stillness, the large crow has inched closer and is now just ten feet away. It tilts its head at my whisper. "I mean, no. Except . . ."

I'm at the first rest stop outside of Vegas. A man just attacked me in the bathroom. He's gone now, but so is Daniel and there's nowhere to hide except . . .

"Except?" Imogene prods, still crisp, still projecting her voice, still playing her part.

Except the phone bleeps in my hand, the triptych chimes of a text coming through, and I look down. Daniel has his phone preferences set to show messages directly on the lock screen—every second counts when you're a trauma surgeon—and that's how I find myself staring at my own name in the sender's box: KRISTINE RUSH.

And in the body of the text?

Say good-bye.
Now.
Or he dies.

///////////

My fingers scrabble over the car's center console, because that's where I left my phone. The dash is empty, my plastic coffee cup

22

lies in the abandoned footwell, and the coffee staining the passenger's seat is nearly dry. No phone. Yet Daniel *has* left something else behind, and I press a hand to my stomach when I see it. My other hand floats up to cover my mouth because my throat is welling up again. It's about to balloon with sound as I watch keys, rocked by my movement, sway beneath the fob in the ignition.

I got rid of Imogene. I told her the hospital was calling through with an emergency while I scanned the backseat for Daniel's travel bag—gone!—but now I'm wishing she were still with me. I could use some kind of connection with the outside world, the one I was a part of just ten minutes ago, and the one that still makes sense. I want someone with me, even a woman who barely tolerates me, yet instead I'm alone.

Except that I'm not.

Bracing against the door, I lever myself upright and face the stunted brown building while the sun attacks my head. This time my gaze is drawn to the five long slats along the restroom's roofline. Assuming the men's room has the same layout as the women's side, someone could stand atop the steel sink, peer through those vented slats, and survey the entire lot while still remaining hidden.

As if roused by the thought, the three chimes sound again.

Drive.

A simple, familiar word . . . one that doesn't compute. I glance around the empty lot, then back toward the interstate. Why doesn't anyone stop? Why doesn't anyone help me? Who's going to help Daniel?

The merry chimes trill once more in the heat.

I said DRIVE.

A hot breath of dust rises off the Mojave floor to swirl around my ankles. Cars tear down the interstate behind me, but I don't move. Daniel is here, and I can't leave him. He certainly wouldn't leave me. Yet I also can't bring myself to step back toward that building.

More chimes.

Drive now. DRIVE. Or you will be driven.

The words slap me so hard that I feel like I'm facing an entirely new direction, staring at the horizon of some hostile new land I don't recognize. I take one tentative step toward the building to try and bring myself back around, and it's not safe—no— but at least it's not entirely unknown. I take another step.

More chimes.

OK.
Have it your way.

Inside the building, Daniel screams.

The agonized cry rolls from the vents in a single, billowing sheet, shooting chills along my limbs despite the blazing sun. I freeze, and the sound cuts off into a series of sharp staccato yips—*ohGodohGod*, what the hell forces that sort of sound?—and then, a blessed pause. Suddenly, another full-throttle screech writhes in the air.

I take a giant step back.

The screaming stops.

And the phone bleeps in my palm.

Good. And no police.

"*Daniel!*" I yell, and five seconds later, more chimes.

Shut up and drive. Or he dies.
Just get on the road or he dies.
No police or he dies.
I'm watching. Believe it. Or . . .

I know. Or he dies.

Now. Drive.

I swivel, whimpering when I crack the open car door with my hip. Chased by a long, thin moan, I fumble my way inside. *Drive,* I think, groping for the keys. Because that will stop his pain. Drive as instructed, and Daniel doesn't get hurt.

I'm sweaty and shaking, and my hand slips three times on the ignition. With each fumble I expect to hear another tortured but muffled scream shoot through the car interior, but cool air finally blasts from the AC vents, and haunting twenties jazz roars from the speakers. Daniel's favorite music. He'd been listening to it while waiting for me. I turn down the volume to practically nothing, shift gears, and press my foot to the gas.

Self-disgust cramps my belly as I back from the lot.

"Daniel . . ." I say one last time, but his name slips away, along with the brown concrete box, until both are left far behind in the rearview mirror.

4

It's a test of endurance.

Less than an hour after Daniel picked me up beneath University Hospital's porte cochere and pressed that indulgent cup of coffee into my hands, I slip back into interstate traffic, alone. I accelerate with my still-throbbing foot while gripping the steering wheel at the ten and two o'clock marks. *Safety first* pops in my head, and a strangled laugh leaps from my throat. Spooked by the sound, I clench my teeth so hard that my head resumes its aching pulse, but I don't cry.

When I'm once again a part of the steady traffic stream, I peer inside the vehicles of my fellow travelers to see if anyone is looking back at me. They're not, and I can't believe it. My fiancé is trapped in the bowels of this desert, injured and terrified, and these people are just trying to reach their destinations without having to stop for gas. My terror, Daniel's torture, doesn't even register in their world. They might as well be from another planet.

When my hands have steadied somewhat, I finally snap off the music playing quietly in the background. Silence replaces the twenties jazz, and I immediately feel guilty. Daniel loves the stuff.

Don't you get enough of this in the OR? I asked when we first started dating, trying hard to sound diplomatic. It was nine months earlier, and we were in this same car, "I Wish I Had You" by Fats Waller scrolling across the LCD screen. The crooning wasn't so bad, but the tinkling of the piano, along with the writhing wail of the horns, grated on my nerves. It was like being tormented by some speakeasy ghost.

"This is a classic," Daniel said, grinning. "It was one of my dad's favorites. Actually, it was playing the first time I saw him splint a kitten."

So it was a healing moment, I'd thought, and one that had clearly imprinted on the son. I'd placed my hand atop his in apology. His father died, like mine, when Daniel was still young, so I understood the desire to bring a cherished memory back to life. I also recognized the strange ways in which the loss of a parent could manifest itself.

For example, I can barely stand to look at a horse to this day.

Now I'm squinting in the rearview mirror, the strong scent of the spilled coffee actually turning my stomach as I scan the vista behind me for a vehicle that's matching my pace. There's only one in the first five miles of this living nightmare; a truck driver who pulls even with me and remains that way for a good thirty seconds before I finally build up enough nerve to lean over into the passenger's seat and catch a glimpse of his face. My movement's too abrupt, though, my angle awkward, and so the driver catches it. He has the gall to smile down at me, and though I jerk back and refocus on the road, my hands are suddenly shaking again.

My hatred for the truck driver is sudden and violent. It's a chemical reaction, something poisonous that I thought was buried deep, but it binds with Daniel's scream to cause my face to flush, and my breathing grows ragged. The roots of my hair feel like they're crackling, and the sole of my aching right foot sends the car jerking forward. I swerve in front of the semi, nearly shaving its front bumper with mine. The move earns me a blast of protest from the trucker, a low-register, high-decibel world-filling *HONNNNNK!* that blares through my body, which is both satisfying and more infuriating still, and I glare at the truck in the rearview as I leave it in the dust.

Then I'm immediately sorry.

This is why I stay out of the desert. This is why I try to remain in control and away from dark places. If I don't, my natural instinct is to explode.

Without looking away from the road, I stretch back, fingers scrambling for the small ice cooler we've brought along for the trip. We had planned to stop along the way and fill it—to do so at the same time that I changed clothes—but my hand still fists when I reach in to find it bone dry and empty. There is nothing to cool me here.

The steady hum of the tires rolling over the road is finally what calms me, and I try to figure out what to do next. I know the man-in-boots is behind me because that's where I've left Daniel, but what do I do with that information? Speed up? Slow down? Both feel wrong.

I glance at the phone I've tossed onto the coffee-stained seat next to me, then reach out to stroke the black rubber case. I can still see it clutched in Daniel's elegant, tapered fingers, skillful hands that stitch and mend and support. Loving hands, that also seek and slip, embrace and knead. How many times has he fallen asleep with this phone in his palm? How often have I taken it gently from him, careful not to wake him?

God, I love those hands.

My attacker has left me this phone for a reason. It tethers me to him. It keeps me yoked. Thing is, it's not just a harness . . . it can be a lifeline too. I'm alone in the car, but I can still call for help, right? Despite what I was told? There's continual police presence along this bleak, Wile E. Coyote stretch of road. Radar-controlled cameras hover over the entire 221-mile stretch leading to San Bernardino, and police helicopters canvass the flat road in throbbing intervals, clocking speeding cars and tagging them for the highway patrol.

And no police.

I don't doubt Daniel will be hurt if I defy whoever this is . . . but how would he really know? I can use the speaker feature to call 911, even though he warned me not to. No phone for someone to see pressed against my ear. I could report the location and time that Daniel was taken and relate it to where I am now. The police would set up a blockade on each side of the highway, a pit of hell for other travelers, but a net for Daniel's captor. They'd triangulate him before the day burns out.

Then *he'll* have to run.

He'd be the one being driven.

I nod to myself and reach for the phone—

The tritone message alert peals through the silent car. "Jesus!"

I jerk my hand away, and the Beemer briefly sails into the fast lane, the Honda next to me bleating disapproval. Ignoring the driver and his limited use of sign language, I grope for the phone, and this time it feels like I'm plunging my hand into an ice bucket. It's a test of endurance. How long can I keep it submerged? How much willpower do I really have?

Car again steady, I force myself to look down.

Buffalo Bill's. Text back when you arrive.

You're thinking 911.

Don't try it or he'll be sorry.

Adrenaline kicks at my heart, but so does slight relief, and I slump back against the leather seat. Buffalo Bill's is a casino in the tiny border town of Primm, Nevada. The man is clearly driving me toward money, most likely one of the casino's ubiquitous ATMs. Once I text back that I've arrived, he's going to order me to empty my bank account and bring the cash to him somewhere in the parking lot. Then he'll release Daniel.

These instructions make sense. Greed makes sense.

I suck in my first full breath since leaving the rest stop. Desperate people do desperate things—I've seen enough proof of that in the OR. For someone poised on a financial cliff, perhaps terrorizing an unsuspecting, unarmed couple at a deserted rest stop is easier than holding up a casino, where cameras and security personnel threaten to foil escape.

Yeah, if terrorizing a young couple already comes easy to you.

That's the thought I have to push away as I increase my speed. It's only ten miles to Primm, and for Daniel's sake, I can hold off calling the police for another eight minutes. Because now I know exactly where the stranger is.

He's on the way there too.

5

Maybe it's just wordplay?

Most state borders are invisible crossings—unseen, unfelt, and insignificant—yet the line separating California from Nevada is stamped atop the earth in neon by not one but three casinos. Buffalo Bill's is the largest, partly because of the outlet mall that sprouts from the property's south side like a randomly attached limb, but mostly because of the bright red roller coaster tracks that soar like unearthed dinosaur bones high above the barn-style roofline. The spine of the ride curves forward, its tethered tracks clacking high before it dives into a dizzying series of impressive sidelong loops.

I am not here for the entertainment, so I ignore both the mall and the roller coaster and keep my eyes on the road as I swing into a parking lot so large that, with a packed casino, it's still only half-full. I search out a space as close to the entrance as possible, knowing the casinos train their security cameras on a property's exterior as vigorously as they do the interior. Daniel's abductor should know this too, though, and that makes me swallow hard.

Why doesn't that seem to worry him?

An elderly couple is backing from a spot just as I round the second row of cars, and I wait for them to clear out before pulling in. I'm hemmed in on two sides this way, but the main entrance stretches out wide before me, and so does the feeder road leading from the highway. Shifting into park, I immediately pick up the phone and text:

I'm here.

A readied reply pops on the screen.

What's another name for bandit, outlaw, cutthroat, gangster, villain?

"You?" I mutter, then glance around, instantly worried that he has somehow heard me. Straight ahead, a family of four hurries past a life-size diorama of a miner pouring coal into a cart. Beyond them, three parking attendants sweat it out at the valet stand, no longer interacting with each other, boredom undisguised. Two teen girls, wearing what would only generously be called Daisy Dukes, sashay across the lot. Not one person looks at me.

So why do I feel watched?

The trio of bells again.

Desperado.

Impatient, the stranger has answered his own riddle. Unfortunately, I have no idea what it means.

I wait, but there's no follow-up text, and I realize I have to leave the car. It's now 4:50 in the afternoon and the desert sun is practically crackling, so when I climb out I have to shield my eyes with both hands just to scan the lot. There's no one in the surrounding cars, no faces or binoculars pointed my way. I study a senior husband and wife as they pass behind me, but the man is wearing loafers, not boots, and the woman is busy digging into a nylon pack tied around her waist.

Desperado. Maybe it's just wordplay? Maybe it simply means desperate, because right now I am most certainly that.

I'm sliding back into the coolness and relative safety of the car to ask for a less ambiguous hint, when I see it. The sign is attached to the soaring vertebrae of the roller coaster, and I follow its arc, craning my neck up, up, up, while Daniel's phone drifts, forgotten, down to my side.

THE DESPERADO, it says.

"No." I shudder as my eyes trace the coaster's enormous spine. But I get it now. The man is buying time. After all, he had to secure Daniel somewhere without being seen, and now he needs to catch up to me. A hot breeze blows a wisp of hair across my face as Daniel's scream ripples again through my mind. I have to do as ordered . . . but I still wonder: does this man know that being hurtled forward, completely out of control, is my personal idea of hell?

I bite my lower lip and think. No, he's only human. And, if he's still driving, how will he know if I just remain in the little bubble of my car and canvass every vehicle that enters the lot from here? Or what if I stand just inside the casino doors, and then flag down security when he does finally arrive? I can tell them—

. . . what?

I have no idea what my attacker looks like, or what kind of car he drives, and if he doesn't show up at all, I'll be stuck trying to explain how I left my beloved fiancé alone at a rest stop and just drove away.

Is that what I've done?

The events occurred in that order, yes, but surely they'd believe me.

Would *I* believe me?

And what happens when Daniel's captor finally does show up and spots security patrolling the lot? What will keep him from just performing a quick U-turn and fleeing right back into the desert to deal with my fiancé?

Daniel's cry scissors again in my mind, but this time it's drowned out by half a dozen mine carts shooting overhead, and the car door is suddenly burning the back of my legs as I sag. I close my eyes and smell blast powder and raw ore. I see a lit cavern filled with matted furs and tattered silk and the Coal Man pointing to a mine cart.

Sit.

Mine carts.

"God." I give my head a violent jerk and blink hard. That's it; I'm going inside. I have to get out of this heat, even if I don't know what I'm going to do beyond that. Ducking back into the car, I use the last of Daniel's bottled water to clean off the blood crusting my face. Then I lock up and knot my long hair atop my head as I limp toward the entrance. Worst-case scenario, I get on the roller coaster. They're not real mine carts—it's just a ride, and Daniel is the one stuck with the stranger. I can endure a silly amusement ride if it means Daniel and I will be back together soon.

I mean, I can endure anything at all for that.

Right?

6

He wants me to know it.

The roller coaster's ticket booth is located at the far end of the casino, flanked by a sprawling food court on one side and a clamorous arcade on the other. I follow the decorative rail tracks that sweep the casino's ceiling to wind past a cashier's cage renamed JUSTICE OF THE PEACE. I know I'm close to my destination when the smell of grease and cheese knots up my stomach.

Linking myself to a line already twenty people deep, I have to work not to snap at those milling aimlessly around me. I'm surrounded by humanity, and even interacting with others—I buy a ticket, I thank the vendor—yet in reality, I'm as alone and helpless as when I was first forced to flee the rest stop.

"How long is the ride?" I ask the pimple-faced boy who rips my ticket at the height of the loading dock. It's fashioned to look like the exterior of a Wild West saloon, weathered pine boards creaking underfoot as I shift my weight.

"Just under two minutes," he answers, not even looking at me as he gestures toward the loaders.

I make a quick calculation as another teen, a girl this time, directs me to my cart. Two minutes on the coaster plus the seven spent in line. Another one or two to buckle everyone in. That makes over ten minutes. Add that to the time I spent scouring the lot, and the stranger has given himself plenty of time to catch up.

Or pass right by, I realize as the safety bar clicks in place over my lap. A jolt that has nothing to do with the ride somersaults through my gut.

The man who has been directed to sit next to me feels my shudder and turns his head. "Exciting, huh?"

I can't help but glance down at his feet. Hairy legs clad in Bermuda shorts, two scuffed tennis shoes. No blue cotton coveralls, no boots. I give a short nod, then grip the safety bar with both hands as a piercing whistle sweeps over the platform.

Down into the mines.

I close my eyes as the carts begin ticking forward. The girl attendant waves cheerily, and then heat pounces, announcing our emergence into the sun. The coaster tips up toward its first apex. I want to remain frozen, I want to pretend this sky-bound ride has nothing to do with me, but I feel like I owe it to Daniel to look, and so I force my eyes wide.

The sun stains the western mountains purple, distance filing their rocky edges smooth. A dry lakebed unfolds to the south, the buff expanse spreading over the land like a stain, and the black scar of the interstate slices right through its belly. Daniel and I would be well past everything in sight, if only we hadn't stopped.

The coaster continues its upward tick, the vertical climb so steep that I'm forced to recline. I'm as helpless as a patient on a gurney. Worse, each time I think the ascent will stop, it continues on. The man next to me giggles, and I look at him sharply, but he's staring straight ahead like an enormous child.

This isn't happening, I think, mind beginning to spin as we finally reach the top. People don't attack others in broad daylight. They don't abduct the male half of a couple and leave the female alone.

They don't say ride a roller coaster when they mean *give me money*.

The front of the coaster drops from view, leaving only the mountain ranges in the distance and me, for an instant, suspended above it all. Then the first anticipatory squeals pivot into raw, curling screams. Pulled by gravity and the weight of the carts, I'm whipped over that invisible edge and hurtled forward so violently I'm sure the safety bar will come loose. I'm in a free fall, and with the vast space of the arid desert around me, it's like being flung into a burning void. When the ground is too close but still rising, the coaster suddenly swerves, the vibrations of the new angle rattling my teeth and spine.

My seatmate throws his thick arms in the air, his weight crushing mine as we pivot and twist, and I wonder if he's bearing down on me on purpose. Then we're flung in the opposite direction, and I level him in turn. We careen around a series of corners and I squeeze my eyes shut. I can't help it, I'm desperate for it to be over. Finally, the machine slows, and I open my eyes again to find the faux train station sliding into view.

"Fuckin' A!" the man yells as we pull even with the platform, and I can't agree more. I have to wait for the bar to release me, and then for the man to clamber out, but I'm pulling myself onto the platform and thinking, *never again,* when I hear, "Ma'am Ma'am!"

The voice, I realize, has been going on for some time, and I turn to find myself facing the girl who loaded me onto the coaster. I glance at her nametag. AMANDA. Okay . . . so why is Amanda reaching for my arm?

"Not so fast," Amanda says, corralling me back the other way. "You stay. You get to go again."

"What?"

But Amanda suddenly freezes. Pointing to her nose, she says, "You have something . . . here. You didn't get that on the ride, did you?"

I realize my disheveled hair can be explained away by the ride, but the blood I feel crusting the side of my nose? "Nope. It's nothing."

The girl's toothy grin widens. Hey, as long as I'm not going to make problems for her, right? "Anyway, a man in line gave up his ticket for you. Said you were enjoying yourself so much that he wanted to treat you to 'another little ride.'"

I spin to search the faces of those waiting behind the stanchions.

"He was just here," Amanda says, seeing my stricken face, but only shrugs when I stare at her. "Probably went to buy another ticket."

He was just here. He'd been watching me the whole time, likely to make sure I followed his cryptic instructions. That means he was closer than I thought . . . and he wants me to know it.

I swallow hard. "I don't think I know him. What did he look like?"

"Um . . . dark hair, fit, but not, like, roided out, you know? Tall." Amanda lifts her hand just above my head. At least six feet, then. "I couldn't really see his face. He had on a trucker's cap and shades, and one of those mechanic jumpsuits, I think."

"You think it was a jumpsuit?"

"I mean, I think mechanics wear them." Amanda smiles. God help me, she's playing matchmaker. "There was some weird name on it. *Malthus*. He made me repeat it."

So that she'd remember. So she'd tell me.

"And brown boots?"

Amanda shakes her head, sending her blond ponytail swinging. "I dunno. But either way, I think he likes you."

No. He doesn't like me at all.

"I'm not going on the ride," I tell Amanda, and whirl toward the exit. If this man—this Malthus—is here, then so is Daniel.

"But then you don't get your prize."

I freeze mid-step, and back up to face Amanda. The girl can't seem to stop smiling. "He made me memorize that too."

Daniel's handsome face flashes in my mind: the bright smile and blue eyes; the smooth, dark hair; and the mole that both mars one eyebrow and makes him perfect. He is—and always has been—my prize. And somehow Malthus knows it.

I square up on Amanda. "How much?"

The girl blinks like an owl.

"How much," I repeat, voice lifting high, "did he pay you to send me back on this ride?"

"Geez. A bill, okay?" Amanda's gaze darts over the platform

to see if anyone else had heard she's taken a hundred dollars to send me on "another little ride." But that's not why my mouth falls open. If this guy has a hundred dollars to pass along to some random minimum-wage casino-ride attendant, then he hasn't sent me here just for ransom money.

But I think a part of me already knew that.

"Well, just . . . get on the ride, you know?" Amanda finally says. "Or don't—I don't care."

Yet if I don't, I won't get my *prize.*

This time, I'm loaded up in the very first cart, and I'm placed there alone. As the coaster begins its slow tick forward, I feel the hot wind like a breath on the back of my neck. A woman knows when she is being stalked, after all . . . especially one who's been stalked before.

And now I am trapped up here—*out* here, I think as we swing into the sun—while this Malthus-man plans to . . . what?

My gaze whips to the dry lakebed where I almost expect to see Daniel being hurtled away from me, but we're slowly gaining the apex, and suddenly I'm surrounded on all sides by aching blue skies.

I see only what Malthus wants me to see.

My body plummets. Screams rise and fall behind me in shrill notes whipped away by the wind, but I'm mute and tense and as immobile as one can be while being flung around in space. It feels like the rushing wind is a part of Malthus's plans too, because it's burying every cry inside of me, shoveling that and my terror atop growing despair until it all bulges in my throat. I don't know how I keep from vomiting.

Do not shut down, I tell myself. *Keep going*. Because if I stop like I did the last time I felt all these things, I might just let go entirely.

So I grip the safety bar with white knuckles and try to think of something else and snag onto the first happy memory that whips past on the fiery air.

Oh, no. I am not ever *letting this go.*

It's Daniel, of course. It was the first time we were really together, and he had just flopped to his back afterward, almost looking shocked. I, too, was marveling—at the way his dark eyes and hair popped against the white of his skin, the way the atmosphere around him appeared diffused, bathing him in gentle light. I'd never even seen him with a hair out of place before, forget breathless and sweaty, and the way those sharp eyes glazed over as he moved inside of me made me glow as well.

I am not ever *letting this go.*

No, he wouldn't, I think, and force my eyes open as the coaster swerves into its final spiral.

Amanda is waiting when the ride finally pulls to a stop. She holds out a hand, but I ignore it and push from the cart on my own.

"I'm not going again," I say, and my voice makes me jolt, because I sound like I'm on the verge of tears. Amanda looks alarmed too, but then she doesn't know that I never, ever cry.

"I can't allow that anyway. Here." She holds out her hand, and I find myself staring at a folded manila envelope. "Your prize."

Not Daniel.

As my fingers close around the envelope, I can't say that I'm surprised. It was clear as soon as I was forced onto that second ride that Malthus was not going to give up my fiancé so easily. Instead he's giving me . . .

"What?" Amanda asks when I gasp.

I try to shake my head, but it jerks as if in spasms.

"That is your name, right?" Amanda points to the envelope. "You're Kristine Rush?"

Yes, I am. And it's clear from the words, neatly centered and typed before me, that Malthus has known it all along.

7

Hurting is what I do.

I need to find a place to open the envelope, one that's away from Amanda and the security cameras, and out of sight from the man named Malthus, who is somewhere nearby. A restroom sign beckons to me in a flashing wink, and I hurry to it, cutting across the clanging din of the casino floor. Inside, the room is clean, over-bright, and bustling with other women, the antithesis of the desert hole where I was attacked just over an hour ago.

Keeping my head down, I use my long hair to cover my face and claim the largest stall, where I press my back against the tiled wall and stare at the envelope in my hands. My typed name peers back up at me in a sharp, blocky taunt. I slip a finger beneath the seal, and out slides a map, the kind that can still be found in dusty roadside gas stations. This too bears my full name across the white band at the top, the squared print drawn in sharp, whittled slashes, little arrows bereft of their tips.

The map rattles crisply as I unfold desert town after desert town—they stretch from one crease to the next, interspersed with feeder roads that branch away like thin, black veins. The dry lakebed I spotted from the peak of the Desperado is called the Ivanpah, a fact I would have happily gone my entire life without knowing. However, I note that the state line and Buffalo Bill's casino are not represented. They've been carefully ripped away. Other than that, and my name at the top, the map appears devoid of markings. No additional arrows. No sharp tips.

Nothing that points to Daniel.

I tuck everything beneath my arm and grab Daniel's phone. Thumbs flying, I enter the name Amanda had been told to memorize into the search engine. *Malthus* is too strange and too specific to be random.

Dozens of entries flood the screen, all related to one of two subjects. I ignore those associated with an eighteenth-century British scholar—some early influencer on Darwin's theory of evolution—and zoom in on the more obvious and ominous choice: a prince of Hell who sent legions of demons into battle.

"Great." A psycho who haunts rest stops *and* studies demonology.

I close my eyes and try to imagine what someone like that looks like, but I can't. I'm also distracted by the unreasonable thought that I should be able to intuit if my fiancé is okay. My love for Daniel is greater than any I've ever harbored for another person, save Abby, so I feel like I should have some sense of his well-being. A good woman, one worthy of a great love, should be able to do that, right?

Yet all I can hear is the blowback of his scream billowing in my mind.

I open my eyes, and before I can overthink it, switch back to the phone's text function.

I'll give you anything . . . just let him go.

I push SEND before I can question the wisdom of letting this man know how desperate I've become. What the hell does it matter? I'm already doing what he asked. All I have to aid me in finding him are a car, a map, and a phone. Great tools in a civilized world, but I'm pretty certain by now that that's not where Malthus lives.

I'm actually jolted when the phone rings in my lap. At most, I expected that chirping tritone message alert again. This is a custom ringtone instead, another of Daniel's favorite old jazz tunes. It's the one he specifically assigned to me.

I answer and say to the man who has my phone, my fiancé: "Where's Daniel?"

"He's with me, of course." The voice is distorted, mechanized via some sort of masking device that turns it metallic. Listening to it is like biting tin.

"And who are you?"

His chuckle sparks in my ear. "You can call me Malthus."

You can call me. Not really a name, then? Just one more way to jerk me around. Keeping my voice low in case anyone else is listening, I force myself to play along. "The demon or the scholar?"

"That would depend on who you ask," he says, sounding pleased. "So. I understand you're off for a visit with your future mother-in-law? Got yourself a nice little Fourth of July party planned?"

"How do you know that?"

"How do you think I know?" The metallic sound snips at my eardrums like sewing shears.

"Don't hurt him."

"But Kristine. Hurting is what I do." His voice goes flat, the humor gone, and I imagine him leaning forward, probably in a car outside, gaze burning like the sun overhead. "Let me ask you. Do you actually care for your fiancé?"

"Of course."

He makes a noise in the back of his throat, unconvinced. "I only ask because I've been watching you for a while now. I've gone to great lengths, in fact. Taps on your phone, bugs on your computer. Cameras . . . those are my favorite."

I bet.

"Understand, Kristine, that I've been desperate to see if there's anything you value above and beyond yourself. Yet even after ten long months, I have to say . . . I keep coming up empty."

I press the back of my hand to my forehead. Ten months. God.

And he's wrong. I care for so many things; for my patients and close friends, for Daniel, and, first and foremost, for Abby. But I'm damn sure not going to tell him *that*.

"You go to the gym to get your tight little ass," he continues in that cutting voice, "and then go shopping to cover it with expensive clothes. You clock hours at an altruistic job, true, but only so you can keep eating and sleeping and waking and shitting and running, running, running on that pathetic treadmill that is your life. All that action, all that running. All of it done so carelessly."

I'm shaking my head, even though Malthus can't see me, and even though I'm glad, so very grateful, that he hasn't mentioned Abby. Ten months . . .

So why hasn't he mentioned Abby?

I lick my lips, trying to think. It's 5:30 p.m. Where is she right now? My fingers begin to tingle with the sudden need to end this call, to ring up Maria instead, to hear Abby's—

"Then I realized, you like *things*." The scissored words sever my thoughts. "You like Daniel's car, for instance . . . so I gave it to you. You can thank me now."

My throat contracts like a clenched fist. "Thank you."

"You like that nice ring on your finger from him too. I've seen you looking at it. You're probably looking at it now."

I grit my teeth and lift my gaze.

"I could have taken it at the rest stop." The mechanized voice lowers. "I could have chopped it off. Kept it for myself."

I can find nothing at all to say to that. The man is talking in complete sentences, trying on reason, but it's like putting a bow on a rabid dog. It simply doesn't fit over his obvious madness.

"But I didn't just leave you with these things because you desired them. I left them so that you could finally see that physical items have very little value when stripped of context. And I think it's time you learn to prioritize, Kristine."

I open my mouth, but no sound emerges.

"Open the map."

I force the tension from my fingers, leaving half-moons carved into my palms. I fumble the map and end up ripping it down the middle, but I hold it together with forced control, same way I'm holding myself together. I stare down at the dusty enclaves of Baker and Barstow, the specter of Death Valley winging off to the north, and Malthus speaks just as I spot it.

"You'll see that I've been thoughtful enough to mark your next destination."

Yes. A tidy black arrow, where there should be none.

The map grows heavy in my hands. Malthus did not mark this in the past fifty minutes. He couldn't have; not while torturing my fiancé, chasing me to Primm, or paying Amanda to deliver this map.

"Yes, ten months is a long time," Malthus says, as if confirming my thoughts, "but do you know what's even longer? The carefully counted minutes in a single twenty-four-hour period."

I'm not even breathing now.

"So after nearly a year of watching your avarice, the way you take everyone in your life for granted, how you have no redeeming quality making you worthy of the good life you're living, I suddenly realized that what you need isn't more time to prove yourself. You need less."

I suck in a breath at that. It's cold against my dry throat. I need water. I need help. I need—

"Twenty-four hours. That's how long you have to prove you actually care for someone outside yourself. And it's plenty of time, Kristine. It's one-thousand-four-hundred-and-forty minutes. It's eighty-six-thousand-four-hundred seconds. But I can promise you that it's an eternity if you're suffering through the whole of it."

He means Daniel.

"And what do I have to do?" I manage, tongue sticking in my dry mouth.

"You have to follow that map."

Chills pop on my arms. "You've only marked one spot."

"Yes, and when you reach it, you'll be given a new map. A new destination." Malthus's words are rote, like he's an actor and he's been rehearsing them for months. Ten whole months, as a matter of fact.

"Who the hell are you?" My whisper is breathy, there's no force behind it, and my question is repetitive, but he knows what I mean.

His chuckle is a sandpaper rasp that's as sharp as anything I've ever heard. "If you want to know the answer to that, you're going to have to wake up."

"Is that what the roller coaster was about?" I ask. "You were trying to wake me up?"

"Did it work?"

"Attacking me in a deserted rest stop worked," I say, and I don't even care if anyone else hears me. This isn't the nutso half of the conversation anyway.

"No, if I recall correctly I left you sleeping there too. Now . . ." He pauses, and even the silence is sliced thin and sharp. "Get the fuck out of that bathroom."

And the line goes dead.

8

That one thing.

The wall at my back is all that keeps me upright. The rides on the coaster exacerbated the injuries to my head and foot, but the pulsing has sunk deeper inside of me now. Instead of throbbing at the surface, the pains are nestled right next to my bones. I feel old, like I've been in this bathroom for years instead of minutes.

I still don't know what this guy Malthus wants. His order to *wake up* tells me nothing, though the admission that he's been stalking me for ten months turns that nothing into something significant. He has Daniel, yes, but it's clear now that this is about me, and I can't even imagine what I could have done to deserve it.

Okay, maybe except for that. That one thing.

But that's long past, and besides, everyone has something in their history that makes them flinch. My memories just happen to spring up like poisonous mushrooms, mealy and rotted and contaminated by my mother's voice.

Try it just once; trust me, baby.

She is soft and encouraging in my sweat-soaked dreams, the way I'd always wished she would be. The way she only was when feeding me total bullshit.

So my real dirty little secret is that while Malthus has been watching me, looking for "redeeming qualities" and wondering why I have such a good life, I've actually been doing the same . . . and I've been searching for the answer a hell of a lot longer than ten months. I know what haunts me and what keeps me only looking forward, but unless I leave this bathroom, I'll never find out what's driving *him*.

I exit the stall and pointedly avoid eye contact with the trio of women at the long row of sinks. Between the music and their self-absorbed chatter, none seem to have heard my conversation in the stall anyway.

I do happen to catch my own reflection as I pass by the full-length mirror, though, and I stumble, shocked by what I see. Other than my too-red nose and wind-tangled hair, I look impossibly normal. It's so at odds with the way I feel that I have to do a double-take before whirling away.

Back in the casino, whipping lights and clanging slot banks mark my progress, cheering me back into the heat. I turn the corner and spot a security stand looming against the wall, and I hope Malthus isn't spying on me now because my steps automatically slow. The stand is placed directly opposite the front entrance, allowing the attending guard a perfect perch from which to observe those who enter and leave. It's also a visual beacon for people who need help.

I consider it. If I tell security what's happened, they can close off the lot before Daniel's abductor leaves. Yet I can already hear the guard's first question. *Instead of immediately reporting that your fiancé was abducted, you drove fifteen miles to the state line and went on an amusement ride?*

Twice?

Because that's exactly what the security cameras will show. That, and a man who isn't my fiancé buying me a ride ticket. And me taking it. And what proof do I have to back up my claims? A few cryptic texts on a missing man's phone?

Ones that've come from *me?*

Sweat pops on my brow despite the frigid casino air. It occurs to me that Malthus has me dead to rights—the psycho can throw anyone in my path now, and I'll have more than just a little explaining to do.

Feeling watched, my heartbeat kicks up again, and my gaze begins to dart. I study the faces poised at the slots, the body language of those strolling between them. Maybe they aren't all simply meandering. Maybe Malthus has an ally.

Blinking hard, I realize that my breath has grown ragged, so I try and steady it, but then I see that the security guard has realized it too.

My movement, or lack of it, has caught his attention, and he leans over his elevated stand, his professionally schooled face gone honed. His close-mouthed smile is edged as he nods at me in invitation, an offer of help if I need it.

Can he help me? Can anyone?

I have no idea what to do with those thoughts, so I whirl toward the exit instead, working to mask my limp. I feel like I'm being pushed toward the doors, invisible palms pressing at my back, and I can't help but run a hand over my head as I risk a backward glance. The guard is fully upright now, unblinking as he tracks me across the floor, and my heart sinks. No matter what I do, or what happens next, I know this man will remember me.

I cut across the casino floor on the diagonal, putting a tall bank of blinking, clanging machines between the guard and me, then remain on that angle until I reach the tinted doors. My hand closes over a gilded handle, and I jolt because it's like ice in my palm. Then, suddenly, I'm back in the heat, quickstepping it away from the covered valet, the sun laser-blasting my body, nearly blinding me as I hurry into the lot. I move as quickly as I can without running and unlock the car by remote before yanking the door wide.

A neat, white package waits for me on the driver's seat.

My head whips up, around. I swear I locked the car when I went inside. How would anyone get in without a key, or breaking a window, or setting off the alarm? Who could break in without even scratching the lock?

Someone who'd been in my house, tapping my phone, bugging my computer. Someone who's been setting this up for ten long months, that's who.

Bending, I touch the edge of the small package. It's sturdy butcher paper, its contents secured by a sliver of yellow tape. I pick it up and find it's surprisingly light. Carefully, I pull back the tape, but when it's laid open I just stare, trying to make sense of what's been sitting there, baking in the heat.

At first I think it's a dead caterpillar, but there's too much blood for that. The liquid fills the rounded pocket, browning at the edges and congealing in the middle. The fuzzy object centered in the gooey mess also had no organs or eyes or head. It has never been alive. Yet a thin layer of tissue surrounds it like the rubbery flesh of a landed stingray, its fluttery elegance gone flat with gravity. Still more puzzled than repelled, I tilt the paper, and my gaze slides to the item's left edge.

And I flash back to an hour earlier, Daniel and me sitting in the car, me kissing his cheek . . . right beneath the small mole I love so much. It sat to the side of his right eyebrow.

Both eyebrow and mole sit carefully gift-wrapped in my hands right now. They are wet, fresh. He is close.

"Excuse me? Ma'am?"

The voice rises behind me at the same time the bile reaches my throat, and I whirl to see the security guard who'd been watching me inside. He's only two cars away.

//////////

I drop the paper—the part of Daniel's face that's been sliced away—and shudder as it hits the seat. Sticky, sun-warmed blood slides across my right palm, and I have to fight a scream as I back from the car. Holding my bloody hand close to my side, I force a smile. I know it's strained, but I'm just trying not to shake.

"You all right, ma'am?" the security guard asks, coming close.

"Of course, why?" My voice is a stranger's, but then this man is a stranger too, so he has no way of knowing that.

He pauses at a professional distance, a few feet away, and tilts his head. "It's just that you looked worried inside the casino, like you were trying to catch my eye. Is someone bothering you?"

"Bothering . . ." My laugh trills, threatens to turn manic, and I throttle it and carefully school my face again. "No. I'm fine."

Squinting, he purses his lips. I shoot a glance around the lot and tuck a lock of hair behind my ear. What security guard follows a woman into a parking lot? It's never happened to me before, not in all my years in Vegas, and it makes me wonder. Is this some sort of test?

"Traveling alone?" he asks, leaning to peer around me.

I angle my body, trying to make it appear as if I'm giving the guard a clear view of the car's interior, but I also slide the door shut to block the slivered eyebrow, the blood on the driver's seat. The tinted windows help. I step closer to the guard like I have nothing to hide, and keep my bloody hand behind me.

What can I tell him? That I'm from Las Vegas and I've driven forty miles to ride a roller coaster? No. What twenty-seven-year-old woman goes on amusement rides all by herself?

Besides, I've heard it's best to keep as close to the truth as possible when weaving a lie.

"I'm headed to Lake Arrowhead," I tell him, both answering the question and not. "Fourth of July party."

I don't say with whom. I don't want him to ask about my fiancé.

"The mountains," the guard says lightly, straightening as he nods. "Get out of the heat for a bit."

Sweat stains his dark blue uniform, and his eyes are narrowed against the sun, which seems to be throwing its rays directly at us in the day's last-ditch assault. The light will soon disappear over the western horizon, but for now the guard has to squint past the glare, and my body, to try and see inside the car. Have I dropped Daniel's brow close enough to the door to keep it from sight?

Is blood dripping from my hand to the asphalt?

"Well, be careful," he finally says. "It's sure not the most interesting drive. People tend to get bored and stop paying attention to what they're doing. They'll text or talk on the phone—"

"I hate that," I say, trying to hurry him along.

He stills again. "Yeah, well . . . as long as you're okay."

Last chance, I suddenly realize. This conversation will come back to haunt me if I say nothing now and try to go to the police later. Surveillance tapes will show I knew that Daniel was already missing at the time I stood in this lot, with this guard, and they'll prove that I lied to someone with the authority to help. They might even show that I had one bloody hand hidden behind my back while amusement ride screams corkscrewed in the air.

"I'm great," I say.

The guard studies me a moment more, but finally shrugs. *I tried, right?* Then he holds out his right hand to shake. He notices my hesitation and his chubby lips part in question, but before his eyes can narrow again, I reach for his forearm with my left instead and give it a heartfelt squeeze.

"You're so sweet. Thank you so much for coming all the way out into this burning parking lot to check on me." Maybe the reminder of the heat will send him scurrying back inside.

He gives me a more open smile, rocks back on his heels. "No problem, it's my job."

"You have a great day," I tell him.

"You too," he replies, but still doesn't leave. He's going to watch me climb into my car. He'll see my hand. He'll see the slivered cross section of my fiancé's face.

A twenties jazz tune bleats through the parking lot. I feel Daniel's phone buzzing in my pocket, and the guard's gaze falls there as well. "Gotta take this," I say, half-turning, but I have to cross over my body to pull out the phone with my left hand.

The guard just stands there, forcing me to turn my back fully, and I'm unable to see where his gaze wanders. I can't risk leaving a crimson handprint on the glossy white door, so I have no choice but to switch Daniel's phone into the hand stained with his blood. Meanwhile, the guard must be wondering why I don't answer.

I glance back as I pull the door wide and catch the way his gaze slides to the car's dark interior. Shoving the butcher paper into the footwell in one smooth motion, I then straddle it with my feet. There's nothing I can do about the blood drops staining the seat, and I imagine them soaking into my light linen shorts as I settle in, a crimson arc stamped there in the shape of Daniel's shorn eyebrow.

I sigh audibly after pulling the door shut, but the guard still doesn't turn away. I'm forced to put my bloody hand to my cheek, tuck my head low, and answer the phone.

Malthus's chuckle burrows into my ear like a metallic worm. "Ready to go for another ride?"

9

No one would blame you.

My head shoots up, and only belatedly do I realize that the movement is too abrupt, and that my eyes are too wide. Fortunately, the guard has already turned and is ambling back to the casino.

"I said, start driving, Kristine."

Did he? I can't remember, or I didn't hear, but I tuck the phone between shoulder and ear, recalling the blood a second too late. *Breathe,* I tell myself, fumbling the keys into the ignition. I can feel my heart throbbing in my palms, and my mouth is tacky, as dry as the desert surrounding me.

"Follow the guard." The strange instructions throw me off just enough to have me acting without question, and I head up the same aisle as the guard, back toward the casino.

"Closer."

"What?" The word snaps from my mouth, cracking like a whip in the otherwise still car.

"Drive faster."

I do, but just a little. I don't want to alarm the guard. He's only been trying to help.

The mechanical voice lowers a degree. "Maybe if I send you another sliver from your fiancé's face, you'll actually do what I say."

I speed up. The guard hears the motor revving and turns. His face goes quizzical when he sees it's me, and he gives a little wave before angling to the side of the row so that I can pass.

"Good," says Malthus, his robotic voice buzzing in my ear. "Now run him down."

I slam the brakes so hard my chest hits the steering wheel. The butcher paper slides forward. The phone falls from my ear. I leave it on the floor and press the BMW's speaker function so I can keep my hands on the wheel, yet I regret it immediately. The man's voice isn't just piped into one ear anymore. It's penned in the cabin of what is now a steel and glass cage, and the sound folds around me like a straitjacket.

"Krist-i-ine . . ." he calls, taunting me. "You'd better do what I say and chase that man down. You don't want to see what I cut off next."

My gaze falls on the butcher paper at my feet. Daniel's face in my mind, I press the accelerator.

The guard saw my car slam to a halt and stopped at the same time I did. He's bent at the waist as he watches me, and this time one hand is inching toward the radio at his belt. *Run*, I think, and angle the car his way. The casino's sidewalk is only twenty yards. All he has to do is reach the end of the row and bolt across the perpendicular street, and he'll be safe.

Safe from *me*.

I grip the wheel with both hands and rev the engine in warning, pumping the accelerator to try to scare him into a jog. It works. His mouth falls open, and he finally whirls.

"*Drive!*" The word thunders through the car like a bomb.

Drive now. Drive or you will be driven.

The BMW shoots forward, straight at the guard, and I think, *Please run.*

But he'll never make it. He's already slowing, lumbering side to side, too large and unused to being chased. He reaches for the gun at his belt, but fumbles it and it skids across the burning blacktop. Moments later, it disappears beneath my wheels.

"Faster," Malthus orders. "Bump the back of his knees."

I lift my foot instead. The guard is close, and he can make it. There's only ten more feet until the aisle ends.

Daniel's scream rips through the speakers.

I punch the gas, the muscles knotting in my thigh, wheels screeching against the burning asphalt. The cry immediately breaks off, while the guard flees, arms pumping like pistons. Yet he can't run fifteen miles an hour or twenty or twenty-five. And I am closing in.

Suddenly, he dodges. Swerving between the cars on the left side of the aisle, he escapes me, and I fight not to cheer. I'll crash into a Toyota and an SUV if I try to follow and have to punch the brakes just to keep from sliding into the cross street.

Hearing my tires screech over the asphalt, the guard half-turns as he continues to flee. Panting visibly, sweat pours down his face as he locks eyes with me one last time.

I scream.

But he never even sees the van that crushes him from behind.

//////////

My cry scissors the air, sawing in tandem with the van's unnatural jolt as it levers over the guard's body. The vehicle rockets past before I even think to look at the driver, and my foot loosens on the brake so that my car inches forward. I know, yet I still need to see, that the guard was really hit.

He's laid flat, prone in the street, a puddle of blood already widening around his skull. A scream ratchets the air, audible even from the car, and for a moment I think it's another of mine. Then a woman half-trips from the curb, followed by a man, and suddenly the guard is disappearing behind a wall of people, bending, kneeling, all trying to help.

I might not know what to do when my fiancé is kidnapped in the middle of nowhere, but I know exactly what to do in a triage situation, and I throw the gear into park.

"Kristine?"

The flat, mechanized voice is a sharp contrast to the screams and squealing tires still floating in the air.

"Kristine. Are you there?"

My hand is on the door, yet for the first time in years, I hesitate in the face of an emergency.

"I think you'd better get out of there. Someone will have seen you stalking that man. Someone will realize that the driver of the BMW and the driver of the white van may have been working together."

My head jerks as if pulled on a string. "W-we weren't."

"Oh, but the security cameras will show otherwise." The words remain even, but there's laughter there too. I hear it when his words go sibilant, an amused hiss. "After all, you lured him outside—"

"What?" I blink. "No, I—"

"You drove him into my path—"

"No!"

"You killed that man, Kristine."

Blood roars in my ears. It stains my palms. It congeals at my feet.

Did I?

Just then, another security guard sprints from the casino, hand to mouth, yelling into his radio. Catching sight of someone with authority, the woman who was first on the scene rises and, as if in slow motion, points in my direction.

I jerk on the gearshift, and my tires screech as I speed off in the same direction as the van. If I am stopped now, they won't just question my strange behavior toward the guard, they'll find out who I am, and that Daniel has gone missing.

And who is the last person to have seen him as well?

Who will be on the phone records as having talked to him last?

Who has assured his mother that everything is okay but is now driving a car decorated with his blood?

I fly out of the sprawling lot, racing yet barely keeping up. I can't help but stare in my rearview mirror. That poor man. I feel the same way as I do when a patient codes, the consolation of knowing there's nothing more I can do melding with queasy guilt because the last thing I should feel is consoled. Worse, this is a direct hit. I attracted the guard's attention, and in doing so, threw him directly into the path of that van.

Oh God. I killed that man.

The feeling that wells in my chest is concussive. I jerk with it as I remember the cries of another doomed man.

"Good girl," the voice says when I blow through a stop sign. "You're learning. Now head back to the I-15, but pull over before the north ramp. Don't you fucking dare get on that freeway."

I blink against the order and the sweat now finding its way into my eyes. I try to focus on the road ahead of me, but shock has my mind going in reverse, replaying the way the guard's eyes widened on mine and pausing on the word that didn't register then.

It screams in memory now.

Please.

The whimper escapes me as I ease to a halt just before the four-way stop that sits between me and the northbound on-ramp. I'm grateful for the reprieve—it's a chance to catch my breath—but these instructions don't make sense. This is the road leading back to Las Vegas. Why would Malthus make me drive all the way out to the state line just to have me turn back again? Why not send me back to Vegas directly after abducting Daniel from the rest stop?

Why kill an innocent man?

Please.

Malthus's voice pokes at me, too soon. "What's the matter? Are you crying, Kristine? Boo hoo hoo?"

"No," I whisper.

I don't tell him that I never cry. This man would see it as a challenge.

"Good. Pick up the map."

I glance over at the passenger's seat, blinking. I'd forgotten about the map. It'd become inconsequential, innocuous, as soon as I saw the carving of Daniel's face. I fumble it twice and finally manage to prop it between steering wheel and thighs.

"Five stops, Kristine. All on I-15, all well in front of your Lake Arrowhead destination, and lucky you, the Desperado was the first. Only four more to go. Make it to the fifth within twenty-four hours, and you'll see Daniel again in just about one piece."

A game. All I can think as the roar builds in my ears is that he wasn't just ready for this trip—he's been planning it for ten long months.

Another thought slaps me: Lake Arrowhead is less than three hours from here by car.

So why so much time?

"You'll stop only where I've indicated. And you'll speak of this to no one. Otherwise, you can count on someone getting hurt."

Someone already had.

"I don't know if you can tell, but I've done this before."

"And if I play this game," I finally ask, swallowing hard. "If I make it out of the desert, you'll let Daniel go?"

"If you make it out of this desert . . . all will be well."

That's no answer, and we both know it. His words are too cryptic to mean what I hope, but what choice do I have?

He reads my mind. "Of course, you can always go home."

My gaze whips to the northbound on-ramp. I can't help it. Home, like I wished. Home with Abby. Home, where I wanted to be all along.

"No one would blame you," Malthus is saying. "And you could go back to sleep. Back to surrounding yourself with all your things, piling them up high so that they bury today's events, numb you to what you did. You'll be able to forget all about it. But . . . "

But.

"You'll have to forget him too."

Daniel, with his unending patience, brilliant mind, clever hands, and kind nature. Daniel, with his lopsided smile, throaty laugh, sweetly curved cock, wide feet, and warm cocooning flesh. Daniel, who lined up the labels in his medicine cabinet, yet forgot coffee cups in every room.

Daniel gone, and I would have to forget him too.

I close my eyes.

"Maybe you need a little help to decide."

"No!" I jerk upright, spine cracking as I listen for Daniel's scream.

But it's Malthus's tinny voice that crawls into the car again. It takes me two whole breaths to realize he's no longer speaking to me. "Yes, hi, I'd like to report a suspicious vehicle."

My gaze darts to my rearview mirror.

"It's a white BMW parked on the side of the road just beyond your property," he goes on, and even though his voice still sounds mechanized to me, I know now that he has two phones, and the masking device is attached only to mine.

"No, I can't make out who's inside," he says, "but there seems to be blood on the front grill. And a big dent."

The lie cuts through my sense of disbelief and I jerk the car into gear.

"Oh, really? He could be dangerous?" My tormentor inhales, the sound sizzling in the car. I catch a break in the oncoming traffic and swing out onto the asphalt. "No. No, I won't go any closer. Of course. You're welcome. Hope you catch them."

I pull even with the stop sign.

"You better hurry," Malthus tells me. "They're coming."

It's a four-way stop, and the driver to my left waves me through. I ease my foot off the brake, inching forward, then panic and jerk to a halt. A horn blares behind me. The cars are stacking up, but if I move even five feet forward, the Las Vegas exit will be lost to me. Shaking his head, the other driver shoots me the finger and lead-foots it through the light. I just stare at the road in front of me, so bright in the afternoon sun that it blinds me.

"C'mon, Kristine. Don't choke now. Not if you want to see him again."

I need more time.

Yellow-white strobes flash into view in the rearview mirror. A white security truck is four cars and five hundred feet behind me. I bite my lip and taste blood.

"How far will you go to save him, Kristine?" Malthus's metal-lic voice taunts. "How much do you really care?"

Something shifts inside of me at that, uncoiling as if abruptly awakened, though it's probably been lying in wait since being prodded by the truck driver back before Primm, the one who set my temper flaring with a mere look. All I know for sure is that it's reptilian in nature and born of this desert, and it rears up now to meet Malthus's liquid-mercury voice with venomous intent.

He does not want to see how far I can go.

I floor the gas anyway.

"Twenty-four hours," Malthus reminds me. And the phone goes dead.

Chasing that voice, I veer onto the I-15, glancing back only once to make sure I'm not being followed. I'm half a mile into

California before the blood stops rushing in my ears and my sight clears enough of that toxic haze to catch Buffalo Bill's Casino disappearing in the rearview mirror. The heat haze shimmers atop the road, as if what lies behind me is something I just made up. Like my whole life has been a dream, but now I've been jolted awake.

Just in time to watch it all fall away.

10

I'm a Big Boy.

Remaining cool under pressure is a prerequisite for a physician assistant, and I am a great PA.

I am water under pressure, liquid and adaptive. As Daniel says, I flow. Maybe that's why, after my breathing has slowed, and the shock has settled more deeply into my bones, I don't drive to Baker as much as I point the car in that direction and just let go. *Check your own pulse.* It's the first axiom I learned in the ER.

Thus, I am not unaware of the way anger has overtaken me twice now in the last hour. I know exactly what's going on here; I have the language for it, because I also put myself through therapy for four years, mostly due to flashes of temper like the one I've just exhibited. This is stress manifesting itself as fury. It's been brought on by terror, and at being thrust back into the god-forsaken desert, where things like water, things that flow, don't get buried. They get absorbed.

I *told* Daniel I couldn't get caught in the fucking desert.

I run a hand over my forehead, swipe at the sweat clinging to my hairline and stamp down the thought. Anger at Daniel is misdirected; he's as much a victim in this as I am. But God, if anything can dismantle the armor I've spent the last decade methodically hammering into place, it is this unforgiving sand trap. There is no flow out here, you cannot be soft. You can only hone yourself on the desert's edges until you are as brittle as flint.

Yet even as I hurtle alone past bright, blooming Indian paintbrush and curled-limbed creosote I am keenly aware that there's something else that would be even worse, a thing that would undo me altogether.

I don't care what Malthus has commanded. Fuck him—I call Maria as soon as my blood slows and my breathing levels out. The need to hear Abby's voice is like metal in my throat, persistent and stabbing. My palms tingle with it, the itch of beetles under the skin. My womb feels hollow and gutted, even though it's been ten long years since my child resided there. Having a baby is like growing a pair of legs for your heart and then letting it walk around outside your body, beating and raw and vulnerable. I have never felt this more than I do now.

Normally I will try out my Spanglish on Maria, piece together my *por favor*s with prepositions that swing wildly into English. It's a game, and Maria corrects me, laughing or stitching together her own Spanglish in reverse, and we stumble our way toward understanding while Abby just sits there and glows.

But this call goes directly to Maria's voicemail, and I growl in frustration, immediately disconnecting and dialing again. I tell myself not to worry—she always takes Abby to cool off at one of the valley's parks, water features spouting liquid relief in the late afternoon. Or maybe they're at the *panadería*, picking out sweet *empanadas* or *pan fino*. My daughter comes home from Maria's sugar-dusted and trilling her Rs.

My hands still shake when I get Maria's voicemail again.

"Abby," is all I manage when it's time for me to leave a message. My voice is as scratchy as rough wool. I struggle to remember what else to say—what else is there?—but I can't even find the words in English now. My worry finally tumbles out of me like bricks. There is no flow. "Maria, it's Kris. I need you to call me as soon as possible. It's important."

I don't add *por favor*. I am not joking this time.

Ten months.

I mean, of course Malthus has to know about Abby. Yet I tell myself that she is out of reach all the way back in Las Vegas, in Maria's bright home with its corner altars, safe in the wingspan of her sturdy brown limbs. Yes, he has planned this journey, the next twenty-four hours, for me, but he can't be in two places at once. Besides, I have proof that she's fine. Daniel snapped a photo with his smartphone when he dropped her off, an overexposed image that captured both nanny and child frowning directly into the afternoon sun. He showed it to me less than twenty minutes later, as we pulled away from the hospital's porte cochere. We were at the rest stop only a half an hour after that. And Malthus was too.

Because Malthus wants me to *prove* my love for Daniel.

Why?

Laughter escapes me in a hoarse bark. I can't even count the times I've heard that exact sentiment from families in the waiting room as they pace, wringing their hands, lips stitching together a prayer drowned out by cable news. God, I hate that room. It reminds me of my mother's lopsided trailer, both places sound-proofed with grief, padded with tears, ghostly regrets priming the walls: *Why her? Why him? Why me?*

Why?

Like those in the waiting room, like my mother, I have no idea.

Thus far, it appears you've gotten by in life on good looks and a lot of lip service.

Untrue. I busted my butt to escape that sorry excuse of a home. I moved to Las Vegas as a single mother and made sure Abby wanted for nothing while I saved up tuition money for med school, one quarter—and one sticky, watered-down cocktail—at a time. And when I was accepted? Between coursework and motherhood and therapy, I found a new maxim to replace that ghostly why: *Primum non nocere.*

First, do no harm.

Yes, every medical student takes the Hippocratic Oath upon graduating, and no, technically I haven't done that. I'm not a doctor. But working alongside trauma surgeons in the OR as a PA is damn close, and I don't need a different degree or piece of paper to swear that oath in my own heart. I've cracked open chest cavities and kept an actual heart pumping with my own bare hands. Moreover, I believe those words—I do. They helped me cement my place in the world, and with them—because of them—I have built a good life.

I've also learned, over time, that *do no harm* extends to me as well.

An image flashes: the guard being flattened beneath the chassis of a speeding van. Daniel's scream visits me too, and I squeeze the glossy steering wheel so hard it should pop in my palm. Forget my mother, forget the question why. I'm even willing to put Abby and Maria aside, just for now. A killer waits for me in Baker, and for whatever insane reason, he believes I need to be taught a life lesson.

I've done this before.

What needs to be my new worry.

What now? What next?

The answer to that, at least, is as clear in my mind as Daniel's face. Both appear whole and solid in my imagination, as yet untouched by Malthus and his sick designs.

What now? I think, shifting in my seat. Whatever it takes.

God knows *I've* done that before.

///////////

I ease into Baker from an off-ramp the length of an airport runway and am greeted by a tumbleweed that skitters alongside my car on a bullwhip of scalding wind. It matches my pace for a few yards before wheeling off to attack a steel fence penning back trailers that are almost violently ugly.

Seconds later, a text:

I'm a Big Boy.

"You're a big psycho," I mutter, and blow out a breath that's round with nerves, but at least this is an obvious clue. Big Boy is a hamburger joint hunkered down on the east side of the street, pinned there like a thumbtack around the time that Googie architecture was a new thing. A motel—seriously, just named *Motel*—springs catercorner to it like an old dusty hinge.

That's where I need to go, I think, attention fixed on that sagging, no-name motel. It has not fared as well as the restaurant, because it doesn't serve burgers, but I'd bet my life savings that the place still smells like rancid grease. Its length shields the majority of the surrounding terrain, save the soaring arch of the next on-ramp, where a freight truck can be seen trying to pick up speed before merging back onto the highway.

Anyone inside that motel has a wide-open view of Baker's main drag, and that makes my fingers twitch on the wheel, my toes flex in my flats. I want to see if a white van with a blood-splattered grille sits on the other side of that building. I want a clear view of the street too. Yet it's obvious from the timing of the text that Malthus is already here, and that he's still watching me somehow, so I obediently wheel into the restaurant's lot instead.

Gravel crackles under the tires as I pull to a stop beneath a scrap of shade supplied by Baker's most notable feature. It is a vertical monstrosity, both eyesore and icon, a scrap of chipped metal billed as the world's largest thermometer. My thighs squeak against the leather seat as I lean forward and squint up at the reading—108 degrees.

Double that if you're being chased by a madman.

I have just curled my fingers around the door handle when I spot the blood dotting my left palm. It's caked beneath my nail beds too. I'd reached back while driving and tucked the sliver of Daniel's face into the empty cooler behind the seat, and a swift glance in the mirror reveals more blood on my cheek, a streaking memento of my run-in with the guard. I lunge for the glove compartment and the wet wipes I know Daniel keeps there, and as I rub away blood and the rest of the dried coffee, I can't help but wonder what else I've almost missed.

What am I missing still?

I grab Daniel's phone and wipe that down too, and when I'm done I knot my sweaty hair atop my head and pat everything into place. There. Both the car and I are once again presentable. Nothing to draw attention to me now. Not unless I start wailing for no reason anyway, and I just might.

Steadying my breath, I have just touched the door again when Daniel's phone rings and Imogene Hawthorne's name flashes up from my lap. Damn it. I'd let it go to voicemail, but she's relentless when it comes to her son. Her possessiveness is such a cliché that I thought she was joking the first time we visited and she asked Daniel to escort her on a lakeside walk of the property. Alone. I wonder how she'd feel knowing that he rolls his eyes at most everything she says. Or that he claims she has a knack for calling at just the wrong time. Given that, do I dare answer?

Do I dare not?

Shifting my eyes to the rearview mirror, I press the speaker function on the phone without lifting it to my ear. That way I am both obeying Malthus—*you will speak of this to no one*—and ridding myself of my future mother-in-law at the same time. I am both answering and not. "Hello?"

The only response is silence.

"Hello?" I repeat, thinking I've missed the call.

"Hello, dear." Imogene's voice, normally aloof, shoots out suddenly, like a cartoon bubble blooming overhead. It sounds

79

swollen with uncertainty, which I understand. I've never an-swered Daniel's phone in the year we've been dating, and now I've done so twice in one afternoon. On the upside, this could dissuade Imogene from calling again, at least for a while.

"Imogene. I—we—were just about to call you. We've had to turn around. Daniel, um, forgot some critical case files at the house and he needs to complete them this weekend."

"Oh dear."

"Yes." *Oh dear.* "I'm afraid we're going to be a while yet."

"I see." More silence stretches over the line and my gaze darts to the motel. Green trim peels from the windows, and black doors dot its long side. It looks like a snake shedding its skin. I search its length for movement. "What are you wearing, dear?"

I have to blink a few times before finding my voice. "I'm sorry, what?"

"I'm asking because some of the party guests have arrived early." Imogene pauses. "So they'll be here for your arrival."

I would laugh at that if I wasn't worried the sound would spiral off into that waiting scream.

I'm wearing shorts with your son's blood staining the backside, you uptight moron. I'm wearing ballet flats I can't run in and a damn bull's-eye on my chest. How about that? "Um . . . linen shorts, a sweater set. Ballet flats."

"Well. That's . . . good."

Seriously, this woman. I don't have time for this. What I have is twenty-four hours and a missing fiancé. "Uh huh. Yes, well, please tell *our* guests we'll be there as quickly as—" The blare of a horn cuts across the line, and I jolt. "Are you driving?"

"Yes. I'm headed to the store," Imogene says quickly.

"You mean the village?"

"Of course." Now she's irritated. "We are fresh out of pitted olives."

"Olives."

"For the martinis."

For cocktails. I close my eyes. "Okay. Good-bye, Imogene."

"Well, drive safe dear, and please tell Daniel—"

I press END CALL, then answer her in the thick silence. "Sorry, Imogene. But if I do this right, you'll be able to tell him yourself."

When I push the door open, all 108 degrees of desert heat pounces on my bare shoulders. I stand under its weight and shade my eyes with one palm. The late afternoon sun makes a mirror of the diner's plate-glass windows, reflecting back the elderly couple who are taking turns posing for photos with the giant plastic figurine out front. He is, literally, a Big Boy.

The man flings one arm over the statue's sunbaked shoulders while pretending to take a bite of the enormous sun-bleached hamburger. The woman squints at the screen of her camera phone, and a stray dog lies there and looks on, likely wishing the burger were real.

I tie the sleeves of my new cashmere sweater around my waist, covering the bloodstains I know are on my shorts, and wait until the couple heads off to their Oldsmobile. I limp to the front door as they pull from the lot, casting a quick glance at the stray mutt as I go. It's some sort of terrier mix, and it shifts its watchful but hopeless brown eyes my way before actually sighing, deeply unimpressed.

I jerk my head at the black crows strutting along the lot's

jagged edge, identical to those that littered the rest stop where Daniel was taken. "Why don't you eat *them*?" I tell it.

The little dog can't even be bothered to lift his head from his paws, and I, too, am without real interest. My mind is already in the diner. I am thinking of maps and clues and Daniel—*DanielDanielDaniel*—and I'm thinking of a killer too. I yank the door open to find out which one waits for me inside.

11

So much for not being noticed.

I pause just inside the diner to acclimate myself. The blast of frozen air and the glare of fluorescent lights are a shock after the hot solitary drive, and the sight of real people doing normal things makes me feel like I've stepped back in time, to when my own life was real. This alienness is amplified by the jaunty tune piping from a vintage jukebox. "Rock Around the Clock." I recognize it from junior high sock hops. That was another lifetime ago too.

A hostess station sits unoccupied in front of me, while a glass wall separates the entry from the main dining area. It doesn't take long to scan each customer. The diner isn't even a quarter full, and my gaze instantly catches on a lone man seated in a booth alongside the long bank of windows. He's thin, and even though he's sitting, I can tell he is tall. He wears sun-cut lines in his face and a severe military buzz cut. He didn't glance up as I entered, and, engrossed in his meal, he doesn't look up now.

The only other single man sits at the diner's long counter, but the expectation falls from his face when he sees only me standing there, shivering in this new-old world. Two other parties are coupled up—could Malthus have a partner?—and a third is busy attending to a trio of sweaty-faced children. No knives. No workman's overalls. No Daniel.

"Booth or counter, sweetie?"

The waitress calls out from behind the counter, and I blinked dumbly. I have no idea. I am like a child suddenly—I need to be told where to sit. So, like a child, I opt for the homey warmth of the counter, where I can hear the fry cook slamming plates and the waitress is never far away. Her nametag reads LACY. Lacy's frilly white apron flares atop her powder pink uniform as she whirls to pour me water without being asked.

No sooner does my bottom hit the red plastic stool than Daniel's phone chimes in my hand. A text.

Order pie.

I spin on my stool, but the man at the window is still engrossed in his meal, no phone in sight. One couple *is* texting, thumbs flying over momentarily forgotten meals, but the other couple uses the timeworn excuse of eating to ignore each other. The kids continue to wiggle in their booster seats.

I turn back around, jumping when I find myself face-to-face with Lacy. She bears a menu in one hand, my water glass in the other, and her dark eyebrows lift high at my reaction. I remember that I can't do anything to make someone remember me here, not like back at Primm, so I fold my hands atop the gold-specked Formica and nod at the tiered plastic pastry stand. "I'll have some pie, please."

Lacy gasps, surprising me. Her eyes light up, dark irises flaring, and she props her elbows atop the counter as she leans forward. A tiny diamond chip winks at me from the left side of her nose. "What kind of pie?"

I don't really care, but it's clear that Lacy does, so I make a show of studying the display case where pies the size of the state rotate on mechanized plates. "Uh, apple, I guess."

Lacy's face falls.

"What?" I ask, as she straightens.

She shakes her head as she swings opens the plastic door and pulls out the apple tin. "Nothing. It's just that I've been waiting for someone. They're supposed to order the cherry pie, though."

"Cherry," I blurt before Lacy can cut into the pie. "I mean, yeah, it's me. I'll take the cherry instead."

Lacy tilts her head, knife hovering. "Then why didn't you order cherry in the first place?"

"I . . . forgot. I-it's been a long day."

"Where are you headed, sweetie?"

She says it like it's the bonus question on a test, and I freeze, wondering what to say. Again, I settle on the truth. "Lake Arrowhead."

"It *is* you!" Lacy's voice goes frothy, whipped and dreamy as she exchanges the apple for the cherry. "Aw, this is all so romantic!"

And for some reason she slides the entire cherry pie in front of me.

"I wish my boyfriend would set up a treasure hunt for *me*." She misses my shudder at the word *boyfriend*, still beaming as she crosses her arms so that her nametag tilts and disappears into her cleavage. "He told me all about it. Said he was leaving you breadcrumbs that would lead you back to him. That it'd be a trip you'd never forget. I mean, how exciting."

You will speak of this to no one.

"Is he . . . here?"

Lacy's hoop earrings swing like a pendulum as she tilts her head. "What do you mean?"

"I mean, you don't see him here now, do you?"

Lacy stares like I'm the one suddenly speaking in riddles. "Don't you know what your own boyfriend looks like?"

I jerk my head. That's not what I mean. "Of course, I was just thinking . . . maybe he's hiding somewhere nearby to make sure I figure out each clue."

"As if I'd tell you." She winks at me like we're partners in this, then instantly shrugs it all away. "Just so you know, and not to ruin anything—I haven't seen him since last week. I been coming in every day since, waiting through the lunch crowd, then the dinner crowd, and still you don't come. Feels like I've been sitting on this pie forever—was hoping it wouldn't go bad before you finally showed up. Well?" Lacy gestured to the pie.

"Oh." I glanced down, then back at Lacy. "Aren't you going to cut it?"

"No, ma'am." The diamond chip winks, the hoops swing, the eyes glow. "He said you'd want to eat it all. His exact words were, and I quote, 'Kristine Rush is an absolute glutton for experience.'"

I deflate right there on that plastic swivel stool. So much for not being noticed.

A long strand of hair has fallen from my topknot, and I tuck it behind my right ear before lifting my fork. Lacy hovers, and I realize she intends to watch me eat every bite. Her hand twitches like she wants to feed me herself, but the man at the other end of the counter holds up his thick coffee mug and asks for a refill. He and Lacy immediately start whispering, stealing glances at me as I begin disassembling the pie.

"Now that's what I like to see," the man finally says, his complexion ruddy as he grins my way. His voice booms, Midwestern friendly. "A woman with an appetite."

I glance at his feet, but they're clad in worn-in runners, not boots, so I look away.

The first few bites are heaven, plump with tart cherries, warm with flaky crust. Yet all I taste after that is glazed lard, corn syrup, and fruit stripped of all nutrition. I shovel it in, stave off a gag, and—I know it's vain, I do; I know this is not the time—but I can't help but think of all the hours I've logged on the treadmill, the calories recorded in the kitchen notebook back home. Like Imogene's phone calls, these various thoughts rear their heads at the wrong time, and that flips over the discipline that I'm so proud of, turning it into vanity. So I ignore the acidic burn in my throat and think of Daniel instead.

"Why are you so vigilant about that?" he once asked, watching me calculate my caloric intake at the end of the day. "You look great. Why obsess over the calories in a pack of Splenda? Even in a pack of Emergen-C?"

We weren't engaged at the time, but I was already dreaming of it: a gasp-inspiring ring, delivered to me with wet eyes, on one knee. A brief period of betrothal, those halcyon days between girlfriend and wife hung like a banner for all to see, and then a white silk dress that would change my life. Change *me*.

I couldn't tell him all of that, though, so I started talking about my mother instead. "Janie Mae Rush," I said, putting down my pencil, "lived on whiskey-and-cigarette breakfasts, and as far as she was concerned, I could do the same. She put a lock on the cupboard and the key around her neck. She said I needed to earn real food for myself."

Daniel gaped, slack-jawed, like I knew he would. Imogene hadn't just provided for him; she'd likely given him every bite of food off of her plate as well.

"How old were you?" he finally managed.

I pursed my lips, cast my gaze up, thinking. "Ten, the first time? Eleven?"

I wasn't sure—all I knew was that I stayed hungry for a while before I started stealing a little and begging a lot. I was babysitting by eleven. I found full-time work before it was legal to do so—small towns don't worry much about that—and I did finally bring home real food.

I even remember the crackle of the bags as I unloaded an entire paycheck's worth of food: whole milk, thick as whipping cream on my parched tongue. Crisp greens that'd never seen a freezer. A bag of apples handpicked by me, each one polished to a deep shine.

When my mother saw the spread, her mouth thinned into nothingness. "You think your food is better than anything I could give you? Is that what you think? Don't you know?"

"Don't I know what?"

"It can all kill you if you let it."

And then she sat me down and made me eat it all at once.

"I had a stomachache for two days," I said, not looking at Daniel. "And I never really got over how food, something vital, something that could sustain you, could also be used against you."

I never forgot how something so basic to survival could hurt you if you let it.

Wiping my mouth, I envision Malthus listening to this story with his wiretaps or bugs or whatever the hell he's used to spy on me. The thought makes my stomach churn, and I'm not even a quarter of the way through the pie. I glance up to find Lacy and the man still smiling at me.

"The whole thing?" I ask, and Lacy just laughs. *How romantic! How exciting!* I clear my throat, dislodging syrup and phlegm. "But then I get something in return, right?"

"Your next map." Lacy's hoop earrings swing again as she nods. Tick-tock.

I eat faster, pondering—for the first time in my life—the merits of bulimia, and how they might apply to me. I'm only vaguely aware of Lacy and the man renewing some previous argument over the motel across the street being haunted. I tune out his babble, something about meeting an online friend there, and automate the process of shoving gooey cherry between my lips. *Chewchewchew.* I swallow past the growing knot of bile in my throat, and I repeat; shove, chew, swallow.

Then, on a hiccup, I realize the man is talking to me.

"What do *you* think? Does the motel look haunted or not? I mean, it's ripe for a ghost orgy, right?"

I wince, and he holds up a hand in apology.

"Sorry. I'm just excited. I've decided to be like those guys on

TV. The ones who travel the country looking for paranormal activity." Every one of his statements curl upward like questions. I am not overly worried for the ghosts. "My buddy and I are gonna stake it out and film all night, as long as it takes. So what do you think?"

I think I'm not in the mood for another stranger with crazy, unanswerable questions.

Sighing, I look back down at my endless pie. Still a third left and my tongue is swollen, the roof of my mouth buzzes, and the sugar high is making my head swim. Meanwhile, my stomach grows heavier with each forced bite. I stare at the fat cherries remaining in the tin until they almost seem to glare back. We are in a contest of wills, the dessert and me, and of course I blink first.

And that's when I see the slip of paper, singed and baked into the bottom of the pie tin.

12

He thinks I'm being friendly.

Pushing aside cherries with my fingers, I tug free one burned edge of the otherwise soggy slip of paper. It's too small to be a map, but my heart still pounds, boosted by the sugar coursing through my blood stream.

This is my next clue, a way to find Daniel, and against all reason it gives me hope. Maybe running over the guard was an aberration, an impulse on Malthus's part. Maybe, if I do as he says and keep to the script, he'll feel no need to act impulsively. Maybe the rest of this journey will be simply a series of notes tucked into cherry pies.

I free the paper and drop it flat, smearing cherry glaze across the counter. I wait until Lacy heads to the dining room, arms full with plates, her attention on soggy fries and bacon strips and chicken paste that's been pressed into nugget shapes, before I peel open the paper. The writing inside is blurred from heat and sugar, but it's still legible. And it's not writing, but numbers.

My fledgling hope plummets, a shot bird inside of my chest, and I have to close my eyes for just one moment. When I open them again, I push aside the paper I no longer need, that I never needed, and pick up Daniel's phone. I don't key in the numbers—I just go to the contacts list, find my name, and push CALL.

"There is a man near you." No salutations. No small talk from that self-assured, altered voice. He doesn't even ask if I enjoyed the pie. "He is alone, wearing a collared work shirt and khaki shorts. Do you see him?"

Of course. I'd been talking to him about ghosts not two minutes earlier . . . but Malthus probably knows that too.

"You're going to approach him." His voice goes gravelly, or maybe it's just the device deepening his tone. Either way, his words rasp over the line, scraping at my eardrum. "Stand before him, and make sure you have his full attention. And then, do you know what I want you to do?"

He tells me, and the cherries and pie crust in my stomach revolt, threatening to wind up back in the tin and all over the counter.

Malthus has somehow guessed at my greatest fear. It's as if he really does know me, but then I imagine you can learn a lot about a person via surveillance for ten long months. As he talks, my too-fast heart lifts and lodges next to my larynx and the cherries, while the adrenaline pounds so loudly in my head that I almost miss his final order: Malthus wants to hear every word.

The silence shifts again, this time into a watching, waiting thing. Lacy returns from the dining room, earrings still marking time. Tick-tock. I wipe my mouth and slowly stand.

Malthus is a silent presence, resting in my palm, phone down at my side. I take the first step, reminding myself that Daniel is traversing the entire Mojave Desert with this madman. A short walk across the diner is nothing.

Lacy's pouring fresh coffee into yet another battered mug, but I feel her glance up when I pass. I imagine that the rest of the room is watching me as well, but I keep my eyes fastened on the thin commercial carpeting, black chains linking busy, bursting blooms. I imagine those chains tightening about my ankles with every step. The only way to keep from being trapped in place, I tell myself, is to keep moving.

I look up only after I reach the man, and then I focus my gaze on the blue and white squares of his work shirt.

Be polite.

After all, Malthus said, it wasn't this man's fault that Daniel had been taken.

I reach out and tap his shoulder. "Excuse me."

The man turns, and so does Lacy, but I don't dare look at her. I try to lick my lips, but my tongue sticks to the roof of my mouth, cemented there by cherries. Humiliation. "I'm sup-posed . . . supposed to . . ."

My voice just fades away, as if someone turned a dial and reduced the volume. Swallowing hard, I jerk my head and try again. "I need to ask your name."

The man's expression shifts into one of surprise before a smile quickly blooms. He thinks I'm being friendly. "It's Henry. Henry Becker."

My nod is a spasm, and I don't offer my own name. Malthus didn't order me to, likely because Lacy already knows it. Now for the hard part. The precise phrasing is important.

Say every single word.

I look down and see that my fingers are white-tipped. They'd be curled into fists were it not for the phone. I force them to relax, take a breath so deep that I could use it to dive into white-water rapids, and then I stare directly into Henry Becker's open, inquisitive face.

"I want to suck you off right on this counter."

The open expression on Henry Becker's face shatters, replaced by incomprehension, shock, and finally a dust-devil look that pitches me back in time, drops me back into another tumbleweed town. If the ability to cry hadn't been cauterized from me eighteen years ago, I swear I'd start wailing right now. Instead, I look at Henry and see another man's face wearing this exact expression as he takes in the length of my body. I lie brown-limbed and candlelit, like a virgin to be sacrificed in exchange for favors from the gods.

I force out the rest of my scripted words in a hard stammer. "Please. You'll be doing me a favor. Let me blow you away."

I clench my jaw, hoping Henry can read in my flat tone, the lost inflection, that I don't mean a word of it. That I don't really want to say this or be here—not in the diner, not in the desert—not in a world where a man like Malthus can exist at all.

It strikes me for the first time, as I try not to sway where I stand, that maybe *that's* what he's after with all of this: the spin on the roller coaster, the maps, the pie. The thrill of it all. He has me boxed in, unable to turn to another person for help even in the clatter of a busy diner, and I certainly can't turn back around.

Destroying my desire to live, I suddenly realize, might be more important to Malthus than destroying my life.

A handful of shocked seconds pass before laughter erupts from Henry, a belly-blast that has him sliding one elbow on the greasy counter as he squares up on me with that decades-old look. I force myself to hold still under the weight of that stare. I am a statue; I am a rock in the desert. I will not be absorbed by those assessing eyes. Meanwhile, the phone at my side crackles under the assault of mechanized laughter. The out-of-body feeling intensifies, and I wonder, am I floating?

"I-I'm not sure what to say." Henry blinks, trying to make sense of my actions. "What are you doing?"

I can't blame him for the question, but I can curse him because I have my orders: if Henry questions me at all, I have to keep talking. And, as I've already noted, Henry makes every goddamn statement sound like a question.

"I want you to dominate me. I want you to slap me as you come on my face."

Poor Henry. He's still operating under real-world assumptions—that the earth is round and that people are basically good and that you are always in control of your own actions. He looks at me with naked concern.

And continues to ask stupid questions.

"Seriously," he says, shaking his head. "What are you doing?"

"I'll fucking kill you if I can't have you inside of me," I say obediently, by rote.

Suddenly, Lacy is there, palms slapping the countertop as she leans over it. "That's enough. No one wants to hear nasty talk like that in here."

Thank God. I blow out a relieved breath, but hunch under the weight of Lacy's glare.

"What's wrong with you? I thought you were a nice lady. You want to sell your body, then go to the truck pit like all them other hookers. But you ain't doing that in this establishment. We have standards."

Yes. I could tell from the plastic statue out front.

"I had to," I whisper.

Lacy crosses her arms. "No one *has* to go round talking like that. Don't you have any self-respect?"

Sure, three hours ago when I still knew who I was, where I was. But that woman, and that reality, feels as far off as Daniel now.

Lacy points to the door. "Get out."

That's the signal that I can disconnect my call, and I do so quickly before slumping where I stand. I can't leave, though, because I still need the next map. Face burning, I force my gaze back up to Lacy's, but she's wearing the look I dread. I haven't seen it for years, but I know it well.

Krissy's momma is an ore whore! Krissy's gonna grow up to be a den hen just like her momma!

I shake off the memory's lilting scorn, a dog shedding water. Forget those girls. If I leave without this map—and that's exactly what Malthus intends—then the pie, the degradation, the entire stop in Baker, will have been for nothing.

Except to accomplish Malthus's real purpose in sending me here.

I remember her well, Henry will be quoted as saying. *She said she'd kill me if she couldn't have me.*

What respectable, sane woman would utter such nastiness in public? Lacy's quote will be accompanied by a photo displaying her own respectably starched pink uniform. She will pose behind a perfect slice of flaky cherry pie. *And who eats a whole pie in one sitting?*

"I had to do it, like a dare," I tell Lacy now that Malthus can't hear. I don't know what he'll do if he finds out, but I don't care about that now. I need that map. "It's part of my . . ." What was the word Lacy had used? "Treasure hunt."

The woman's hands were in fists atop her pink polyester-clad hips. "You're telling me your boyfriend wanted you to use that foul language on a total stranger?"

I wince. "Yes."

Lacy shakes her head, points to the door again. "Out."

I don't remember moving. All I know is that one moment I'm standing atop bright blooms and black chains, and the next I'm at the counter that Lacy thinks she owns. I could slap her twice before she backs away. "Give me the map."

The face I should have already hit now twists. The diamond sparks as her nostrils flare. "I ain't giving you nothing, 'cept one last chance to walk out that door."

I run my hands over my head and have to fight not to pull at my hair. Another old feeling comes back to me, another blast from my dusty youth. It's an urge to respond as I did to those barren schoolyard taunts, long before I worked in health care, before I swore to do no harm. Instead, I clench the phone in front of me, preventing fists. "Okay, I'm gone. But just tell me what the man who gave you the map looked like. Any defining features? Did he give you a name? Anything?"

Lacy shakes her head side to side, so slowly, so considered, that this time her earrings don't sway. I remember that Henry is next to me, hanging on every word. I feel his gaze still raking my body, breaking it into usable parts. I feel Lacy noting that too.

"Lacy," I say, closing my eyes, searching for control.

"What?"

Ore whore, ore whore, ore . . .

My eyelids flip open. "Give me the fucking map!"

The curse whips out, a lash of fury so loud that Lacy actually takes a step back. Then a matching tempest flares in her eyes, though instead of forming fists, she reaches for the phone.

I hold up my hands, surrendering as I back away. No way will anyone in this diner forget me now. And I know small towns. The sheriff can be here in moments. I can't imagine a worse way to blow the bulk of the next twenty-four hours than trapped in county jail.

I pause just long enough to toss some cash on the counter next to the pie with a crater carved in its red middle. Fifties music blares, telling me to return to sender, but instead I find myself fleeing under the heavy weight of Lacy's exacting stare, under Henry's thunderstruck one, and just as Malthus had intended all along: totally empty-handed.

13

I see exactly how this is going to go now.

Bursting from the diner in a near-run, I have to fight to control my limbs, my reeling mind. It's hard when I'm as hot on the inside as it is outside, and when the summer heat attacks once again, I feel like I could ignite. *I'm such an idiot*, I think, my thoughts red, all my long-dormant rage turning inward as I begin to pace.

I wonder what I could've done differently, what I can do next. Only now can I see how I fell right into Malthus's trap. He never had any intention of letting me leave that diner, or Baker, unnoticed.

I cover my face with my hands, breathing deeply, trying to regroup. I feel watched—either by Malthus or by someone in the diner—but I don't care. I just block out the searing sunlight, reducing my five senses to four. It might appear to an onlooker that I'm about to cry—but that's a thought that's laughable in itself.

I once told Daniel this during scrub-up, just off-handedly mentioning it in order to reassure him that the eight-year-old trauma victim we were about to operate on wouldn't affect me, not professionally. Not the way he thought.

He was startled by my words, though, and he angled himself to try and force my gaze. Only then did I remember that people didn't say such things, which made me regret saying anything at all. The water steamed, his hands reddening as I watched, yet he held them steady beneath the gushing stream of water, as if that could hold me steady too. I appreciated it, but I still squirmed beneath his worried gaze.

"What do you mean you don't cry?" he asked softly.

"I mean tears will well in my eyes if you pinch me, but that's just a reaction to physical discomfort. I'll tear up if my eyes are too dry or if I'm facing a cold wind or something like that, but my eyes don't get moist just from emotion."

"Never?" he pressed, amazed.

I shook my head. "I can't remember the last time."

That's a lie. I can bring back that shattered night in razor-edged detail, right down to the scent of blasted sulfur and the hot spatter of my father's blood on my skin. Yet it's as if that experience somehow cauterized my tear ducts, searing them so that they remain forever divorced from my emotions. I haven't shed a tear in the eighteen years since. Not when my mother died. Not even when Abby was born. I'd worry about the latter except that I also remember eventually taking great pride in her fierce, lusty newborn wails.

That's right, I thought, staring into that perfect, pink face. *Rage against the world for its injustices. Rail against all that's unfair. Weep for us both.*

Yet I hadn't been sure enough of Daniel at this time—or convinced that he was sure enough of *me*—to say any of that. And when he finally moved, pulling hands as red as lobsters from beneath that streaming water, he shook his head as he stared down at me. "Why, that's just . . ."

Unnatural, I thought. *Unfeminine, unbelievable, unattractive.* I looked away, but Daniel reached out, and in a move that's since become habit, pressed his fingertips along my jaw and forced my gaze back to his. "Incredible."

Yes, I have a past that can rear up to send me into spiraling silences. Sure, I take the graveyard shift for the sole purpose of turning the hated darkness of night back into day. But Daniel's acceptance of all that is how I face down the censure I see flickering in Imogene's gaze. It's how I combat my mother's intrusive, ghostly scorn. And it's why I can think of the future with hopefulness rather than the black bloom of emptiness that'd been there before, as dark and deep as an abandoned mine.

With Daniel at my side, why would I ever need to cry again?

Exhaling hard now, I empty the hot breath from my belly and try to be present, try to think. Daniel claims I'm at my best in an emergency, so I recast this crisis and pretend I'm in the OR.

What's the diagnosis for someone who has attracted a madman? What's the cure, I wonder, when being chased by pure evil?

I glance over to find that the stray terrier has settled into the shade provided by my car. Attuned to threat, it tilts its head the moment my eyes alight on its wiry fur. I have a sudden vision, a flash of me showing up to the estate, Daniel safely at my side, and this drooling black mutt tucked beneath my arm. Imogene Hawthorne has something called an Affenpinscher that she carries that way. It, too, is wiry, though inbreeding has given it a superiority complex this pitiful creature will never possess. It snapped at me every time I looked at it.

"Purebred," Imogene said then, staring directly at me with her arctic eyes. I didn't blink, so she decided to elucidate. "Those with superior pedigree possess a sensory perception that operates on a plane ordinary beings cannot begin to intuit."

It was a lot of words for a simple put-down, and they all came back to me under the steady gaze of the skinny, dehydrated, flea-bitten beast hunched in the shade of my car. This dog might not exist on the same rarified plane as Imogene's fanged furball, but I bet its shit smells the same on her antique Persian rug.

I bend to it, holding out a hand, but the move shifts the terrain and brings the background into relief—specifically the thick screw piercing my rear tire. It's kissing the treads right where they meet the sidewall, its angle precise, thoughtfully placed to cause a blowout at seventy miles an hour. The dog remains put as I reach out and test the screw's depth, and after a moment, one of us whimpers.

I see exactly how this is going to go now. Even if I can get Lacy to give me the map, changing this tire is going to eat up precious time, and Baker is only the second stop of Malthus's scheduled five. For each step I take, Malthus will push me back another two. The twenty-four-hour deadline will march on, and instead of moving closer to Daniel, I will inadvertently end up moving farther and farther away.

I drop my head, and a hand seizes my shoulder.

Whirling, jerking back at the same time, I almost fall right on top of the dog.

"Whoa, hold on there!" The man from the diner—Henry?—catches me in strong arms. I yank away, and he holds up his hands, easing back like I'm the one to fear.

Palm to my chest, I stagger to my feet and relearn how to breathe.

"Sorry! I didn't mean to scare you."

I take a moment, braced against the trunk of my car, then finally look up. "I'm sorry too. I mean, for—"

I motion back to the diner.

"I know." Henry smiles, and it's almost startling. The expression changes him completely. He suddenly looks fresh out of high school, and I picture him on the television show he mentioned, a ghost hunter in a robe and mortarboard cap. I bet it would get good ratings. "I could tell that wasn't really you."

"You could?" I swallow back hot surprise, but know I still sound suspicious. Is someone actually being kind to me?

Has it only taken three hours in Malthus's desert for me to be surprised at that?

"Sure." He shoves his hands into the front pockets of his jeans as he shrugs. "Too weird."

I jerk my chin at the giant plate-glass window where Lacy is leaning across a booth to glare into the lot. "What about her?"

"She's not happy," Henry admits, but his smile widens. "But she gave me this."

"Oh my God." I snatch the map from Henry's hands, rude and greedy.

He just continues to smile.

My hands, so steady with a scalpel, reliable at work, shake as I open it, and sure enough, there is a big, black X staring back up at me. *A dead man's eye.* I shake off the thought as I look back up at Henry and exhale so loudly that his smile swerves into a laugh. "I don't know how to thank you."

"Based on our short history? Let's just settle on a friendly handshake," he says, offering his palm.

"Thank you." I take it. It is warm and large and firm. His strength and kindness wash over me. "So much."

Henry just waves, then tucks his hands into his front pockets as he turns and heads across the street toward the motel that might or might not be haunted. I smile after him, even though I can still feel Lacy's eyes on me, watching and judging behind the diner's sun-seared glass. I sense the weight of someone else's regard as well, and it's even hotter than the tricky pilot light inside of me. However, between the dog that saved me from a seventy-five-mile-an-hour crash and the man now disappearing in the center of that sagging motel, I am momentarily fortified.

I may not be able to cry, but I can fix what has been broken. I've done it before. And then I will drive on.

14

I do not want to get out of this car.

It takes me an entire hour to change the tire, and when I finally exit Baker I am so grimy I feel like I'm taking half the shitbox town with me. Sweat-soaked, I gorge on a bottle of water I scored from the adjacent convenience store, downing it so quickly that it sloshes in my stomach as I gain the on-ramp. At least the highway is now absent of its heat haze. The sun has tucked itself into a rocky pocket, and a robe of purple lays over the heavy shoulders of the distant Cronese range. A hushed pink stain sweeps the sky above it, but in between those sherbet mountains and me are miles of low, ratty brush that turn the desert into Martian terrain.

"You can get lost out here, baby doll." My mother's voice, wispy with dreams and dehydration, rises to fill the silence. These were her words the day after she dumped our clothes into black plastic bags, folded those into the trunk of our old Chevy Caprice, and started driving. We were middle-thick in the desert by then, speeding through the anus of Death Valley. I remember being spooked by the name. I didn't know yet that it was the unnamed places that you had to worry about.

"I don't want to be lost," I said, my voice still high and amorphous, unharnessed so that it was easy for my mother to continue on like I hadn't spoken. This was the beginning of her not-hearing. It was right before the not-caring that followed.

"Ain't nothing to anchor yourself to out here," she said, voice as airy as the wind outside our windows. "Nothing at all to weigh you down in these crevices and cracks. Why, I bet we could probably just float away. . . ."

I wanted to ask what she thought was anchoring us down anyway. Our home was gone, the postage stamp pastures repossessed, soon to be auctioned off. I knew this because I was there, hiding behind the couch as the insurance agent patiently explained that there was no provision in the policy for suicide. Not that it mattered. You couldn't exactly have a horse farm with no horses.

We began driving the next day. My mother refused to tell me where we were going or how long before we got there, and it wasn't until we'd slipped in and out of three increasingly dusty towns that I realized we weren't actually going anywhere. We were just leaving.

The Mojave Desert asserted itself like a striking rattler. A grave-dry arroyo herded us toward a mountain range that then dumped us onto two-lane Route 6. Not long after, a hundred-year-old mining town popped up like a grizzled specter, pock-marked and defaced. We stopped to fuel up and stretch our legs at a sandy service station on Main Street, which was where we met Mr. Waylon Rhodes.

"What's Mizpah?" my mother asked, jerking her head at the station sign over his head, absolutely no curiosity in her voice. A greasy lock of hair slid over her forehead, and I resisted the urge to reach up and tuck it back behind her ear. It made her look forlorn, and somehow indecent. I smoothed my matching black hair down behind my own ears instead.

"Why, that's what Tonopah is famous for. Our silver mines. Mizpah was the biggest." Waylon's baritone was as broad as the blue sky above and as rough as the scarred earth below. I edged back toward the car when he looked at me.

Imogene Hawthorne would say that my sensory perception was attuned to a plane my mother could not intuit.

She sent him a single-eyed squint over the rusted hood of the Caprice, sweat dotting her hairline, her shirt sticking to her back where it'd touched the seat. "So why, if them mines are so famous, ain't I never heard of Tonopah before?"

"Well," Waylon drawled, putting on an accent I didn't even know they made in central Nevada. "We're more famous for our legal brothels now."

I didn't know exactly what a brothel was, but I could feel Waylon's eyes on me, searching for a reaction, and I kept my gaze down, kicking dirt with the toes of my Chucks. His laughter oiled the air at that. Then his attention shifted to my mother. I looked up too.

She felt Waylon's gaze on her too, but in a different way than I had. Without even moving, she bloomed under his eye, and suddenly the two of them appeared closer, a wildflower pressed up against a dead mesquite. For a moment she looked like her old self, the woman my dad had left sleeping in bed while he embarked on a midnight bloodbath. Then she arched her back, sucked in a great gulp of the dry desert air, and turned back into a husk of herself. "I'd sure like to see them mines."

The Caprice didn't see a full tank of gas for another eight years.

Right now, I stick to a steady seventy-five miles an hour, even as other travelers bolt past me, racing one another to separate destinations. Even an ambulance whizzes by in a rocking gust, right past Zzyzx Road, a sharp-as-shears moniker for another path leading nowhere. There are a lot of them out here: Arrowhead Trail, Rasor. I focus on the ambulance's taillights as if they're all that's anchoring me to the road, but it's soon gone too. It was a good reminder, at least. Mine isn't the only emergency in the world.

///////////

It's after eight by the time I roll up to Malthus's second appointed stop, now over four hours after Daniel's disappearance. I turn off the engine, and the burgeoning night rushes to press oily fingertips against the windows, peering in. I have the sudden urge to fill the newborn hush with a scream. Dusk is no more than fifteen minutes away.

"The Rock-A-Hoola Water Park." I say the words aloud to cut the silence and stop the scream, and because I still can't quite believe that *this* is what was buried beneath the tight X on the second map. I am parallel to the main highway, and a nine-foot fence looms between it and the access road I had to take to reach the abandoned park. The dual curbs that mark the park's entrance look like deserted islands, and its graded lot is the size of a football field, flat and only partially paved.

The water park itself is just a smattering of crumbling pastel cubes with lidless doorways that note my arrival with unblinking gazes. A lumpy man-made hill rises behind them, concrete pillars—the scaffolding that once held slick blue waterslides—spiking from its rugged back. The slides are long gone, likely salvaged and sold for scrap, so what remains looks like the ribs of a beached whale, stripped of its blubber and gnawed on for good measure. I must look like an ant from the top of those dusk-fogged hills.

I do not want to get out of this car.

I must get out of this car.

Instead, I feed the dog next to me another Slim Jim.

Yes. The dog.

The stray mongrel has taken my place in the passenger's seat and doesn't look eager to relinquish it anytime soon. I know, I know. The last thing I need is to take care of something else. But one moment I was having a daydream of arriving at Lake Arrowhead with this mangy, panting beast in tow, and the next—after the tire was changed—I was suddenly coaxing the dog inside the car with whistling noises and a processed meat snack. It doesn't make sense, but I give my hopefulness, and myself, a pass considering the rest of my day.

Feeding the little terrier another rope of jerky, I watch the sky shrug off one more layer of light. My belly cramps with cherries and nerves. The sense of abandonment is total out here, but that's dead wrong. I am neither alone nor forgotten.

In the gloom of the onrushing dusk, I lean past the dog and open the glove compartment. It's strange, and a little sad, but I'm not even surprised when I push aside the wet wipes to find that the pocket flashlight, just like Daniel's bag, is gone. Slapping the bin shut so that the dog jumps, I drop my hand atop its furry head.

"I don't want to be lost," I tell it, my voice still small, still ten. But I am twenty-seven now, and I have to climb out of this car into the desert and the dark that I hate so much because some maniac has decided I need to prove I care.

"Don't mess the seats any more than I have already," I tell the dog as I reach for the door. "Daniel will kill you."

It's a bad joke. I don't laugh, and the dog doesn't even look up. I think it knows I'm about to leave because it begins licking its front paws, pretending I'm already gone. I climb from the car.

And then I'm truly gone.

15

It's like being plugged into a socket.

A dusky wind slings gravel against my bare ankles and whips my hair against my face as I step onto the jagged end of a once-pink sidewalk. I pocket Daniel's phone and keys as I walk, then roll my hair back into a knot to keep it out of the way. I've left the car door gaping so that the dome light remains lit behind me. No sense in locking it. Malthus clearly has access, and besides, the heat's still up, even though the sun is down. I don't want to return to a car full of microwaved mutt.

It's also a reminder that there's still light in this world, no matter how dark it may seem.

I pick my way forward into the water park, hurrying but not, wanting to duck from view of that scarred hilltop, yet not really wanting to arrive. The sun-bleached pastels are being dipped into twilight gloom with my every step. The stars have yet to tap their way into the wan, swollen sky, but when I glance back the

111

way I came I can see headlights floating on the I-15, steering forward on a lake of looming shadows.

The smart thing would be to cut an angle to the nearest building but for some reason I find myself following the washed-out pathway, obedient and dumb, like I'm lining up in a queue. My progress is marked by a handful of overgrown pepper trees flanking the path's sides. I have no idea how they're even alive, but the wilting branches are stung with green, even as they cringe against the heavy heat.

Painted arrows appear next, rising from the cracked pavement beneath my feet, all helpfully aimed at a crevice between the concrete buildings. I reach the first structure and try to sense movement within, but the only thing that leaps out at me is unimaginative graffiti, obligatory curse words and spray-paint scarring every surface. The scrawled lettering drips in globules off the buildings, coalescing on a sole thought, *fuck, fuck, fuck. . . .*

My pace slows, but my breathing picks up, at the park's edge. Unhinged signage slashes the splintered rooflines, and I squint through empty window frames and naked thresholds to find that the buildings are just empty shells but for the insulation drooping from the ceiling in tufts. I itch just looking at it. I imagine asbestos cross-stitching the air in an invisible, poisonous web, and find myself holding my breath.

Wedged between the first two buildings, I keep my back to one as I inch forward in the heavy gloom. My ears pop with the silence. I can be ambushed from ahead or behind now, and instead of wishing for more light, I surprise myself by longing for a weapon. My personal oath to do no harm has lasted four whole hours in this desiccated wasteland. I feel almost righteous as I realize how quickly I have lost myself. I want to say I told you so, but there's no one around to hear.

At least, no one who cares.

The cinderblock walls of a restroom slide into view, and a handful of green Martians wave at me from odd angles as I approach. Someone with rudimentary art skills has paid homage to Area 51, but other than that creative deviation, it's penises everywhere. Large and vertical, small and horizontal. They are modern-day cave drawings, but without the interesting context or, ironically, the passion. Even the cracked concrete beneath my feet blossoms with small, flat dicks, and I quickstep along a series of phallic footprints to what used to be a ticket booth but is now just a urine-stained shell festooned in trash. Pressed against it, I peer around the corner.

The core of the water park is so dark it's entombed. Hot wind races through it unchecked, rattling the corners of flattened cardboard boxes, setting little sails of toilet paper to flutter. Dead grasses sprout in dry tufts, cushioning shattered glass and cigarette butts. Steel gates loom mid-clearing, where an arch sports the word WATERPARK, though another promising artist has made jism of the cartoonish water spray. The turnstiles below it are stripped of bars, and the remaining metal stanchions stick up like medieval blockades, sharp and ready to spread infection.

I stand motionless, ears pricked, eyes wide. I have no idea where to start looking for the map.

There's a souvenir shop directly across from me, its face tattooed with black-and-white tiles, a checkered flag urging me on. I veer to its north side, where I can slip around the back and traverse the park's perimeter rather than cut across the spilled, open bowels of its center. I peer around another corner, gain it, and am about to do the same with the next when I stop.

There, near my feet, sits a tight coil of twisted rebar. It's rusted and attached to the brick wall by a spiderweb so large it crackles like tinfoil when I lift the rod. It's perfectly weighted to my palm.

It might even be all that keeps me from floating away, because now it is full dark.

I've been bathed in lights and neon for too long. I know this because my technology-soaked, twenty-first-century mind instinctively swings toward the cell phone in my pocket, and I'm reaching for it before I realize that the glowing screen will turn me into a shining target. Instead, I force myself to remember that I once had the ability to tunnel through pure darkness.

Yet I've spent too many years avoiding it, and it isn't long before I stumble. My good foot cracks against something stunted, the sound a shotgun blast in the aching silence. I force myself to swallow my grunt as pain blooms above my toes. I can barely see the ground in front of me, but when I bend to touch the bridge of my foot, my fingers come away wet. I should have slipped back into my tennis shoes before leaving the car. Silly me. I was too busy being terrified.

I remain bent low just in case the sound has attracted anyone, but begin inching forward again. I keep to the crab-like crouch as I reach the far side of the building, pausing because I can't quite make sense of the shadows before me. It's like facing a dark stage between acts, the blocky outline of the scenery in the foreground made known only by the backdrop of solid sets and filmy scrims.

A concrete bridge finally takes form beneath my squint, and after another moment, I recognize the tube of concrete below it. It's a lazy river, now caked with dust, and on the far side of its concrete shore is a slim row of hollow concession stands. It is the deepest section of the park, lying right below the waterslide peaks, and as the wind wheezes around me, I am suddenly dead certain that I am meant to go up there.

I bolt for the bridge, gripping the steel bar so tightly that the tendons in my hands ache. The darkness barely makes room for me, allowing me sight of the ground only an instant before my foot hits, and threatening to capture my heels if I don't move fast. I imagine the blackness rushing into my open mouth, crushing my breath when I need it most, and I know I'm going too fast as I come off the bridge, but somehow I make it to the other side, and then I'm racing past the concession stands—one, two, three . . . then five—and then I'm finally, finally pressed against the last one, where I sink to my heels to catch my breath, eyes peeled to the night.

I cannot see the car. There is no beacon in sight.

That's it. My mind jerks away, no longer my own. I drop into myself like I'm lowering into a silver-mine drift, five hundred feet straight down. The rasping wind doesn't seem to touch me anymore.

The Coal Man's voice reaches out and drags me deeper.

Krist-i-ine . . . are you ready? Cause I'm going to show you how long a night can really be.

"God."

When I come back around, sweat is stinging my eyes, and I have palsy hands. The rebar has fallen, useless at my feet. It was stupid to have picked it up anyway. When it comes to danger, I am always flight over fight, yet even running isn't enough this time. I have only managed to climb deeper into darkness, and now I'm jammed up against a forgotten building waiting for something bad to happen to me. Again.

I close my eyes, lower my head, and hear, *Mommy*.

It's like being plugged into a socket. I get a flash of Abby at bedtime, when I'm tucking her in and she turns to me, even though her knees are tucked almost to her chin. She pulls me close, her head crushing my breasts like she's trying to burrow back into my core. I ignore her sharp angles, those elbows and knees. In those moments I am her singular need, and so I wrap her up, a little gift to me.

And there, suddenly, is my beacon.

It's enough to get me on my feet.

I think of Daniel as I rise, and I pick up the rebar again. Between the two of them, I'm able to remember who I am, even in the dark. I am not a woman lost in the ruins of this park or in the haunted memory of a pitted mine. I am not trapped in the darkness of the present or the past. I am just a work in progress, a journeyman who just hasn't reached the apex of those hills yet. But I will.

And then I'll work my way down, top to bottom, until I find that godforsaken map.

As if responding to that thought, there is a snap. It's actually a light, and its greedy edges reach around my little corner like grasping fingers. I cringe from it, the very thing I was desperate for only seconds before, but I feel exposed as I blink hard against the sudden glow. Something hums on the wheezing wind, something I know, but the surreal depths of the park have disoriented me and I can't immediately place it. All I know is that it's coming from the same place as the light.

The desert flats tilt as I peer around the corner of the concession stand, yet tip back the other way and dump the park back into place when I finally make sense of what I see. Staring back at me, in the middle of a wasted playground—caught between a seesaw stump and a tilted merry-go-round—is a pair of headlights. They're attached to a pristine and softly idling ambulance.

16

The damage is done.

The ambulance, I think, letting out a long breath. Of course, the ambulance.

Only upon seeing it here, empty and placed as purposefully as a car in a showroom, do I remember that the CHP uses aerial patrol to canvass these wasted flats. I was too stunned to realize it before—wondering what was happening, what was going to happen next—that the oddity of an ambulance zipping by me on the long stretch of highway hadn't even registered.

My gaze snags on the Nevada license plates, confirming it as one of the private franchises affiliated with my hospital. My familiarity with both the ambulance and the logo illuminated on its side must have also numbed me to its presence, but that numbness grows tentacles now, which unravel to vibrate through my limbs along with the vehicle's motor, which hums lightly on the wild winds. The planning that had to go into acquiring this vehicle, taking it, driving it . . . the knowledge just shakes through me.

Yet a strange comfort washes over me too. Malthus isn't some all-knowing demigod. He's just a man, a sleight-of-hand magician using smoke and mirrors and *ten whole months* of preparation to terrify me. More importantly, I now know where we've crossed paths: the hospital where I do good work. Where I do no harm.

I ease back behind the concession stand, mind flipping through a mental scrapbook of all the EMTs I know from University. A medic is the most obvious choice—how else would Malthus have gotten hold of a rig?—yet my interaction with emergency services has always come in short, intense bursts. There's no water-cooler talk, just verbal punches, a fast patter of medical shorthand: vitals, BP, and HR on the way to the resuscitation bay. The exchanges are necessarily brusque, but if someone were particularly sensitive? If I'd bruised an ego on a bad day? There's no telling which road jockey I've managed to piss off.

But Malthus is more than just a little pissed off, isn't he? And forget his identity, right now the message is clear: the map I need in order to save Daniel is inside that glowing, idling cab.

My thighs twitch with the need for action, but the way Malthus prepared for me at the diner keeps me in place, and despite the heat, I shiver. Twice now, I have stopped at his command. Twice my name has been revealed in a way that won't easily be forgotten. Twice I was blindsided in the glare of full daylight, in public . . . and it sure as hell isn't daylight anymore.

I realize suddenly . . . I don't want to see what Malthus has left for me in that rig.

No sooner do I have the thought, than *baarrriiing*, a trill rips from my pocket. It falls over the park like an axe, slicing the hot air and cutting my breath short again.

Green-fucking-Acres. Again.

I yank Daniel's phone from my pocket, the ringtone blaring through the wind-washed park like a blow horn, and I fumble the mute button so badly that the entire thing clatters to the ground. My heart makes a drum of my chest, and my ears roar with blood. I lift my leg to stomp it into silence, but it has already fallen quiet.

The damage is done.

I don't just cower—I back into the doorway, that slitted eye of my concession stand, and listen for the arrival of another presence on the wind. I wait for a flashlight to blaze in my face and blind me to my fate. I crouch like a battered woman, gripping the rebar as if I haven't already gone jelly-limbed, like I could actually lift it.

The clicking sound reaches me first. Inching farther into the shell, I rattle an empty soda can at my feet. I am too loud, I've gone clumsy, and the light from the ambulance seems suddenly determined to reach me. I imagine the headlight beams winnowing into bright arrows pointing right at me, and that's when the clicking sound is joined by a quick, heavy pant. I rise into a half-crouch, grasp the rebar like a bat, and get ready to swing.

It's all so fast. The hunched shape appears, smaller and darker than I expect, and it's between my legs, and licking my face before my hand even loosens on the steel. "Shit."

The dog shakes with excitement, thrilled at our reunion. It's still smelly and flea-bitten, but I pet its warm, shivering side as I relearn how to breathe. "You," I tell it in a whisper, "are hard to see in the dark."

I scuttle back to the phone, which has been saved by its hard shell case and blinks up at me from the ground with a single red eye. Imogene has left a message. I snag it and thumb the audio to mute as I return to the shadows, but then I pause.

Because then, I realize, I can do more.

//////////

Malthus waited until I was close to flood the playground with light. He's letting me know I'm expected, and that he knows exactly where I am. He's planned this journey so carefully that he knows what steps I'm going to take before I do.

But I know something too. There are gaps in the high desert, and places where even the best plans can fall through. I bet Malthus has no idea how great the divide can be between what you expect and what you get in the forbidden Mojave. Yes, he has driven me out here, literally, but all that means is that *he* is out here now as well.

I *tap-tap-tap* into the face of the phone, then drop it on the ground just outside the stand. I can't go head-to-head with him, I know that for sure. I am strong and capable for a woman, and I am a scrappy desert rat at heart, but the psychosis that drives this kind of man—and one wrapped up in a stronger male body—is too much for me. I've lived in Vegas long enough to know I have to play the odds.

Right now, that means crawling back into the darkness.

I run back the way I came, emboldened by the fringe of light from the ambulance's beams, counting on the engine's low hum to smother the sound of my progress. One-one thousand, two-one thousand . . . I reach the gap between the second and the third stands, then swerve. The angle is great enough that I can reach the base of the hillside holding those not-slides without being seen. Once there, I will dart from pillar to pillar in the dark and come up on the rig from behind.

But I know I've made the wrong move the moment I break from behind the shielding stalls. Even with the rebar in my hands, and the dog at my feet, I feel the vastness of the park around me like a circling wolf pack. I am totally vulnerable to attack, completely exposed. Then, too early, the phone that I left back at the stand rings again, and it's farther away than it should be. I am falling into a wild gap.

To the tune of "Green Acres."

I reach the last concrete stanchion, realizing I should've told Imogene in my text to wait two minutes before calling back. The idea was to draw Malthus, or at least his attention, to the concession stand while I approach the ambulance from behind. Even murderous psychos can't be two places at once. Yet it cost me the phone, my connection to the outside world . . . and my only connection to Daniel too, since Malthus can't reach me without it.

The park falls into that ear-popping silence. I don't know if Imogene hung up or if Malthus found the phone, but I can't worry about it. Instead, I charge the rig like an Olympian. My delicate flats scratch at the rocky earth, the motor continues humming atop the swirling wind, the sound of the terrier's ragged breath fill my ears, and still I think, *It's tooquiettooquiettooquiet.*

The vehicle is self-contained, privacy curtains pulled tight, but light edges out from the sides in a warm, faint glow. I glance back to make sure no one is coming up behind me as I reach for the door handle. It's warm, almost hot, but I yank it down with my left hand, the dense length of rebar rising in my right.

I expect Malthus to be there, and my muscles brace for a charge that will knock me to my back. I ready a breath, anticipating the air whooshing from my chest, but what I'm not prepared for is how empty an ambulance can be. Even when washed in liters of fresh blood.

It looks like someone has hosed down the walls with a gushing vein. I'd seen a carotid artery burst before, only on video, but it could happen. A big artery like that? It could explode.

The glass on the supply compartment is streaked, and splatter marks festoon the ceiling. There's enough for it to have pooled at the corners, and rivulets drip over the plastic cabinetry. The emergency fittings—cot, medic's chair—have been removed, but a long bench remains, blood browning over the sides but still pooling crimson on the seat.

Above it hang rugged restraints that shouldn't be there. It's a custom-fit, meant to stretch a chest high and lay a person wide, and the leather buckles have gone stiff beneath the layers of blood. I look down, vision spotted red, and see a fresh smear along the bumper and a dark pool blotting that ground near my feet.

The sight sears my mind. It's a red Polaroid flashing, and it finds a home in the gray folds of my memory, wedging in next to two other crimson snapshots: my father, falling to his back in a field that smells of gunpowder and manure, and my mother, convulsing with mad laughter as she disappears around a rocky corner of feldspar and trachyte.

I whirl from the blood and the memories just as the figure rushes me from the right. My vision is scrambled, my irises not yet shrunken from staring into the blazing lights, so all I see is shape—man-shape. Something hard thwacks my cheek to send me spinning, and I careen back into the ambulance's open doors. My forehead smacks the bumper and my knees buckle as a snarl crackles like fire in the hot air. I'm blinded by pain and squinting against the light, but a surprised yelp helps me pinpoint my attacker. Left.

I swing out into the void with the iron bar I've somehow managed to keep hold of, adrenaline sizzling in my ears, momentarily overtaking the throb of the blow. I am thrown off balance when I hit nothing, then flail the other way, my movements both stiff and wild. I'm still blinded, but I don't dare hold still. I'm backlit like a Vegas headliner, and I can imagine Malthus grinning as he circles me, timing his next attack.

Another wild growl saws at the night—my little terrier friend has grown teeth!—and I am emboldened, until the first gunshot sounds. My cringe is pure instinct, knees up, head down as I brace for the white-hot flash of pain indicating I'm hit, that I'm already dead.

Instead, another shot rings out, spitting gravel over my ankles. A pained yip sounds near my feet, and then the rig jostles behind me. The dog has run for cover. Good idea. And so I lunge for the most immediate protection, leaping up and yanking the ambulance doors shut behind me.

I lock myself inside the blood-soaked box, alone.

17

And then there is laughter.

I avoid darkness for a reason, did I mention that yet? I can't remember. But I always have some sort of light to round out the gloomy corners of my home, even in the daytime, which used to be the only time I slept. I stopped taking the graveyard shift after Daniel and I started dating, at his request, which surprised and thrilled Abby. She'd never had me home in the evenings before.

I woke in the middle of every night those first few months. My restlessness roused Daniel too, a light sleeper since med school, and that's when I finally told him about the mines. I explained that where some people see the boogeyman, I see jagged walls with chopped, empty veins. I smell the hot tin of blasting caps. I taste the dust that haunts the old gap-toothed drifts. I didn't say exactly what happened down there, but I told him enough that he came home with night-lights for every room the very next day, and between those and the comforting circle of his arms, I began sleeping again.

With Daniel next to me, the darkness just receded.

But now I need it back.

My feet slap and stick to the floor as I rush the passageway separating the ambulance's cab from the MICU. Reaching across the bucket seats, I slap down the locks, then snap off the dome light before Malthus can circle round. I twirl the wiper handle's end cap and extinguish the headlights too, then grab the keys from the ignition and pocket them.

But the knowledge that Malthus has a gun forces me back into the rig's shell, where I huddle, shaking, and trying not to touch anything. My face stings where Malthus hit me and where I'd smacked my forehead against the bumper. I can hear the dog whimpering somewhere beneath the chassis, and I want to shush it or say it will be okay, but I can't even tell myself that. We are both small, hunted things.

The silence outside is front-loaded and full. I feel like it's going to pop, and I drop the rebar and place my hands over my ears to block out all that nothing. Poised in darkness and stillness and blood, the world closes in around me. I am so disoriented that I actually fall on all fours, my hands bracing against the sticky floor before making a sucking sound as I yank them away. I need to gain my balance, I am off-kilter, pitched over on the inside, but then I realize that, no, that's not it.

Instead, the ambulance is rocking.

My hip slams into a built-in shelf, and I have to brace against the wall to right myself. Turning, I grip the bucket seat up front and angle my eyes in the direction of the side mirror. The optics take shape after a moment, and then I spot it: a silhouette outlined in the night, shoulders bunched high, head low. A man using his full body weight to shift the rig from side to side.

I whirl again, fumbling in the sticky darkness for the rebar. I bang it against the side of the vehicle where I saw Malthus, imagining it hurtling through the steel and directly into his skull. The shaking stops abruptly, and I peer again out front. I see that Malthus's shadow is gone just as a scraping sound rises behind me. It's a serrated shimmy, a metallic slice that goes on and on until it reaches inside of me to spindle at the top of my spine. Movement flashes in the driver's side mirror, and I catch a shadow inching forward in a troll's crouch, one hand trailing the quarter panel in a caress that narrows into an unnaturally sharp point.

Malthus pauses . . . then unexpectedly dodges from sight.

One of us has fallen into a gap.

I stare out the windshield at a yawning maw of darkness that rings with stars, the pinpricks of bright light a raucous and white-hot chorus accompanying the heartbeat drumming in my ears. My veins pulse beneath my skin, threatening to break through. Suddenly, bramble, brush, and stunted cacti jut from the ground like startled corpses, and the deserted park floods with light. The flat terrain turns whitewashed, as if bleached.

Where's the light coming from, and where the hell is he?

I fight my instinct to back away, but it feels like I'm extending my neck for him as I scan the sharp angles and steel bones of the playground. It feels like I'm just asking for a blow. Yet, outside of wind-rustled debris, nothing moves.

Studying the angle of the shadows, I realize the light source is slanted and I'll have to climb into the front seat if I want to see the topmost part of the hunchbacked hill.

It's the shirt that I recognize first. I'm not even settled in the passenger's seat when the realization hits, sizzled. The blue-and-white checkerboard is a festive reminder of the holiday weekend, and I see it and feel stars burst behind my eyes. I'm not religious, so maybe that's why I fixate on the shirt, and nothing else, for a too-long moment. Or maybe my mind just won't let me process the sight of a body hanging from a cross, pinned to a hillside. Or maybe I'm drawn to the checkered shirt because I'm the one who bought it.

"Daniel."

I leap from the ambulance, tumble into the night, and start clawing up that bright, bramble-wracked hillside. I don't look around me, I don't look behind. I fall twice on the rocky slope, and both times I expect to feel strong hands encircling my waist to yank me back. Instead I hear another gunshot, the report of it pinballing off the entrails of the park. Two more follow, but I keep running, sharp rocks slicing new lines into my palms when I fall, bottle shards skewering my fingertips and cutting into my knees. I rise as if drawn up by strings, stumbling past the concrete girders and tripping over chip-toothed stairs.

I pass a portable generator, its rumble deafening. I keep climbing, and suddenly I am what's featured in all that light, caught in a blaze meant for movie premieres and screen sirens. Blinded, I barrel up and up, keeping my mind off what's behind me, what will happen if I stop, and focus only on what's in front of me. Same way I did the last time I was fleeing upward, long ago in the Mizpah mine.

I risk one sky-bound glance that costs me a much-needed breath, but I have to be sure my eyes didn't deceive me back in the rig. No, the figure is still there, enshrined in the spotlight, sprawled across a backdrop of stars, hanging like Jesus on the cross.

Hanging for my sins.

Then I spot a loafer on the jagged slope and a strange keening sound sails from my body. Loafer in hand, I reach flat ground on hands and knees and have to strain my neck to look up at the bare bloody feet dangling from the steel cross. The world flips, and suddenly all the scary silence is inside of me, and outside the wind whistles by and a crow caws in the distance and Daniel makes a gurgling sound in the back of his throat.

He is still alive.

I reach for him without thinking and have to press my body against his, which is so cold in the hot night, icy under that burning light. I have to lift to my toes in order to unhook the nail buried in his spine. A sound wheezes from him, then warmth pools over my shoulder as his head flops onto my neck. I collapse, knees hitting first as I topple under Daniel's weight. The crossbar falls with him, still binding his arms and spreading them eagle-wide, and it pins me flat too. Then there is silence.

And then there is laughter.

Forced and far off, it rises over the battered park, all the way up the spiny hill. I twist my head and immediately sight Malthus. After all, he is illuminated too, blazing in the distant headlights of Daniel's car. Lifting one arm, he gives me a little wave. With the other, he holds up the tiny terrier. I can't see the expression on either of their faces—the dog is black, Malthus wears a cap—but I can't miss the exaggerated windup as he rears back, and then uncoils and punches the little dog right in its muzzle.

Maybe I only imagine the crack. Maybe the sound comes from inside of me.

Before I can figure it out, Malthus tosses the dog into the BMW and climbs in behind it. He starts the car and the tires spit gravel as he reverses through the immense lot. I feel another wail rise inside of me but push it back down as he speeds away.

Hurting is what I do.

And there's one more thing I have to do. Turning my face, I untangle my limbs from Daniel's at the same time I push away. Flipping him over, I brace myself to stare down into his lifeless, destroyed, and beloved face.

And that's when I see it's not Daniel at all.

18

They look like they've been dipped in red wax.

I know this man. This not-Daniel.

It takes a moment because the light is blinding me, and the blood is drying on my neck slowly, as if his last breath lingers there. His eyes are also unfocused, like they've been slightly unscrewed in their sockets. It's a sharp contrast to the last time I'd seen them, when they'd been lit from within, a matching smile right below it. That is now off-kilter too.

But it's definitely Henry. The guy who followed me from the diner in Baker, the one who handed me the map and dismissed my dirty language and behavior with nothing more than a wave. The one who disappeared into the middle of the sagging motel to meet an online friend and look for ghosts. I push back to my knees, wondering if Henry was forced into Daniel's clothes in that motel room—me just outside, obliviously changing my tire—or if Malthus dressed him in the ambulance before trussing him up and brushing the walls with his blood.

I lift the hem of Daniel's shirt, already stiff with dried blood. I've cut open bodies before—I know what it's like to slice through the skin and fatty tissue and muscle of a living, breathing man. I've dug past the raw nerves and twangy tendons to get at a distressed organ. Using precision, study, and a hell of a lot of nerve, I've saved a body from itself.

Yet I am transfixed by this sight. There's no precision here. Malthus might know where to find the largest arteries, but he has the finesse of an angry toddler. I'd wonder what exactly he used to slice Henry wide, but I think I already know that answer by now: whatever he thinks will best set me up.

I'll fucking kill you if I can't have you inside of me.

I flash on an image of Lacy, dark eyes flashing at me above the frilled collar of her apron. Daniel's phone crackling with laughter at my side.

Pushing to my feet, I stumble downhill and back to the blazing spotlight. The klieg lights whitewash the tan from my arms when I reach out, causing my stained hands to pop. They look like they've been dipped in red wax. I'm sweating by the time I find the switch, eyes stinging from the beam, and when I snap it off its abrupt absence makes the night actually feel cool. My limbs go slack, and a sharp rock pierces my left butt cheek as I fall back. It keeps me keen in the dark.

But I can't stave it off anymore. I am too deep in the desert and it's too damn dark and the Coal Man's voice is what throbs brightly now, pulsing through me unchecked.

You don't know who you are, Krissy-Girl. Not until you been pushed to the edge.

Who I am? Perched on a hill in an abandoned water park,

covered in a dead man's blood, I am prey. With no way of fleeing this place, no change of clothes even if I did, and no money or ID, I am a stooge. Having sat by and watched as another man was run down while my own fiancé was missing, I am a woman stripped to nothing.

I rise, slow and heavy-boned, to pick my way back up the hillside. My eyes have adjusted to the dark, and I can see by the light of the piercing stars, but I keep an even pace. There's nothing else out here in this swollen darkness. There's no hurry now. The absence of danger is as round as the night itself.

It's easier to look at Henry in the dark. It eats up his features and allows me to pretend he's just another John Doe in need of my help. Someone who will be moved from the OR long before I learn his name. Still, I apologize as I place one stabilizing hand on his chest, and then yank on the giant spike nailed to his rib cage. His chest heaves upward as I pull, and his body expels the death rattle, one final exhalation shaken free. Henry finally has his answer about ghosts.

I wipe my hands on the khakis that've taken the place of his cargo shorts, the ones Daniel was wearing when he disappeared. I flash on him chained in some van, naked and red, and have to make myself stop. That's another problem with darkness. You can superimpose whatever your imagination can conjure upon it, and when day turns to night? My imagination is bold.

Once my hands are dry, if not clean, I finally pick up the map Malthus left nailed to Henry's chest. I don't look at it, but tuck it between my shorts and shirt instead. I can't leave Henry out here for the crows and coyotes to find, and I need both hands to carry him back down the hillside. I owe him that much.

Angling myself at the head of his body, I bend my knees and lift him beneath the shoulders like I learned in the OR. Gravel slips beneath my feet as I begin backing away, pebbles spurting downhill in tiny landslides. Pulling Henry behind me, I make good progress and am halfway down when my ankle suddenly twists in my stupid leopard flat. I instinctively hop to keep my weight from rolling over, and gravity gives Henry a great push and flips him off the narrow trail. I have to let go in order to keep from pitching over too, and guilt twists my gut as he disappears down the steep hillside. It's like he's running from me, and each dull thump makes me wince. Arms empty, I pant in the silence, then force myself to move again.

I locate Henry again at the hill's bottom, facedown, like he's refusing to look at me. His neck is bent at an odd angle, which makes me feel for a second like I'm falling too, and I back up a step to make sure I'm not about to empty out cherries and bile and regret on top of the dead man's broken neck. Then I grab his feet. There is no best way to pick him up, so I just pull.

The flat drag to the ambulance has sweat popping along my hairline, but it's an easy trek compared to the hillside. I leave the lights off as I heft Henry back into the MICU, and finally, even though he can't hear me, I apologize softly as I shut the doors behind him.

///////////

Malthus blew out the tires. That explains the gunshots that rang out behind me as I rushed the hill, thinking that I'd killed Daniel, and that I was about to be killed too. It doesn't matter. I lost the keys to the ambulance somewhere on the saw-toothed hillside.

I climb into the driver's seat anyway, locking myself away from the wilds outside before dropping my head back to the seat. I wait to cry. Surely witnessing a crucifixion is enough to convince my body it's time for tears. After a full minute, I open my dry eyes, flip on the overhead light, and stare into the rearview mirror instead.

My eyes are black holes, sunken ravines above the rise of blood-specked cheeks. I want to wipe those red freckles away—maybe I can wipe myself blank—but my hands are even worse. There's blood all over them now, and as three images flash in quick succession—Henry's open smile, the security guard flattened in a burning parking lot, the little dog going limp in Malthus's outstretched hand—my palms itch. If I still had the spike Malthus hammered into Henry's side, I would scrape the blood from my hands. I would slice off my tingling skin. Tearing my gaze away from the destructive force reflected back at me in that mirror, I look around for something to clean them with instead.

And spot Daniel's phone propped on the passenger's seat.

For a moment, I just stare. Then I reach for it, but I have been whipped from glaring light to near darkness and my vision is scrambled, hot and runny like eggs. My hand goes wide and I have to redirect it.

Turning the phone over, I try to make myself believe that it isn't the same phone I left ringing outside the concession stall in my foolish attempt to beat Malthus at his own game. My itchy palm knows this phone though. I'm slipping a nail into the groove gained when Daniel once dropped it, even as I press the HOME button to check.

I expect the factory icons to flash up at me, small blocks superimposed atop a photo of Daniel and me taken at the beginning of the summer. It's a great picture, the night of our engagement, and the screen stretches with our smiles. We are cheek-to-cheek, and Daniel still has his whole face.

That's not what waits for me on the home screen. Instead, the little square icons are stamped atop a photo of Daniel alone, and he's seated in the MICU behind me, though it's pre-blood, pre-Henry. A bandage is draped across his right eyebrow—or where it used to be—and a long, solid stain pops out at me like a red bloom. It's covering one eye, but the other stares back with unblinking terror. His beautiful lips are stretched into a flat grin by a too-tight gag that digs into his cheeks and effectively divides his face in two. His hands are lifted in surrender, the leather buckles holding them up, just out of frame, and I can't shake the feeling as I stare down at the photo that it doesn't just look like he's pulling away from the camera. It looks like he's cowering from me.

I do not cry.

I fall out of the ambulance from the driver's side, hit the ground hard, and vomit into the black night. I empty myself out, my soured, cherry retching echoing across the playground, my head pounding with each heave. Afterward, though, I feel light. I float back to the ambulance's cabin. Bloodied and stinking, I shut myself in tight.

I can't stay here. Even if I hadn't seen Malthus drive away, this photo alone tells me he's moving on.

I've done this before.

If I had to guess, I'd say that Daniel was being secured in the Beemer while I was picking my way through the park. The trunk is now likely stained with his DNA, and this returned phone is my warning. *Keep going*.

How many hours do I have left? Twenty? Nineteen?

I thumb the touch screen, looking for more photos. The rest of my body feels hollowed, but nerves crowd my fingertips, and my palms still buzz with that red itch. Then, *whoosh!* I flick the touch screen again, and it's like my heart pops into view.

It's the photo that Daniel took of Abby earlier today. *Was it really only today?* It's actually a terrible image. Abby and Maria aren't smiling as much as fending off the sun's glare with a squint, but it's the last photo taken of Abby, and so that makes it meaningful. I flick my finger over the touch screen, maximize it, and yes, even blurred, my daughter is beautiful. She's a bloom of a child, a strong floret that has blossomed despite being raised in the arid, barren desert.

Was I ever like that?

I stare at her knees, too large for her skinny legs, sticking out like doorknobs beneath striped running shorts. I don't think so, and it's not just because I was underfed. Her curiosity is a ball of twine. It knots in her gaze, an energy that makes her freckles pulse. She wants to know everything, why bees buzz, what the lines on her palm are for. How water can flow up pipes. I never opened myself to those sort of questions because if I did I'd have to open myself to all the why-what-how's of the world, including my father's death: Why is he outside at midnight? What is he doing with the horses? How did he get that gun?

I'd have to open myself to it all.

No, I was never like my daughter, but the vitality staring back at me from this image is proof that I'm not my mother either.

This child thrives because of, and not in spite of, me. And forget my father. Unlike him, the sight of *my* child makes me want to live.

I reach under my shirt and pull out Malthus's next map. He has thoughtfully laminated this one so that blood didn't soak through the thin folds. I run my finger around the hole piercing its middle, the concentric circles widening until I finally stumble upon an X. It's been Sharpie-d atop Barstow, a town best known for a sprawling outlet mall, only sixteen miles away. Not far . . . unless you have to walk.

I take a minute to compose myself, then use Daniel's phone to call Maria again. I get the machine once more and hang up and climb from the ambulance before I can overthink it. I'll call back later. For now, I just sidestep my puke, apologize again to Henry, and begin to walk.

19

It feels imperative that I don't move first.

Malthus's deadline is now twenty hours away, and I'm on my way to the second-to-last stop. I tell myself this to be reassuring as I cross back through the center of the water park, even though I know now that anything can happen any time at all.

Using the scant light from the far-off interstate to guide my steps, I imagine rattlers side-weaving away from me in the dark. I hear the sharp scrabble of scorpions skittering away as the gravel of the vast parking lot crunches beneath my feet. I do not look backward at the hunched ruins of the abandoned park. In my mind, Henry's ghost already wavers there, sadly unable to speak, his questions now living in his eyes as he watches me walk away. Swallowing hard, I wonder instead if Malthus will keep his word that Daniel and I will be reunited if I reach the final stop.

I try not to imagine what will happen if I do not.

By the time I reach the feeder road, the wind that swirled so mutinously in the deserted park has died away. Like Malthus, it too seems temporarily sated by the night's violence. Grateful for the flat surface after the park's jagged edges, I stick to the road's center. It is a smooth black ribbon that runs for miles in both directions, and my heart thumps as I look at it, because I'm not sure if there's an inlet back onto the freeway up ahead or not. So I stop and shine the light from the cell phone's home screen along the roadside ditch that runs parallel to the feeder. Beyond that, the fence is the only thing penning back the freeway.

I am just outside the periphery of the headlights of the traffic whisking by, but near enough to feel the dust stirred up by the commercial semis and larger trucks. One of those would be my best bet. A truck driver would be used to seeing hitchers and more likely to stop. If they don't see all the blood on me, I can catch a ride all the way into Barstow. If they do, I figure I can just play victim. I already know a good story.

I tuck the phone away, and look for some place to breach the ditch and jump the fence. I'm so immune to the sound of traffic that I don't pick up the rumble behind me until it's too late. When I turn, my first instinct is to run, but then I gauge the oncoming vehicle's size by its headlights, and the big cat motor that takes on a deeper purr as it nears. It's a semi, for sure.

I turn my back to the oncoming vehicle to hide the blood staining my front, though my thrust-out thumb is a little red flag. Brakes squeal behind me and I toss what I hope is a reassuring look over my shoulder. *I am female. No threat here.*

Just ignore the blood.

"Need a lift?"

The voice that rings out is so dulcet and high that I actually jump. I'm so desperate too, that I've taken two steps toward the driver's window before I realize I've slipped into view of the side beams. The woman who stares down at me is built as squarely as her truck, though her hair is soft. It frames her face in clean, bouncing tufts. She gives me a night-owl blink from her high seat, as if it's natural to find another woman hiking on a desert road. Then she gets a really good look and her dark eyes flare and stay round.

Her gasp volleys right into me. "Holy hell."

I surprise us both by laughing crazily.

She's reconsidering. I can see it as I cover my mouth, nails digging in my cheeks to press the sound back down into my throat. Gripping the window of the truck hard, she draws back, turns her head, and squints at the road in front of her. I want to throw myself on my knees before the truck, but remain quiet instead, hare-like in those headlights. Somehow it feels imperative that I don't move first.

She finally sighs and motions me around. "I'll take you as far as I can."

"I'm just going to Barstow," I reassure her.

"Good."

I get in the truck before she can change her mind, and it's like climbing into a spaceship. The real world, the orderly one, has become totally alien to me. The AC vents wash me in sweet, cool air, and the dashboard glows with satellite radio listings, a GPS, a clock. I buckle in with a reassuring snap, and notice I was wrong about the time. There are only nineteen hours left to reach Daniel. I sat in the ambulance with a dead man for longer than I thought.

I can feel the driver's eyes on me, digesting my appearance

and trying to make sense of all that blood. She's waiting for me to speak, to explain myself, but I wait her out. She doesn't know what she's asking with that look. Or maybe she does, because she finally just says, "My name's Crystal. Crystal Parnell."

"Thanks for stopping," I say, keeping my gaze down and my own name to myself. The silence in the cabin draws out so long I feel like it'll snap. Crystal could still kick me out. She hasn't started driving yet, but I wait, hoping she'll leave it at that. Malthus has made a danger of banter.

She finally motions to the cubby tucked near the footwell by my door. "There are, uh, wet wipes in there. Use as many as you need."

The truck throttles forward as I locate the wipes and begin to scrub the dried blood from my hands as best I can. I deposit the soiled ones into a wastebasket Crystal has pulled between us, hoping she's not keeping count, not that that's stopping me. I attack my face and neck next, scrub so hard I feel myself momentarily vanish beneath the rub. When I stop, I smell like an astringent rose. Better. However the cashmere shell Daniel bought me is shot. I could turn it inside out, but it'll never be the same. Just like me.

We regain the highway just as I finish, and Crystal gives the basket a shove so that it disappears beneath the dash. A reflective sign winks into view. Barstow is only sixteen miles away, and I need to figure out what the hell I'm going to do when I get there.

The obvious answer is to call my own phone, but that worries me. Every intended action I've taken thus far has set something else into motion, something that will do me—and anyone around me—harm.

Crystal leans forward to survey traffic through her side mirror as we speed up, and I take the opportunity to look around at
her safe, insular world. The overhead cabinets are smooth and
locked. A netting ribbons the roofline to keep objects from falling: a deck of cards, a flashlight. Notepads and tampons. She's
fastened fanciful butterflies and ribbons to it too; they have wings
that glitter, tassels that swing. There are two bunks behind us,
one high and curtained off, likely used as storage, and the other
low and smoothed with bed linens. I bet if I lift the comforter
I'll see a Crystal-shaped outline, a dented silhouette like there's
another passenger along for the ride.

"You're shaking like a leaf."

I realize she's been watching me, eyes as dark as lava rocks in
the glow of the dash. She's right. My hands wobble uncontrolla-
bly in my lap. They don't even stop when I place one on top of
the other. How long have they been doing that?

"Can you talk about it?" she asks.

I shake my head.

"Not even with the police?"

I jolt, my gaze winging to the radio on the dash. The fingers
on my wobbly hands flare.

"Relax." Crystal soothes. "You're not the first young girl I've
picked up from the side of the road, okay? Here." She lifts a ther-
mos. "Try some of this. It's medicinal."

"I don't drink much."

"Don't want to be out of control?"

Don't want to be like my mother, I think, but just shake my head
again.

Crystal props her elbows on the steering wheel, unscrews the top, and pours anyway. "I don't either. It's too dangerous while I'm on the road, and not worth losing a minute with my girls when I'm at home. This is just green tea and ginger root. I make it myself. It keeps me caffeinated, but without the jitters."

I take the cup, and despite the heat that has acted like a second assailant throughout the day's journey, the warmth actually feels good in my palms. It is reassuring and grounding, civilization seeping back into my pores.

"Those them?" I ask, nodding at the photo taped to her dash. Two pre-teens gaze back at us, arms thrown over each other's shoulders, matching gap-toothed grins marking them as sisters, and dusky skin and eyes marking them as Crystal's.

Her face transforms as she looks at the photo. It's the most beautiful thing I've seen all day, and thus jarring. "Yeah. LeAnne and Jann. It's nice to have a bit of home with you on a long haul, you know?"

She nods at the photo and then at the tea, and so I sip to be polite, though I can't hide my resultant shudder.

"I know. It's bitter. I normally add honey, but . . ." Crystal makes a face and grabs at her belly.

I nod once, as if that's my greatest concern in the world too. The tea eases out when I sip again, and its warmth couples with the ginger to relax my knotted muscles. I'm shocked to feel the back of my throat stretch into a yawn, but then give in to it. *Just for a moment*, I think, stretching with it. We'll be in Barstow soon enough.

"So, what's your story?" Crystal tries again, both hands back on the wheel. "Looks like a doozy, if you don't mind me saying."

I know she thinks she can help. She thinks she's already

heard it all, as evidenced by her non-reaction to picking up a woman covered in blood. I wonder how unimpressed she'd be if I told her that almost everyone who has helped me today has ended up dead.

"It's more of a cliché," I tell her instead. "I met a man."

"Husband?" Crystal presses, nodding at my ring.

"God, no." I shudder, and cup my mug more tightly. "This is someone who's . . . taken an interest in me. We—*I* ran into him on the road."

I glance over to see if she caught my slip, but her eyes are on the road, face cut in hard profile as she lets out a hard puff of air. "Yeah, isn't that the way it happens? One person bumps into another, and off they go, their lives spinning in totally different directions."

Lives spinning like tops. I see hard red swirls behind my eyes and think maybe she can understand. I yawn again.

"You can sleep, you know," Crystal says, catching it. "It's only a few more miles to Barstow, but a ten-minute cat nap can do wonders."

Yes, I take power naps at the hospital all the time, so I slide lower in my seat before I even know I've agreed and nestle my head into the space between it and the window. A perfect fit. The rumble of the rig's motor vibrates through my body and my cheek is cool against the glass.

I am just drifting off when Crystal's soft whisper slips around me. "I'm sorry, Kristine."

It takes three tries to lift my eyelids. When I finally do, Crystal's profile wavers like she's floating in a fishbowl. I try to frown, but my eyebrows don't move. I lift my hand and feel the burn of hot tea sluicing over my thighs. Crystal nimbly plucks the cup from my limp and open hands.

"No—" But my voice sounds only inside my head. On the outside, Crystal says my name again . . . and I know I never gave it to her.

"I don't know what you did to him," Crystal is saying. She's been talking this whole time, her lava-stone eyes hard, her voice rippling around them so that each syllable widens before being pushed away by the next. "But I have a family too."

The tea is working. I don't know exactly what was in it, but I know I'll be out soon, and then Crystal—and Malthus—will be able to do whatever they want with me. "Please," I mumble. "He's . . . an animal."

Crystal doesn't ask who. She just lifts her hand and pushes on a panel behind the cabin lights. It springs open, and suddenly there's a gun in her hands. A secret compartment. "I know he's an animal. That's why I have this."

I want to warn her. I want to say that he knows more about her than she could ever believe and that no matter what we do he's always two steps ahead, but my tongue is swollen and dry. I breathe through my nose, and all I can manage is, "He'll kill . . ."

You. Me.

But so what? Crystal has turned out to be his ally, and I've been waiting to die since I was nine years old anyway.

Daniel.

That's what I think instead. He's the one I care about. So my final thought is of him as the red swirls behind my eyelids shift. They wheel suddenly in the opposite direction. They ripple out and expand, and then they wash me away in a dark and sweeping tide.

20

Daniel . . . Daniel . . .

"Why the fuck is she saying that?"

The voice is a snake, its scales made of razors. They slice through my brain, tunneling down.

"Don't worry. She's out."

"She'd better be."

I am. That should worry me. That should . . .

And I think—

Daniel . . .

21

Who knew I had room for one last shock?

Daniel.

His voice, his touch, his smile as he gazes down on me in the hours of early morning—this is what floats through my thick mind first upon waking. They are foggy images, soft and memory-filtered, and I linger on them like an observer, like I'm spying on someone else's dreams.

Then I smell the blood.

My heart thumps so hard it grazes my spine. I open my eyes, but my vision is semi-blurred, and it takes a moment to orient myself and realize that I'm not staring at an abstract painting on the wall. I'm on my back, and that's blood splatter on the ceiling. I bolt straight up at the waist and rise to run in one motion, but the drugs in my system send me spiraling to the floor.

I don't catch myself in time. My chin hits first, and my vision flashes in and out like an old film reel. I finally manage to push to my hands and knees, and the stains on the carpeting gradually take shape. A musty smell pushes into my mouth next to the tin-red tint. I know I'm indoors . . . am I alone?

I lift my head slower this time, and though the world lists to the side, the space finally finds its shape around me and gradually stills.

I'm in a motel room. I've never been here before, but everything about it is familiar. Dingy, spackled walls adorned in landscape photos with zero sense of place. A beat-up particleboard dresser beneath a mirror framed in the same. Through it, I spot a single ceramic lamp. Its white shade flares before a window with curtains thrown alarmingly wide.

I stagger to my feet and manage to remain upright with the help of the battered dresser. It wobbles beneath my weight, and I lunge to brace against the wall instead. My palms are streaking red across the wall, and the marks I leave are brighter and more evocative than any of the framed art.

I do a quick body check. Just because I don't feel pain doesn't mean I'm not injured. I once saw a man walk into the ER, calmly taking a seat so that we could finish up what we were doing before attending to the jousting sword that was harpooning his stomach to his spine.

It isn't only my hands that are blood-caked. There's a red hole in the middle of my shirt, so blood-saturated that it's as if the center of my body has been pried open. Air wheezes from me as I lift the ruined cashmere, and I am actually surprised to see the skin on my stomach still smoothed in place, right where it's supposed to be. Relief floods me, even though the sweater is plastered to my back as well. My awareness is strengthened by the iron-bright scent pricking my nose. I study the dark, burgundy circle staining my middle and wonder, *Whose blood is it?*

I turn back to the bed and feel my hip crack into the dresser's side. I back-palm it, bracing it, bracing myself, but the sight jolts my irises from their sockets. They jitter in my skull, and for a moment I think, *Maybe the sheets have always been that red. Maybe that dirty mattress has always sagged with blood.* It's just a shitty motel with exceptionally bad housekeeping, and it really has nothing at all to do with me.

It has everything to do with me. I was placed there while passed out, a fledgling in a nest of blood. Atop the rim of the crimson cradle is a cotton pillow, so white in comparison that it almost glows, and it's piled with a mound of long black hair.

The dizziness wanes, even as I whirl back to the mirror. The fog from the drug lifts as I catch my reflection, evaporating as slowly and invisibly as steam, yet the room gives one last shake, causing what's left of my hair to skitter across my cheeks. The jagged ends whisper against my earlobes, individual strands shushing, telling me who did this. Unfortunately, I am distracted by the knife lying perpendicular to the mirror, clean and bright, and pointed directly at my image. One long strand of hair trails from the bone handle.

My legs wobble, but I fight the slump. My skin starts to itch again, buzzing in the sticky places, all plastered with blood. A vision flashes: me picking up the blade and running it across all the places that tingle, peeling away that humming skin. I reach down and lift the cashmere tank over my head instead. I am not one to self-injure. I have always had plenty of other people for that.

My ruined shirt crackles in some places, the blood dry as tissue paper, but sags in others, and I shudder as I toss it to the floor. At least I don't have to worry about bedhead. A laugh zigzags from my open mouth, jagged and high like my mother's was at the end, and I clamp my hands over it to stem the sound, but that just brings back the scent of blood, and my belly finally revolts. I'm retching before I reach the toilet.

My head throbs as I empty out raw bile and ginger tea. I am hot, so hot, inside, and the dirty tile floor feels cool and solid beneath my palms. The toilet seat is an ice cube beneath my burning cheek, and I leave it pressed there while my bowels twist back into place. When I am cool enough, and able, I stand.

And there it is. I face the sink, wonder flooding me. Who knew I had room for one last shock?

A loose red scrawl has been drawn just above the swell of my stained bra, numerals and one word staining my skin, thoughtfully placed backward for easy reading through a mirrored image.

13 HOURS

Crystal's tea has cost me six whole hours.

Without looking at the bed or in the mirror, I wobble back into the bedroom. Clothed only in my shorts and bra, I open the front door enough to peer out into the deep night. The air is cool, but dry, which means I'm still in the high desert. I squint past the unpaved lot of the motel and make out signage glaring at me in a hard orange scrawl.

Then, blinking, I mentally flip the landscape around. I place myself directly in front of the opposing building. In my mind, I stand right next to the giant plastic boy and his oversize hamburger. Behind that mental me is a thermometer that soars upward to prick the night sky. It now reads 89 degrees.

I am back in Baker. I am in the same room Henry disappeared into while I changed a tire . . . and my DNA now mingles beautifully with his blood. I lean my forehead against the doorframe, slump, and close my eyes.

Behind me, the phone rings.

22

I begin a slow search.

I track the sound of twenties jazz and locate Daniel's phone tucked beneath that pristine pillow. I have to push aside the mound of my shorn hair to answer it, but I back up and close the curtains on the window first. Malthus is near.

"You called me an animal." It's the first thing he says, and he does it in a voice that is so normal—outside of its mechanized buzz—that I reply before thinking.

"What?"

"Crystal told me," he goes on, as if it's natural to have a conversation at 4:30 a.m. with a woman you've been chasing through the desert. Maybe it is normal for him. Maybe he's done this thousands of times before. "She said you called me an animal. I find that offensive."

I look at the bed straining under the weight of gallons of blood.

"Animals are not mentally adaptive, Kristine," he goes on as

157

if he knows what I'm thinking. "They're beasts of habit and instinct. They're concerned only with survival, not evolution. Most of them only exist to satisfy the predatory longings of stronger, more noble creatures."

"Like yourself, you mean."

He chuckles at that. "Admit it. I am one flexible predator."

I sink into the chair in the corner, an olive green weave that scratches the back of my bare thighs. "You kill innocent people. Those men did nothing to you. That guard was innocent, just doing his job, and Henry was just looking for a bit of fun. You stole their *lives*."

That brings the crazy in his mechanized voice back to life. "Give me a break. That guard didn't have a life. He had a status update. An existence summed up in one hundred and forty characters or less. His being on this earth changed nothing for the better. His leaving won't make it worse."

I set my jaw. "And Henry?"

"Yes. Our friendly neighborhood ghost hunter." A note of wonder, like he'd just remembered. "You should know by now that I'm all for some fun"—like hilltop crucifixions, nails in the side—"but there has to be a reason for it. Henry talked only of escapism from the mundane, and so I gave it to him. He had no real purpose on his own, and without purpose, Kris, there's no evolution."

It's strange. I have no idea what Malthus looks like beneath his trucker's cap and blue jumpsuit, yet I can still picture him now, nodding to himself, so sure.

"No," Malthus continues, "Henry was yet one more redundant voice, and if allowed to procreate, he'd have spawned creatures even dumber than he was. Don't you see? It's natural selection, Kristine. It's survival of the fittest. Small things must die for a more evolved class to thrive."

"So you just kill them?"

"I remove the superfluous, the unnecessary, from this earth. In that way, the strong are preserved, the weak destroyed, and a new species evolves. Perfection," he says, voice gone honed, "is my purpose."

Hurting is what I do.

I blink. I think. This guy believes he's some sort of evolutionary theorist. A man of the ages putting grand theories into practice. Daniel always said that he couldn't be happy if he wasn't growing and learning, and I feel the same way to a degree, but this psycho has taken Darwinism to a new level.

The smile re-enters his voice. "Are you waking up yet, Kristine?"

No . . . there's no fish-shaped bumper sticker that can neatly sum up these beliefs.

"I want my fiancé back," I tell Darwin's twisted devotee.

"And I want you to get him." His voice is artificial sweetener, an engineered approximation of something pleasant. "But remember, defective creatures have no place in my world, Kristine. So if you want to see Daniel again . . ."

He waits for me to finish the sentence. He's testing to see if I'm evolved enough to keep up with him.

"I'll have to be perfect," I answer, swallowing hard.

"See, and now you actually have a shot at it, because I've given you a purpose too." He says it like he's presenting me with a gift. Then his voice swings wildly, a gavel cracking in a courtroom. "You have thirty minutes. Starting now. Then I call the police."

And, with that, the phone goes dead.

///////////

Two minutes later I am still sitting there, a silent phone in my hand, my heartbeat pulsing through my ears. I know I am acting just like one of Malthus's small, dumb animals, but I can't seem to make myself think and move at the same time. The coolheadedness that I'm so well known for in the OR—my flow—has fled me after twelve hard hours of being chased, and I sit rigid while my options fan before me like playing cards.

Clean the room? *Impossible in thirty minutes.* Just get rid of my hair? *It's in the shower drain, in the sink.* I know it. I'd bet money that investigators will fish something out later, and with only twenty-eight minutes left to me, I can't even imagine what that might be. So I just sit there, and eventually I realize that I'm waiting for the police to arrive.

They will take me out of the desert. No one else will have to die. Abby will have to visit me in prison, but let's face it, wouldn't she be better off without a mother who carts home tragedy like it's something she picked up off the sales rack? I scoff at that, and my gaze floats over to the knife on the dresser. Maybe I'll just put it to my wrists. *My mother*, I think, *would approve.*

You're just tired, says a saner part of my brain, and I close my eyes.

Yes, I've been tired ever since I heard the horses scr—

A noise skitters through the room. The scratchy chair claws at my back as I jolt. I listen again for the sound, a shushing of weight against carpet, a whisper of willful movement. All is still.

I rise and retrieve the knife. Then I begin a slow search. The only thing under the bed is more blood caught on the haunches of dust bunnies. I straighten again. I've already been in the bathroom, but I didn't check the shower. I'm heading back there when I realize I also didn't check the closet.

The one with the spot of blood on its handle.

I take it slowly, palm on the door's center, ready to push back at whatever might be in there. The door squeaks open to reveal a space that's narrow, but deep, and totally dark. The lamplight from across the room seeps in enough to reveal a clean, cream T-shirt draped on a hanger, along with khaki shorts which, in another life, I'd packed for this trip. The tee looks like a white flag announcing surrender, and I quickly look away. Then I squint my eyes.

I'm sorry . . . but he'll kill me too.

The words hiss at me from the closet floor.

I moan back and sag against the wall, and the question pops out of me. *How?*

How did Crystal think she could deal with a man like Malthus and just walk away? How did she get messed up with him to begin with? And how the hell could she believe he'd allow her to return to her daughters, to her life, unscathed?

How could she not know that Malthus has secret compartments too, all of them tucked deep inside of his sick, sick brain?

One person bumps into another, and off they go, their lives spinning in totally different directions.

But how could Crystal really know? How could I?

She has been discarded, her head pushed forward by her

forced slump. Her dark hair is matted with blood and obscures her face so that it seems her skull was removed and put on backward, and for a moment I believe that's what Malthus has done.

What wouldn't that man do?

But maybe not. Maybe she's still alive. Because I heard something move.

I straddle her body, the scent of blood and bowel matter reaching out to me as I grab for the string swaying overhead. I yank at it, the bare fluorescent bulb blazes to life, and I go cold as I sag against the mildewed wall.

Crystal's midsection, the part that birthed the girls she wanted so desperately to return to, has been carved out of her. The uterus is atop her chest now, fully intact, and her arms have been wrapped around the blackly bloodied organ like she's cradling it. I can't make sense of the rest. It's both concave and mounding, the coil of her intestines looping like ribbon along her left hip, the rest piled back inside, enormous worms in a bucket.

This is Malthus, evolved. This is him pursuing his *purpose.*

Stretching into a lunge, I reach out and ease back Crystal's head. I know she's dead, but I'm beginning to think like Malthus now, and I know he has left her here for a reason. He's left her for me.

Crystal does her best to ignore my ministrations, her milky gaze staring right through me, but her mouth still has a message for me. It's stretched wide with words and with the world . . . or at least the greater Mojave. Grimacing, I work the map from her throat. It's absent of blood or saliva, inserted post-mortem then, but when I unfold it, I am met with another surprise. Words scrawled like fire across the middle.

THERE'S AN ANIMAL INSIDE US ALL.

And the noise sounds again, accompanied by a twitch of that bloodied belly.

"Oh my God."

I am in the resuscitation bay. That's what I have to tell myself in order to bend, just so I can steel myself against the odor and slick wobble of the cold entrails. This is just another gangbanger, a car crash victim, a failed suicide attempt. I push the coiled bowels aside. And I see a little black body buried inside Crystal's swollen core. I see another face covered in blood and two little brown eyes gazing up at me in unblinking shock.

My wail smothers the dog's dazed whimper, and I lift it from inside Crystal in one smooth motion. Even once it's against my chest, I can't tell if it's okay. There's too much blood. So much of it.

I race back to the bathroom, slipping on viscera, causing the dog to whimper. I fling back the curtain and start the shower, and I step inside, shoes and all, murmuring assurances to the dog, or maybe to myself. Yet every time I shift, more blood circles the drain. I find a white washcloth and gingerly rinse the dog's face clean, avoiding its misshapen jaw as I work my way down its body. Its front left shoulder is slashed where the missed bullet scraped and burned, but the water soon runs pink.

I make a bed of wet, dingy towels at the shower's far end and set the dog down. It drops its head and plays dead.

For a moment, I just stare. As water falls over my body, I think maybe I'll finally cry. I feel the ability there, rising like a thought bubble inside of me, but then I think, *What if I start and can't stop? What if the authorities arrive before I can sort my hot tears from the lukewarm water? What if my mouth fills with them, preventing me from explaining the inexplicable?*

Then Malthus will not be stopped. He'll keep removing every life he sees as superfluous from the earth. He'll certainly kill Daniel. And while I still have no idea why he's targeting me specifically—why after ten months of study he thinks I need to learn to prioritize; why I need to show I care—I do know that he'll continue killing others long after I'm locked away.

Hurting is what he does.

And then, *snap*, I suddenly remember what I've spent a decade trying to forget: I've stopped a man like this before.

I lunge for the free bar of soap, peel off the soaked wrapper, and let it drop to the drain. I coat my body and hair with the cheap, sticky bar and watch death sluice from my skin. Something else falls away with it, a feeling I can't yet name, but I've worn it for so long that I feel naked without it. Lighter too. I scrub and dip my face beneath the hard water spray, and I'm not sure how much time has passed by the time I open my eyes again, but the bathroom is fogged, almost glowy.

"Me too."

It pops from my mouth as I snap off the shower, an exhumed, belated reply. It's what I should have said to Malthus back when he first took Daniel, back when he hinted at his true purpose.

Hurting is what I do.

And you're right, I silently tell him as I towel myself off and meet my gaze in the fogged mirror. I can see that now. There really is an animal inside us all.

23

For a moment, nothing can touch me.

I leave the room with five minutes to spare. I carry the knife that Malthus used on Crystal in my right hand and hide it beneath the towels I've wrapped around the dog. I've swaddled him like a baby. I don't want him to spook once we're outside and injure himself even more, but his gaze is glassy, and when the yellow glow of the industrial porch light hits us, he doesn't even blink. His thoughts are still lost somewhere inside Crystal.

I'm wearing the clothes Malthus left hanging for me, and as I lock the door behind me—knowing he's there, watching—I wonder if I look compliant. I hope so. At the very least I won't spook anyone. I've smoothed my newly shorn hair behind my ears, and my cheeks are pink from scrubbing. I smell like overripe lemon instead of dust and sweat and decay.

I cross the street quickly and skitter past the large hamburger boy to enter the vestibule of the diner where Malthus sent me earlier, yesterday, to eat pie. It's open twenty-four hours, but I'm not going in. I just need a safe place from which to view Baker Boulevard, but I know I can't stay long. Malthus could still call the police.

For now, I'm betting it's enough that he's watching. That he'll drink in the sight of me, knees bent inward, looking unsure, just making his deadline. He'll devour the way my gaze scrabbles for purchase like a roach. He'll think I'm searching for him . . . but I already know where he is. He's lurking in the infinite darkness that I avoid. My awareness of its depth makes him easy to visualize within it.

A lone motorcyclist finally pulls up at the gas station down the street. The pump lanes are exuberantly lit, and I wait until the cyclist has removed his helmet before rushing from the diner, my dirtied flats slapping against the pavement and causing the man to turn while I listen for the sound of an engine gunning behind me. Nothing.

I cry out and let the sound ignite real terror in me. It's not hard. *"Help . . . dog . . . found . . . I don't know . . . please!"*

The rider looks down at the towels, then back up into my face. I can tell by the way his jaw drops that he's a dog lover. He simply opens his arms as I push the little terrier toward him. The knife I'm carrying disappears behind my back before he can see it, and, along with it, so do his keys. The fumbled exchange for dog and towels—fingertips scrabbling—has made it shamefully easy.

Go on and git that six-pack off the Martin's tailgate for me, Krissy-Girl. They got two coolers, that fancy portable grill. They'll never miss it. 'Sides, why should they get so much when we have so little?

I follow the man into the service station, wondering what

Malthus is thinking as I disappear inside. He's probably picking through inventive new ways to kill the cyclist, likely considering doing it in front of me, and nodding as he tells himself it'll be both lesson and entertainment, a way to whittle another horror into the folds of my heart.

After all, hurting is what he does.

I wait until the cyclist and the cashier have gone into the back office with the dog, then whirl and hit the front door with both hands, palms stinging as I flee. If Malthus is watching from where I think he is, then the pump blocks me from view as I dump the knife in the saddlebag and strap on the helmet. The roar of the cycle's engine splits open the night, I can't do anything about that, but I'm hoping he's so surprised by my ability to even operate the bike that he's the one left flat-footed and gape-jawed for a change.

The rider pushes open the doors to the station just as I swerve from the pump lane, his face tinged red by the taillights as I shoot into the night. I'd feel bad, except that I've just assured his well-being. He's worth more to Malthus alive now that I've stolen his ride. It's one more person to implicate me in all the wrongdoings in Baker.

My back is exposed, the white of my clean T-shirt as taunting as a red cape, but when I dare to look, I find the road behind me is clear. I relax, but not much. Malthus knows exactly where I'm going, of course. The map he shoved in Crystal's mouth has a big red X where Victorville was supposed to be. My goal is to get there first, to be the one lying in wait for him for a change. I want Malthus to be the one who totters uncertainly into sight. There are just over twelve hours left to end this game, so let's see what happens when someone tests his beloved adaptability.

//////////

The mountains are hunchbacked masses around me, blanketed by the night sky and slumbering along with the heat. Traffic is light too, and for long stretches all I see is the road just in front of me, highlighted by the bike's beam. Driving this way is almost like melting. The wind hits my skin, and it feels like it's lifting it free. It then does the same with my muscles, my bone. I become weightless and arid.

The cycle's side mirror only suggests at my outline, making a silhouette of my hunched shoulders. It's a portrait of coiled energy, straining forward. My features are obscured by the helmet, and I wonder if Daniel would recognize me right now, or if Abby would. I certainly don't . . . though I have a feeling my mother would, if she were still alive.

Don't forget the Coal Man.

No, I've never been able to do that. Out here, I'm remembering him more than ever.

I gun the engine and duck lower, and the thought skitters behind me on the wind, but without leaving its usual oily coating of shame. Leaning into the next curve, I use reflexes and an aggression I thought long forgotten and realize I'm tired of that. Of working so hard not to remember things. I wait for what I think is a straight shot of road, then bend forward and give myself over to the desert's bosom. *My true mother*, I think. *My childhood home*. For a moment I decide to trust the road and the bike and the desert and the world around me, and I close my eyes and just let myself be.

It's good. Like sinking to the bottom of a pool while the world rages above the water. For a moment, nothing can touch me. The road leaps away from me like I'm flying, the bike thunders between my thighs, and I realize this is the best I've felt since leaving work the day before.

A smile breaks out beneath my visor, and I take in such a deep breath of the desert air that one of my ribs actually pops. Then I open my eyes.

Just in time to catch the cop car swinging onto the interstate behind me.

24

Please, please, pl—

The police cruiser's lights whirl in a strip that yanks the desert away from the night and send chills racing through my body. I am no longer melting. For another quarter mile or so, I consider not stopping and if I thought I could outrun the car, or that the officer inside wasn't already on his radio, I'd gun it.

Instead, I let up on the gas, and the bike jolts atop the gravel of the wide shoulder as it slows. The emergency beacons spin behind me, painting alternating shots of red and blue light against the desert. Shifting my weight to one side, I lower the kickstand but leave the motorcycle idling and my helmet on as I watch the door to the patrol car swing open through the side mirror. The officer steps from the vehicle and suddenly I think, *White van, ambulance, BMW . . . police cruiser?*

My heart kicks hard. I watch the officer stride into view, I look for a weapon at his side. *I'm not sure, I'm not sure.* Another car whisks by, and I can see two occupants, one slumped and the driver with his neck craned our way, but of course they don't stop.

Glancing back through the mirror, I see the officer's step hitch as he realizes I haven't turned off the bike. Half turning, I pretend to fiddle with my helmet as I take stock of him too. His bulk is illuminated by the headlights of another car, though it flickers once the car flashes by, then flares again in front of the beams of an oncoming semi.

I have to shield my eyes from the high-beam glare, but relax a little. The officer is too large to be Malthus. The man who waved to me in the water park was slighter, and agile compared to this man's bow-legged saunter. The officer seems to swell, getting even bigger as he nears, but that's probably just a trick of light. The phosphorescence from the oncoming headlights splay around him like heat, and he looks like he's fuming, fuming and then bouncing as the semi slips just slightly to the gravel shoulder.

I catch a flash of concern on the officer's face, or maybe I just imagine it in the whitewash of the semi's beams. Either way, we both turn at the same time, him toward the oncoming rig, me away, and I right the bike and heel-kick the stand so hard my left flat pops off my foot. The semi —*Crystal's* semi—roars behind me.

Nerves shoot through my limbs like fireworks and I grip the clutch too fast. The bike shoots out from under me, burning my left calf with the exhaust pipe, and the pain blinds me along with those onrushing headlights. I cannot let this bike fall. The muscles in my arms scream as I cling to the handlebars, and I launch myself at the wobbly seat while a collision shatters the still night behind me. I shoot forward, leaning low. *Please, please, pl—*

I think I'm gunning the motor, but I can't hear it over the screeching metal behind me, and all I see in the side mirror is a wad of tin being catapulted toward me, growing larger and larger still, until it almost resembles a patrol car again. I might be shrieking. My throat burns as I gain traction, and then everything speeds up again as the cruiser whips the cycle's back tire from under me.

I can't keep it from falling this time. In my mind, I curl my limbs in tight as I'm flung around, a stone skipping over asphalt. The road punches my breath from my chest as I skim the blacktop, and a searing heat lights up along my left leg, flaming as I slide into the roadside bramble.

My vision goes speckled, but I realize my helmet remains on. I'd be thankful, but I can't catch a full breath in the small space. I can't lift a hand to remove the visor yet either. My hearing shorts out, ears buzzing, and my pulse throbs in strange places, twitching beneath my left armpit, and in one inner thigh, but my body is in that shocked nothing place. I am feeling very little at all.

It's dumb luck that I've come to a stop facing the wreckage. The smoke and dust thrown up by the crash has dropped a forbidding scrim over the whole scene, but the semi's headlights pierce the haze like spotlights on a prison wall. Burning rubber suffuses the air, and I cough and try to force myself into a sitting position. The immediate burn in my left leg incinerates my breath.

Miraculously, though, my limbs are straight, and after I work out my right side from my left, I rise and limp back to the bike, which lies tottering between me and the semi. The saddlebag is on top, and I'm hoping the knife is still inside. Barring that, it'd be nice if another car could pass by right now. I'm moving well, but only out of shock and adrenaline. Once those two things wear off, I'm going to be paralyzed with pain, and I need to be far away from Malthus before then.

Or do I? Knife acquired, I pause. Why chase Malthus to Victorville if he's right behind me? And Daniel has to be in that semi too, right? Malthus has kept Daniel close all along. He's used him to keep me going.

Before the smoke clears, before I can change my mind, I unlatch my helmet and let it clatter to the pavement. Then I limp across the wide, empty road, away from the revealing headlights and straight into a black abyss. I can't help but whimper as the pain and the darkness team up, like doorbell and mat, to welcome me back home.

25

My injured leg flares in warning.

I need to keep moving.

That's all I'm thinking as I crouch in the creosote and sagebrush behind the semi, though this need to act fast and move forward is linked to a more dubious fortune: I now know exactly where Malthus is.

He cut the truck's headlights thirty seconds ago, and I haven't heard a sound since, which means he both wants to avoid attracting the attention of other drivers for as long as possible, and that he's still inside the cab of that truck.

I hesitate in the swollen darkness and squint down the road, hoping for a set of headlights to emerge over the soft decline. It's a selfish wish. Nearly everyone who's tried to help me, down to the little terrier, has ended up terrorized or dead. Malthus has done a stellar job of letting me know that I'm all alone out here, and that if I want my life back, if I want Daniel, I need to go after him myself.

The abrasion along my left leg is beginning to scream, and my joints ache and wobble, like they're held together by screws that've come partially loose. My fingertips tingle as I grip the blade, and I have to focus on the mechanics of breathing, in-and-out, as I scrabble to the other side of the road.

I search for movement around the semi, then drop to a low squat and scuttle forward like that, all of my senses snapped tight. I make good progress until I brace against the ground near the back tire and something soft breaks open beneath my hand. I can't really make it out, but I feel something fleshy bubble up between my fingers, and when I jerk my hand back, I know it comes away red.

The desert sways. I have to grip the bumper for balance and grit my teeth to keep the tightness in the back of my throat from unraveling into sound. That would be dangerous, and I'm not even sure at this point what would come out. Before my legs can give, and before my mind tries to begin working out what part of the police officer I've just touched, I force myself to stagger forward, ready to swing out with the knife.

I know I can do it too. Forget my motto, the maxim that saves me while I save others in the OR. I know I can do harm.

I can do it without shedding a tear.

I ease around to the right, away from the officer's remains, keeping low to the ground to minimize my movements in the side mirror. Yet my footsteps stutter on the sharp gravel, as if the dead cop's body parts have coalesced, and he's now gripping me by the ankles, holding me back. There is a soft blocky glow hovering two feet from the ground up in front of me, and I waver as I realize the passenger's side door has been flung wide open.

My injured leg flares in warning. Was the door jerked open at impact? Did Malthus climb out after dimming the headlights? Or—hope springs now—maybe Daniel was able to overtake him after the crash. Maybe my fiancé is free, escaped into the wild night.

Bending, I place my palms on the ground, still warm despite the absence of the sun, and search beneath the chassis for movement. I then swivel to peer at the darkness looming up behind me, expecting a horror-movie moment, and am almost disappointed when I see nothing there. There's nothing anywhere except for that door, only fifteen feet away.

I'm coming for you, Kristine. I'm following close. I'm right . . .

I tear forward, jerking free of the Coal Man's voice. I can only handle one madman at a time.

I launch myself atop the stairwell, and the truck tilts beneath my weight. The shocks go off like a cannon across the flat terrain as I swing into the cab, eyes wide against the dark, ears pricked, so tight they ache. I sight the figure behind the driver's seat and yelp before familiarity registers, right before I lash out with the blade.

I'm not sure what tips me off first . . . the slim, unwinding frame that's tilted away from me. The strong, square jaw rendered mute beneath duct tape. Maybe the beautiful hands, sloppily bound at the wrists, shaking as they flare in defense. Perhaps it's the sole soft, brown eye staring back at me, the other lost beneath a blood-soaked bandage.

But then I think, *No. It's just me.* I don't recognize Daniel because of the way he looks. I recognize him because the emptiness that has been Malthus's accomplice on this journey, ever since

Daniel was first taken from me, is suddenly gone. The world rounds out and is recognizable now that Daniel is once again beside me.

I reach for him, yet Daniel makes a sound that's both ululant and wild, and even though he can't speak, the smothered cry tells me all I need to know.

Malthus is still here.

I lower my blade and tear back around, catching the rubber edge of my remaining shoe in the doorframe as I yank it shut behind me. I slam down the lock and lunge to do the same to the driver's side door, then blindly search the ignition for keys as I squint through the dusty windshield. Nothing.

I push back between the seats and rest a hand on Daniel's knee as I catch my breath. I can't reassure him fully, because I'm still scanning the vista outside our troubled cocoon, and I'm spooked by what I see. The entire desert is visible from up here. I certainly would have been visible from this vantage point. So where is Malthus?

I shift close to Daniel, my breath lifting his hair. I place a hand on his neck and find it hot and slick with sweat. "Does he still have a gun?"

Daniel nods.

"That's okay. I have this." I lift the knife, causing Daniel's sole eye to flare, and I motion for him to hold out his hands. Provided he's uninjured—outside of his carved-off eyebrow, that is—it is now two against one.

"See that?" I rasp once I manage to saw through the tape without cutting his palms or wrists. I try on a smile for him, for both of us, but it doesn't quite fit yet. Even in the dark, I can see that he's been forced to don Henry's old clothes. "You're not the only one who's good with something sharp."

I drop it to the bench between us and yank the tape from his wrists while glancing at his ankles. They aren't restrained. I ball up the tape and scan the dark outside as I throw it on the floor of the cab, before I realize Daniel's breath is as labored as mine.

"God. Sorry." I rip the tape from his mouth in one go, and Daniel turns his head from me, hissing from the sting. Immediately, though, he's gulping in air, filling his lungs like he hasn't breathed in a year. I wonder how long that air passage has been covered, as he looks me directly in the eye and exhales. "Ahhhh. . . ."

Then he's in my arms. That's it. I'm done being stoic, at least for a moment, and I begin to rock, holding him close. We're chest to chest, heartbeats thumping like alternating pistons, *boomboomboom*, and I realize too late that I'm making another weird sound in my throat. I cut it off if only because we still need to hear what's going on outside.

Daniel finally slumps, his breath hot against my neck, and I let out my own jagged exhalation before letting go. Drawing back to search his face, I can't help but flinch. The bandages render him unfamiliar, a half mask that splits his face into two warring factions: the smooth, kind side that I know so well versus the blank-slate part I can only guess at. This close, almost nose to nose, even his good eye looks shattered near the iris, and I think of Henry and Crystal and the dog and can't help but wonder at all the things Daniel's been forced to see since his abduction at that rest stop hours earlier.

He must be thinking the same thing, because his face shifts

and crumples in on itself, and the collapse works its way down his spine until his whole body shakes. I bring my hand to his cheek. "Don't cry. Please. . . ."

He shifts beneath my touch, his first voluntary movement since I've entered the truck, and I feel a prick beneath my left armpit. I freeze as his alien gaze catches mine again. The burn on my leg throbs so hard I see red.

Daniel's not crying. He's laughing.

His other hand tightens on my forearm, jerking me still when I try to shake my head. "No."

Nononononono . . .

"Yes."

Then his forehead is crashing down. The first strike just jars me, but the second one hits my temple, and in a flash I see it: that gap that pops up so readily and often out here in the Mojave. The divide between what you expect and what you really get. A rattle reaches up to me from the depths of that unexpected arroyo, and I know it's the Coal Man shifting. Sitting up, attentive after more than a decade of lying in pieces at the bottom of a mineshaft.

He's laughing too.

26

We are both panting hard.

The charge nurse at University is named Ann Roy, a no-nonsense name, though it's downright fancy compared to her grim attitude. She doesn't even look up when I duck behind her station for my files. I've been here an entire month and she hasn't looked me in the eye yet. "So what color are you?"

I frown and glance down at my hands, the only part of my body visible in the coat draped over my scrubs. It's borrowed and too big. The one with my name—Kristine Rush, PA-C—is still on order.

"No, honey. I mean, up here." Ann waves her hand at the rotation board where the doctors on call are listed in handwriting so blocky it looks carved. The PAs, myself included, are lined up just as evenly below that. "You're going to reveal your true colors soon enough, but in order to save us both some time, I figure I'd just ask. Which one are you?"

There are three colors: black, red, and blue. "What do they mean?"

"Black means you've got a god complex of the first degree. You think you're better than us, twice as good as your peers, and your patients are

181

only there to provide proof of that." She eyes me as she says it, looking for signs of offense. I keep my face clear as slate. I'm not going to give her anything until I can see where this is going. But I read the onyx name topping the list and murmur, "Dr. Matthews."

I've already assisted him in the OR, and he's certainly earned his black mark. I tried to close an incision without being asked on my first assist with him, and he responded by throwing a retractor at my head. The woman we were operating on was open and bleeding out, CTD—circling the drain—yet he stopped to yell at me mid-clamp. He then saved the patient with as much skill and as neat a closure as I've ever seen, but the way his fingertips brushed her skin, the way he pushed inside her body without really touching her, that alone would have told me exactly how much he thought of himself.

Dr. Schiff and Dr. Rogan have also earned black marks.

"What's red mean?"

"Moody. They're hit-and-miss." Ann shrugs a heavy shoulder. "But certainly not interested in the patients. Not unless they're wrist-deep inside of them."

There's the same number of reds as blacks. I'm so new that I don't yet know if the doctors on staff are really this thoughtless or if Ann just doesn't think very much of them. I hope for the latter.

My gaze drops lower, pins on a name that pops in blue. "Hawthorne," I say, and one corner of Ann's mouth quirks up. She explains that blue means the physician holds a healthy dose of respect and acknowledgment for everyone he works with, and the way she says it, I'm surprised she hasn't drawn little hearts around his name. Then there's the way a twitch develops next to her left eye. I glance back at the blue, and a memory sizzles. A little solar flare behind my eyelids.

It's two weeks earlier and I'm checking on a patient I closed up not swerve

an hour before: SWM, mid-twenties, inked up, with a stab wound to the abdomen. We learn later that his name is Torrey Thatcher, a guitarist who specialized in classic rock covers, and who happened to sidle up to the bar after his set right next to a patron who was feeling proprietary over a bowl of nearby pretzels.

Thatcher is last on my rounds before I can leave the windowless recovery room for my regular Sunday breakfast date with Maria and Abby, and I fling back the curtain in the observation room like the huevos are already frying in the pan. My eyes narrow into slits when I see this new-to-me physician looming over Thatcher, and when he whirls, my gaze falls to his name stitched across the right breast pocket of his jacket. DANIEL HAWTHORNE, MD. I don't see the rest of him, not just then. All I see is him looming above my patient, oxygen mask in hand.

"What are you doing?"

I remember it now, the panic flashing before his ice-blue gaze resettles, a monster in a lake, diving back under. It must have been such a foreign emotion for him, that fear. Still, his answer was ready. "I heard the pulse ox monitor ringing. There seems to be some breathing difficulty, and it was reading an unstable eighty percent. His skin was blue-gray; he was desatting."

It's a solid reply. I think even Ann would have mumbled an apology and left. After all, Daniel's name is written in blue.

Yet I stabilized this patient myself. Thatcher's color had already pinked up when I left his bay not an hour earlier.

Daniel returns my stare with a heavy gaze. I feel it like a weight, and if I'd known of Ann's system at the time, my gut would have told me his name belonged in black.

"What's your name?"

"Kristine Rush," I answer, though I'm the one who should be asking *the questions. Was he dumping the oxygen flow rate? Why was he even here, instead of writing up notes in the lounge? "Why—"*

"New," he says, nodding, and so I find myself nodding too. Then to himself, "I'd have noticed."

I frown, looking at him now, and I see the spark come into that cobalt gaze. I can't hide my eye roll. I bet that line—along with those looks, the MD on his pocket, and probably some car that costs six figures in the staff parking lot—serve him well.

"Do you mind?" I ask, more rudely than if he hadn't unnerved me. I sidestep him to reach the oxygen inlet, and adjust the flow up to five liters before checking the monitors for pulse and BP. Thatcher is stable, so I make a note on his chart to check his oxygen flow more frequently. The entire time, Daniel stands silent and unmoving across from me, and I force myself not to look at him as I finish the chart. He's waiting for something, I can feel it, and I finally look up to see what it is.

It's me.

"Kristine Rush," he murmurs, as if memorizing it. "I'd like to take you out for a drink."

"No."

It's knee-jerk, the pat answer of a woman who doesn't date co-workers and has no intention of introducing a man into the life of her ten-year-old daughter. What isn't pat is the shift I feel inside of me, like wax going hot to find a new shape. The altering flame comes less from those words than the way Daniel says them. They're a command, same as in the OR, and God help me, I'm responding to it.

Later, I'll think that this is how my father's death really marked me. His weakness, his inability to see me standing there, right in front of him, or choose me over the demons in his own mind—this has made me a sitting duck for a decisive man. Especially one who decisively chooses me. One commanding sentence, and the rest of my nos fall trampled underfoot, unvoiced.

Daniel levels me with that ice-blue gaze, and I shift some more. "Go out with me."

Insistence pulses behind every word, but it doesn't make him sound unshakable or privileged. No god complex here, but something. It turns basic requests into non-refutable orders. "Scalpel . . . suction . . . dab . . . go out with me . . . on your knees . . . marry me."

I stare at Daniel and pretend I still have a choice. I know it's not true, even though I do turn and leave, and I do go fill the rest of my day with huevos rancheros and green chiles and laughter with trilled Rs. It still takes another couple of weeks, but after seeing Ann's chart, after assisting Daniel in the OR and watching the magic he can work with those talented hands, after he demands it of me again—go out with me—I finally say yes.

I don't just have dinner with him; I let him buy me breakfast too. I let him reach in and upend my world from the inside. I fall so completely in love with Dr. Daniel Hawthorne that never once—never again—do I see the black mark of a man with a god complex on him.

///////////

But Daniel doesn't fancy himself a god, does he? Daniel believes he's something else entirely. Daniel is an *evolutionist*.

At that, the blue light pulsing in front of my eyes turns yellow and sharp. It bleeds through my lids, and then I'm back. World upended again.

///////////

"Torrey Thatcher." The words emerge in a dehydrated croak, but I don't care. I can feel Daniel's gaze on me, as heavy as it was that first time, and I speak without looking at him. "You were about to asphyxiate him when I rounded."

Fats Waller is blaring from the radio, his throat just as scratchy as mine, and from the corner of my eye I spot Daniel's iPod hooked into the semi's dashboard. The technology—along with the roar of the wheels over the road—makes the tinkling piano keys feel otherworldly and out of place.

"Yes."

My head lolls as Fats continues to croon, my right cheek bumping against the window with each dip in the road. The sky outside is hot and blue, the hue so pale that it's both a color and not. The night has been bleached away. My hands and ankles and knees are now tightly bound by the tape that I cut through in order to "save" Daniel. He also detached the semi's load while I was out. I can see through the side mirror that we fly over the highway on stubby stunted wings.

"You're a goddamn murderer."

"At least look at me when you say it." Daniel scoffs, the sound a slap. "I hate it when you pout."

I don't want to look at him. I have this image of him in my mind as a healer in a white coat, a hero, and as soon as I look at him I know it's going to burst. I turn my head anyway . . . and have to blink twice. He is surprisingly normal.

He's wearing different clothes—not Henry's, as when I found him in the semi. Looking at his pink collar, his khakis, I wonder where the jumpsuit went. He probably soiled it while shoving Crystal into a closet, or while tearing out her uterus, or while fitting a living dog inside her core.

Wondering this makes me feel so lost, so stupid and blind,

that I'm almost thankful for the pain this road trip has inflicted on my body. It almost blunts the edge of betrayal slicing through my heart. Almost.

The sloppy bandage slanting over his left eye is gone, replaced by a wide, neater one, a thin membrane of carefully cut mesh peeking out from underneath. My God, he really did carve away a piece of his perfect face. Even if he has a skin graft, he'll bear a scar. I wonder what he'll remember when he looks at it.

I stop wondering because of what that means for me.

He catches me frowning at him and rolls his eyes. "Ugh, I knew I should've shoved you inside the bench seat. But you hate enclosed spaces, right?"

He knows I do. I told him about the mines.

Oh God. I told him *everything*.

"I enjoy watching you sleep, though." Daniel leans back and plucks a water bottle from behind him. He guides the steering wheel with his forearms, the same way Crystal did when offering me the drugged tea. "You're very restless."

He says this like I've been snoozing. As if we've resumed the roles we were playing when we left Vegas, back before he sent me on a deadly treasure hunt and he was still hiding who he really was.

"You almost threw me back there, though. The thing with the bike?" He rubs his chin as if contemplating a chess move, like he'd forgotten about my queen. "I mean, wow. You never told me you could ride."

You never told me you could kill.

But Daniel is injured too. He is wincing with every other breath, unconsciously touching his rib cage where it aligns with the giant steering wheel. It's not hard to imagine him pitching forward over it, all of his weight bearing down on one fragile rib as he rams into a police cruiser. It would also explain the redness around his nose. He has bled, courtesy of the dashboard and the officer he left splattered atop the asphalt behind us.

"I guess I should have known you'd put up a fight. Not because you're anything special, but because of me. I seek challenge, yet invite provocation. I brought out the best in you." He looks at me to make sure I understand, then shakes his head and sighs. "No? Well, Mother always said I had a tendency to make things harder on myself than they needed to be."

Yeah, I can relate.

"Maybe I do." Daniel is nodding to himself now, and his voice has turned low and soured. "Still, the harder I work for something, the more valuable it feels when I finally get it."

And Daniel is nothing if not a hard worker. Graduate, magna cum laude, residency at Johns Hopkins, trauma surgery and critical care fellowship at Emory. A research fellowship at Tulane. His attentiveness to detail has helped him publish extensively, his ability to think on his feet makes him a fascinating lecturer.

Funny that those are the things that I used to admire about him most.

The highway bends, the morning sun slashes over my body, and the road burn on my raw left leg flares to life. I can feel Daniel staring at me again, studying me with that unfamiliar gaze and following my backward-reeling thoughts. "So, you figure it out yet?"

My nod comes out in an uncontrolled jerk. "You're covering your tracks. You're setting me up."

"For?"

The road burn pulses along the left side of my body. I can't even begin to guess. All I know is that there were never any wiretaps or cameras, no bugs in my house. Why would there be? I gave it *all* to him.

"I really was attracted to you, just so you know," Daniel says now, eyes back on the road. "Your physique . . . *speaks* to me. Even the way we worked together in the OR was like a dance, and nobody even had to teach us the moves. We really do have fantastic chemistry."

My stomach heaves, causing me to shudder. Daniel pretends not to notice.

"But then I started to crave your presence outside of the bedroom too. I'd be fine, sated and calm, all the buzzing inside of me momentarily silenced. Suddenly, it was, 'What's Kristine doing?' Or worse, 'I wish I could share this with her.'" He tilts his head. "Don't you think that's strange? I mean, what the hell was the matter with me?"

I look at his preppy pastels and still-pretty face. He thinks the normal is strange. That the strange is normal. This is the man I fell in love with. This is who I introduced to *Abby*.

Abby.

I close my eyes. All the time I spent trying to keep from mentioning my daughter to "Malthus" and it turns out he not only knows about her, but he *lives* with her. He knows her routine— and he could have injured or killed her a million times over. I wonder why he didn't. Shifting, I try to think of her as Daniel might. Does he hear the lilt of her unformed soprano and think of her voice as redundant? Does he watch her bend over her homework, or cartwheel through the yard, and miss the meaning and beauty in it?

Does he see her as superfluous?

I don't, and can't, know. But she's with Maria, far away, back in Vegas, and she's safe as long as Daniel is with me. As long we're on this road together, he can't touch her.

"I hated it," Daniel says suddenly, jerking my attention back to him. The wonder has fled his voice, and he is sullen again. "Why should I care what you think? Why should anyone? You're nothing."

My gaze jerks to my engagement ring of its own accord. The solitaire winks at me, flashing falsely in the sun.

"Besides," he goes on, "if you really loved me, loved me the way you always claimed you did, you would have *seen*, way sooner than now. Instead, I had to draw you a fucking map."

"There's no way I could have known what you really are."

God. How could I not have known?

He points out: "Oh, come on. You were with me at work, at *home*, Kristine. Yet you only saw what you wanted me to be . . . for you."

But that's what people did when they fell in love, right? They superimposed their dreams on another person, and if they fit—if that person was willing to *pretend* they fit—they didn't look any further. Why would they? Why would I?

His name was in *blue*.

"And what would you have done if I had finally seen?" I finally ask.

He shrugs. "Same thing."

"Propose to me?"

"Pro—*propose?*" He fans his eyes wide in disbelief. His beautiful, ruined face stretches. "Oh, I was never going to *marry* you, Kristine. I just needed to keep you close. Marry you? No, no. You are *broken*. We both know that. Despite your physicality, which I truly *will* miss, you are faulty. Here."

He pokes himself in the skull so hard it makes a dull thud, then gives a sad shake of his head.

"I can stabilize an entire ER overflowing with victims of a multiple vehicle accident, but there are limits even to my healing abilities. Yes, you're pretty. Relatively intelligent. You're certainly aspirational. But you are defective. *You* cannot be made better or fixed. A doctor," he scoffs, remembering my dream. And then he shudders, remembering something else. "Besides, the last thing the world needs is *two* Mrs. Hawthornes."

I look away. Outside, heat haze is already rising from the highway as it slices through the desert. Crusty hillocks lift and fall on each side of the road, undulating as if the desert is breathing. Larger mountains, the San Bernardinos, loom in the distance. For a moment, I think I'm going to cry. It's a strange sensation, but outside of Abby, this relationship with Daniel is the truest thing I've ever known. The truest thing that has ever been false.

My parents laugh at me from their graves.

Daniel suddenly sighs beside me before a hand, familiar in its gentleness, alights on my leg. The touch ignites my road burn, and pain sweeps through me, licking bone as he runs his hand up and down my shredded thigh. I cry out, eyes tearing up from the pain, and turn to find Daniel's completely ignoring the road, attention fixed on me, something akin to pity softening his gaze.

Something hungry too.

"Look, I know it's difficult," he says gently. "But don't worry. You won't have to live with all your imperfections for too much longer."

He rubs some more, stealing my breath. I grit my teeth, even though it sends the lightning bolts at my temples into overdrive. I whimper but fight the urge to wail as he presses his thumbs into my ruined skin. I will not give him the reaction he's seeking with that ravenous look, yet I can still only sit there, bound and writhing, and wait until he chooses to remove his touch.

When he does, we are both panting hard.

"Well? Aren't you going to say anything?" he finally asks.

I have to wait until I've caught my breath to answer.

"Yes," I say. My fists are clenched in my lap. I am no longer close to tears. "I *really* hate this fucking music."

27

Let's review the incriminating evidence.

No more talking. These are Daniel's final words to me before he turns up the volume on Fats, and a whole hour sails by without communication as we rocket down the 15. That's fine. This brief conversation with the monster I was going to marry just one day ago has turned my mind into unknowable terrain. Gaze drifting, I let it wander away.

The desert is still a scribble of unpaved side roads and buff bramble, but we're nearing Victorville, which sits tucked in a valley, an unlikely green dip that surprises me every time. After that, come the mountains.

You can go crazy in an hour, even under the best of circumstances, and since this isn't that—this isn't even close to what I have imagined as the best of times with my fiancé—my mind is bursting. Bright flashes of realization keep going off behind my eyelids, same as the fireworks that'll rupture the night sky tonight.

Independence Day. What a joke.

Meanwhile, my body aches from my many collisions with Daniel over the last day, and he's bound my hands and feet so tightly that my skin bulges around the tape. My palms are red balloons, my fingertips numb and pulpy. I shift, but between the ties and the fire banked along my left leg, I can't get comfortable.

Daniel, though, is perfectly still. He's so relaxed his eyes are even half-closed, lids shielding the ice in his gaze, though his jaw remains rigid. It's so unnerving that I almost wish he'd start palming my raw, road-burned leg again. Anything to help me figure out what's going on behind that placid facade. Anything to tell me what's coming next.

Because there *is* something more. As much pain as I'm in, I'm acutely aware that he hasn't yet tried to crucify me or made any moves to disembowel me or run me down with a twenty-ton vehicle. We are no longer following his cryptic maps, yet I am certain this placidness means he has a firm destination fixed in mind. He's saving me for that. He needs me for something that requires him to put his feelings for me—none of them positive, I now know—on ice.

But that's not the only thing keeping me alert.

I know he's an animal. That's why I have this.

Crystal's gun.

The memory of it in her palm flashes in neon through my brain, and I sneak a glance at Daniel, as if my thoughts alone could draw his attention. I have to bite the inside of my cheek to keep my gaze from lifting to the hidden panel. Surely he's inspected this truck.

But the panel is a custom fit, and if he hasn't found the

weapon—and I haven't seen any indication that he has—then it must still be there. Besides, Crystal would have used it on him if given the chance. I saw the look in her eyes when she spoke of her girls, and remembering it, I don't even blame her for what she did to me. Who knows what he threatened to do to those children. I think of Abby, think of this Daniel even in the same room as her, breathing the same air, and it doesn't just make me want to lunge for the gun—it makes me want to do *grievous* harm.

Yet I realize in one of those searing flashes of clarity that if I shoot Daniel now, it'll look as though I've done everything that he set in motion. And let's review the incriminating evidence: the security cameras back at Buffalo Bill's show me riding a roller coaster, carefree and fun, before chasing down a security guard and driving him to his death. Just down the interstate, in the next town over, is a waitress named Lacy who will be happy to tell her story to the first cable news crew to shine a camera her way. Lacy's earrings will swing, winking in the flash of bulbs as she sadly shakes her head. *Kristine Rush propositioned that man, and told him, verbatim: I'll effing kill you if I can't have you inside of me.*

Henry will then be found in a blood-soaked ambulance linked to my hospital.

Crystal will be found in a closet, holding her most intimate organs.

A motorcyclist, holding a stray dog with a broken jaw, will be linked to the bike found near a crushed patrol car and the bits of the officer who'd been driving it.

Some of this has likely already happened. Some of it is yet to come. But all of it will be pinned on me.

Maybe that's why Daniel cruises on, silent and still, knowing there's no way out for me, even if I were to escape this truck. I suppose I know it too, and I'm tired enough and hurt enough and shocked enough by my stupidity and my not-fiancé's evilness to give up hope altogether . . . but for one thing.

Abby.

So, broken and burning, I bide my time while Daniel drives me toward some unknown impending doom. Fats Waller has been replaced by Ella, who warbles from the console between us: *Trouble, trouble, I've had it all my days. It seems that trouble's going to follow me to my grave.*

//////////

Daniel sails through Victorville like it's not even there. I'm not wearing shoes, and I'm still tied up, but I have to fight to keep from giving in to the despair that sweeps over me as I watch the small town recede in the rearview mirror. I tell myself it's stupid to feel bad about losing options you never had. Still, I think Victorville was my best shot at freedom.

Then, seven miles later, Daniel suddenly swerves, and my head jerks up. I search for signage along the rocky feeder road and in another twenty-five feet I see it: KOA. We roll past billboards touting showers and free Wi-Fi and right into the campground, kicking more dust atop a limp hedge of hack bush separating the parking lot from an empty playground clutching two swings and a torn teepee. I look over at Daniel, note the light press of his thumbs on the steering wheel, and know that—just like Buffalo Bill's and the motel in Baker and the abandoned water park—he has been here before.

Daniel edges the stunted semi around a cluster of campers, eyeing them icily from under the low brim of the cap he donned as he swung onto the off-ramp. At the far end of the compound is a concrete picnic table already baking in the morning sun, and he wedges the cab between it and the rest of the campground before killing the engine. Ella falls silent.

The leather seat squeaks as Daniel turns to me and pulls out the knife he used to kill Crystal. "Kick me in the face and you know exactly where this blade is going."

Forget moving, I don't even breathe. I've assisted Daniel in the OR. This is a hunter's knife, but he is amazing with a blade of any kind.

He rises, looming over me in the crowded space as he edges into the footwell where I sit, and then kneels before me. Placing his left hand atop my knee, he shifts on his haunches and begins working on the tape that binds my knees together first. His thumb slides along my inner thigh as it gives. The blade's point leads the way as he works the tape, and his fingers widen on my thigh, massaging just above the crook of my knee. My muscles tense beneath his touch, and for a moment his grip tightens. He makes a familiar noise deep in the back of his throat. I close my eyes because I know that sound. It means he's hard.

The tape gives with a jerk and the blade tip nicks my left calf. I hiss, jerking reflexively, and my knee barely misses Daniel's nose. He glares up at me, but after a moment he frees my ankles, and then pushes back into the driver's seat. He does not undo my hands.

Turning, he lifts a cooler into his lap and deposits the knife inside. "If you yell for help, if you scream, if you call attention to yourself in any way at all—"

"Yeah, I know." I say before he can finish. I won't make it twenty feet on this blistered earth without my shoes, and I'm certainly not going to cry out to the unsuspecting campers for help. Not after the security guard and Henry. Crystal. Besides, I want to sound compliant. I am still thinking of Crystal's gun. "Okay, yes."

My ready agreement seems to satisfy Daniel, and he nods. "Good, I'm fairly sure we understand each other by now."

He points to the passenger's side door, and crowds me so that I don't even have a chance to reach up and test the panel. The gun will have to wait. Now my bare feet are hitting hot ground and I'm wincing at the stretch to my road burn, already crusting over. I'm stiff and sore enough not to have to exaggerate the moan that escapes me as I shuffle forward. Daniel sails past me to claim the small square of shade bestowed on the concrete bench from our truck's shadow. No one else is in sight.

Thighs burning, I tuck into the bench and draw my feet up beneath me as I squint past the morning sun to study Daniel. His cap is drawn low to hide his features, and his shoulders are tense and drawn back like a bow gone taut with arrow. It is a new stance to go with his new face, yet it fits him perfectly. He opens the cooler and begins to unpack: cheese and bread and grapes.

"Were you planning on killing Henry all along?" I blurt as he lines up the food just inside that square of shade. Out come bottles of water beaded with ice. Apples, already sliced.

"Who?" He does not pause in his unpacking. A cloth napkin. A reusable plate.

"Henry," I say slowly, and have to elaborate when he only flashes me a blank look. "The man you crucified back at that abandoned water park?"

Daniel rolls his eyes, like I'm crazy to expect him to remember the names of everyone he has killed.

I loved this man, I think, too stunned to even shake my head. *This* was the man I had loved. The other—the kind man with talented, healing hands—was like the heat haze on this godforsaken road. He was an illusion brought to life by the perfect conditions. He was a shimmering fantasy that only appeared tangible from a distance. He wasn't real at all.

"Hold on a minute," the new Daniel—whom I do *not* love—says now. "I mean, *you* killed Henry. You lured him into the parking lot with that map. Same way you lured the guard to follow you from the casino."

"You can't blame that on me."

"Nobody else was there," he says, uncapping one of the icy bottles. Water drips down his wrist. He tilts it back, emptying it in almost one gulp, watching me the whole time. He knows exactly what dehydration is doing to my body, and that my mouth is made of cotton. He watches me like he can see the honed pulse at my temples. Small lightning bolts continue to batter my skull.

"*You* were there."

"No," Daniel wipes at his mouth. "I was in the motel."

"Where Henry was butchered."

"Where you so carelessly sent him to his death. The one now littered with your DNA. Geez, Kristine." He pops a cold grape in his mouth. "Get your facts straight."

I try to swallow, but can't manage it past the dryness of my throat. The sun is starting to burn on my shoulders and arms. My injured leg festers. Yes, that's exactly what it'll look like. Ten months of planning has given Daniel enough time to envision every scenario. He has my back pushed so far against the ropes he might as well be wearing gloves. But what I still can't figure is . . .

"Why?"

"*Why.*" Daniel flares his eyes. "That's such a boring question. I've always hated it. Sometimes there is no *why.* Sometimes 'natural selection' simply needs a little hand. A slight flick of the scalpel and, oops, that drunk driver did himself in. A microscopic slice to an artery and, damn, the suicide was successful. A sliver of something infectious pushed deep into the body, just because, and when you sew it all back up, nature takes its course."

I think back through all my assists, studying his past behavior through the clear lens of hindsight. It's a mental blooper reel of everything I missed.

But I don't believe him. Daniel's need to set me up didn't spring from nowhere. This "treasure hunt" is an escalation. Something set him off.

Come on, you were there. You should have seen.

I mentally skim the last few weeks like a dragonfly over water, until something jumps out at me. His disappearance two weeks earlier. My eyes pop open. "The splenic laceration."

Daniel just smiles. He's been waiting for me to put it together.

"He had that comminuted femur fracture too, remember?" Daniel gives a short nod, head tilting just slightly. "His CT scan looked like blown glass."

"We didn't lose him." We'd fought for nine hours to repair the spleen and stop the bleeding in the femoral artery. We busted ass to save the guy. Or, at least, I had.

"He was a big guy. But people often forget that, you know?" He frowns. "How fragile even the big ones are."

You were there. You should have seen.

I was *right* there. I applied the C-spine collar while Daniel assessed the blood loss from the fracture.

I should have seen.

"I didn't plan it," he says, as if it matters now. "Every once in a while, there's one I'm not sure of, you know? They're perched right there on the fence between life and death. Those are the ones that really test me. I can pitch them over into the darkness or pull them back to safety . . . but how to cut the fat from society without slicing too close to the bone? I was almost done triaging when the charge nurse came in with the report."

Ann, who drew Daniel's name in blue. *"Twenty-two-year-old, white male, who—obviously—spent the evening performing Olympics-caliber dives from his roof into his backyard pool. Guess the deck is harder to avoid with a blood alcohol of point-two-one."*

I remembered.

Daniel gives a little laugh. "I couldn't get it out of my mind, you know? The wastefulness of it, the stupidity. You turned your back and my hand was right there, right on top of the retroperitoneal space. It was done before I even willed it."

Yes, he would have to be fast with me in the room. Just a few misplaced sutures. I even closed the surgery for him. "God."

Daniel nods, like he's thinking the same thing. "I've never been that impulsive before. It shook me."

"That's why you left." And it was when he set all this up. The note in the pie. The maps. Three days, refusing my phone calls, just intermittent texts telling me to hold tight. That he'd arranged a leave of absence with the hospital. That he'd be back soon.

Then, when he finally showed up again—exhausted, eyes bloodshot, wearing wrinkled clothes I'd never seen before, smelling musty and aged like he'd been gone years instead of days—he'd looked right through me, same as now, before going to bed and sleeping for twelve hours straight.

When he woke, he had some cereal and acted as though nothing had happened. At first, when I questioned him, he evaded, saying only that he had to get away. When I pressed, he grew sullen, then angry, before switching suddenly to sorrow. It was the anniversary of his father's death, he explained. He'd needed to go home, alone, and face the day in the arms of his childhood home. Then he'd wept while I held him, and that was enough for me. After all, I'd loved him, I'd believed him.

Besides, what did I know of tears?

"I had to get my head on straight," he says now, and I gape, dumbfounded, because he thinks it's on straight now. "Make sure my impulses were under control. I mean, can you imagine being caught like that? By you? Over a man whose name I'd already forgotten?"

"You mean a kid. He was a kid. He was just goofing off."

"He was *oblivious*." Daniel's voice falls flat. "Ignorant to his purpose on the planet. Thoughtless, though most people are. The world is filled with redundancies."

Torrey Thatcher, who played the guitar and nearly died because he stole some pretzels. The big kid . . . what was his name? God, I didn't know his name either, but he died because he was foolish and took a swan dive from his roof.

No, he died because *Daniel* thought he was foolish to swan dive from his roof.

Daniel figured I'd eventually put it all together. That's why he's taken such great pains to set me up, but I can't help thinking he gives me too much credit. I saw none of it, and that's what really makes my head spin. It makes me believe I am as broken as he thought.

At least I'm not a killer.

Liar.

"You're hot," I whisper under my breath. That's what the experts call it, right? When a killer's violent compulsion flares?

Daniel, being a medical professional—oh, and a *serial killer*— is familiar with the term. He leans forward, slipping into the sun. "Kristine? I am *molten.*"

He stands so suddenly that I flinch, and wipes his mouth with a near-dainty pat before dropping the napkin to the ground.

Then he reaches into his pocket and pulls out a syringe.

28

**If pain means you're alive,
then I've never been more so.**

Daniel doesn't stab me with the syringe. I expect it—he holds it aloft like a threat—yet instead he whirls and heads back to the truck, leaving my heart thumping in my throat as he strides away.

I stay where I am, thankful for the distance, though I stare as he clambers into the passenger's seat and starts fiddling with the storage bench beneath the bunk. He pushes the mattress aside, grunting with the effort, and I lean forward, lifting my hands to block the sun. I try to blink, but my eyes are sandblasted by dryness and heat, so I bend my head, just briefly while he's still away, and close them.

When I reopen them, I catch Daniel in a half-turn, yet the knowing part of me, the forward-thinking part, cracks inside my head. I blink again, but the mirage is still there . . . a tangle of knobbed knees and tanned legs ending in pale pink shorts.

Something wild and cornered roars in me, and I feel the echo of it lower, in my chest, but I keep my gaze wide and pinned on Daniel and the four limbs now sprouting from his arms. Daniel eases down the semi's deep steps, and then he turns to face me fully.

The syringe is pointed directly at the carotid artery in my daughter's neck.

The past sixteen hours flash, and the bright bulb of understanding pops—that head/heart call-and-response—reordering events in my mind. This is why "Malthus" never mentioned Abby. It's why he never referred to anything outside of me or my selfish nature, and the relief I felt at that now comes back to taunt me. *Fool.*

No one exists in a vacuum. Everyone has at least one vital connection to the planet, either through blood or love. His is through blood. Through everyone he kills.

And mine?

I strain to see my daughter's face, but her hair is forest wild and splayed so I can't see her features, which panics me. As if that alone can erase her from existence. Yet the tangled strands are damp with sweat, and that gives me hope. I think I see her chest moving. I think.

"Please . . ." I finally, barely, whisper.

Daniel smiles. The desert floor quakes beneath me.

"Wow," he says, devouring my expression. "Look at you. You're just going crazy inside, aren't you? Do you even feel your feet burning?"

I don't even remember standing.

"You're shaking too. That's strange. I mean, she's such a little thing." He bounces, jiggling Abby so that her little limbs flail.

I feel things unsnap inside of me, careful stays and long-closed latches come undone, and the thing I've buried deep, the killing thing, the thing that makes me a *liarliarliar* rises, sensing release.

Oblivious, Daniel goes on.

"A little person . . . so much like every other little person out there. She's done nothing of import yet, and likely won't. I guess every mother convinces herself that her offspring is unique, a special snowflake . . . but when they're this young? They're still unformed. Still empty and pliant, as interchangeable as a set of tires."

I see my bound hands curling into fists. I see myself lunging, intercepting the syringe and plunging it through the place where Daniel's heart is supposed to be. I see my hand pressing on the hidden panel in the semi and a gun dropping down, fitted perfectly in my palm. I place the barrel in Daniel's ear and I squeeze off a shot that scatters that psychotic brain over the high desert and I don't even blink.

But that's all in my mind. Outside, I just bake in the sun and pray. Please, let him have big plans for me. Something bigger than crucifixion or vehicular manslaughter. Please, God, let him have a horrible use for me that is worth keeping my daughter alive.

"Why, you look positively feral, Kristine. Like you could literally attack. Not a great idea under the circumstances, but still. Impressive. Interesting."

It should worry me that he sees this, but instead I feel a snarl rise like a charge from an electrical current. A switch was thrown inside of me as soon as I spotted Abby. Let Daniel have his tools and plans and maps and scalpels . . . I can tear him apart with my teeth and nails. I will consume him in small, even bites.

But I can't do it without causing Abby grievous harm . . . and Daniel knows it.

"It's okay," he says, smiling as me like he used to. He is happy again, taunting me, angling the sharp needle toward the soft, smooth flesh at Abby's neck. He winks coyly. "As you might suspect, I'm very fond of animals."

And he plunges the needle deep.

I am a rocket, launching from the hot earth, boosters roaring red, but Daniel is ready for me. He falls back and braces against the truck, and the straight kick to my chest drops me flat. My heart stutters, but jacks right back, pumped by the sight of Abby. My eyes never leave her, and if pain means you're alive, then I've never been more so.

Daniel drops her. He just lets his arms fall so that her limbs tangle and her body thuds, and then he steps over her, even as I scramble forward.

"Interchangeable," I hear him mutter as he returns to the concrete table.

Bramble and gravel scrape my palms and knees, stabbing my forearms as I face-plant, but I immediately rise again on a tri-pod of flesh. My bound palms slow me, Daniel's laughter is a hollow-train echo in my ears, but my daughter's legs and hair and face are ten feet away, no five, then they're looping up beneath me, weight familiar and rightly balanced in my arms. My unsafe arms.

I bow my head to her and hold and rock, rock and then re-learn how to breathe, but only after I feel the soft puff of her breath feathering my neck. It's faint, but it's there. I have to smooth back her hair, sweaty at the hairline, with my forearms and blow aside errant strands, but I finally see the familiar features I've already memorized—the tight, bow-like mouth, the flushed cheeks, and curling wisp of her black lashes. Whole, intact, perfect. Her eyebrow has not been carved away. Nothing vital is missing.

But her neck—*oh no, her neck, you bastard*—is littered with needle marks.

"God, God . . ." I press my lips to the injuries and wish I could just suck out the venom, same as if she'd been ambushed by a snake.

The one I brought into our home.

///////////

Maybe it's the tape binding my hands, or maybe it's the needle marks on the column of my baby's neck, stamping a trail all the way into my past, but I am suddenly whisked back to a not-quite-abandoned mineshaft, absent of today's searing sun though just as hot, stuffed with open candles, and the lung burn caused by spent fuel.

The old opium den had been repurposed. A new designer drug had taken over with the new millennium, and new addicts filled the old niches and bunks. Like Abby today, I was not there of my own will. I stared at the fire topping the black, oily kerosene wicks and willed myself someplace else. I thought instead of the damp, cool stalls of the horse farm, which helped me ignore the pinch of the needle forced into my arm. I recalled the waft of fresh-cut hay and that helped blow back the hot salami stench of Waylon Rhodes's breath on my face and neck and finally my chest. Then my brain unhinged and I soared.

My mother was never there to suck the sting away.

"So dramatic," Daniel says now from his square of shadow on the bench, and I startle, realizing I'd fallen still. He watches me over the top of that final water bottle, neck now dotted with perspiration like he has a fever, eyes cut in a hard squint, even beneath the brim of his cap. The water is not all he is drinking up.

"What did you give her?" I ask, trying for a normal voice, but it comes out like a wisp of steam. Daniel can see right through it . . . and through me too. Like I'm made of glass.

And I am. When it comes to Abby, I am infinitely fragile.

"Versed."

I go light-headed with one great sigh. The sedative is safe . . . if the dosage is properly monitored. I try to gauge via her breath exactly how much of the drug pulses through her sixty-five-pound body.

"Aren't you going to ask what happened to Maria?"

The wild thing inside me now howls, but holding Abby, I don't answer. I know damn well what happened to Maria, and if I stop to think about it, I might just cease moving altogether. I can feel fear already slowing me down. Giving up would be so easy.

But I can't give up. Abby is *here*. So I just pray that Maria's death was quick and painless, driven by a need to grab Abby and hurry to me.

I count the tiny holes in Abby's neck.

I keep praying in puzzle-piece fragments.

And I focus on a way to get that gun in my hands.

29

I can still hear the sizzle.

We're headed to the estate, just as we planned from the beginning. I think I've known this all along. The Fourth of July is Lake Arrowhead's biggest holiday, and Daniel will want an explosive end to his treasure hunt. Maybe something he can commemorate annually for years to come.

Daniel, I know now, wants to take me out with a big bang.

I simply can't get to the gun. I'm hunched over on the back bunk, and Daniel has rigged the storage bench so that I'm wearing bicycle chains on my wrists, my custom shackles. Abby is chained too, her restraints welded to the rig's back wall, but at least I get to hold her . . . though Daniel's not allowing it for comfort. I can tell because there's a sneer in his gaze as he watches through the reflective square of the rearview mirror. He knows how much it's going to hurt when he makes me let her go.

Hurting is what he does.

Yet there's an upside to my daughter being drugged. Besides

being a sedative, Versed is an amnesiatic, which means Abby very likely won't remember much of the past day's journey while under the influence of the drug. My mind still spins with questions: How did he seize her? Did she know what was happening? Did she struggle and try to run off? I finally give up and just hope Abby was drugged the entire way.

Daniel uses a back entrance to climb from the desert into the sky, approaching Lake Arrowhead from the quieter east side. The road stitches back and forth in a slow switchback journey, allowing Daniel to altogether avoid the Los Angeles crowd fleeing the smog and congestion from the mountain's other side. The only travelers we risk encountering now are those continuing on to the even more reclusive Big Bear.

I glance over the metal guardrail at the undulating vista, spread out around us like a picnic over a blanket. We've moved out of the greater Mojave, for which I should be thankful, but every minute we continue uphill is a rise into a world that I don't know. Trees with cones now crowd the landscape. Needles pad a ground that actually cools underfoot. These mountains sport evergreens that can be turned into timber or used as paper, fauna with a purpose, and most of which I can only guess at. Where the arid desert makes me feel small with its vast openness and stretching sky, this terrain dwarfs me with its unending layers of life.

Then there are the animals. Deer and elk. Bears. Things that can survive snow and cold. I know why the desert creatures have their scales and their shells, but fur hides the fangs and claws up here, and the trees whisper when rustled, their mildewed secrets scenting the air.

The answer to how Daniel grew into what he's become is in that wind song. The sweeping winds that rocked the desert kept me from being able to see this before, but my eyes are open now. The terrain reveals it to me with bright green urgency.

"You started with animals," I finally say.

Through the mirror, his eyes find mine. After a moment, he nods. "You can't just fall into this line of work, Kristine. I had to study very hard to become the great surgeon I am today."

I feel my fingers clench and have to actively unwind them from the warm roots of Abby's hair. "My God. Your father was a vet."

It was just a dry fact before, one I connected to Daniel only because it was proof that healing hands ran in the family, and because it was another bond between us. Both of us were young at the time of our respective fathers' deaths. Yet now it blooms like an ache . . . the knowledge that the senior Dr. Hawthorne had a home office. The way Daniel had made a point of showing it to me the last time we visited. Imogene had long turned it into what she called the "billiards parlor," but Daniel had ignored the pool table entirely. The green felt looked like it'd never been touched. Instead, he lingered over an old bloodstain on the wood paneling encasing the wall. He ran his fingers over the antique medical cabinet still outfitted with apothecary jars and jabbing instruments.

Nostalgic, but not for the reasons I imagined.

"Father said touching the animals made him feel connected to the greater world. That in working on them he felt more a part of it." Daniel smiles. "He was a hundred percent right."

As foreign as this new-Daniel is to me, it takes very little to imagine the passage of instruction, father to son. It's so clear that I can't believe I didn't see it before. "Oh God . . . he *mended* the animals you tortured."

"While I watched," Daniel says, words so cool for someone so hot. A psychology class I took as an undergrad covered the phases in a killer's cycle, the trolling and luring and killing. The cooling off period. And right before the next killing? Agitation. Escalation. Loss of control.

Yet serial murderers reportedly always had some sort of childhood trauma, and I just couldn't see the senior Dr. Hawthorne caring for animals, yet abusing his own son.

"It pleased him to heal them," Daniel continues, and he shakes his head, whether at me or his father I can't tell. "So I started leaving him little gifts. A squirrel. A rabbit. Dozens of birds. He worked so hard. Sweated so much. He never complained about the long hours or the blood or the number of animals I brought him."

Because he *knew*, I thought. He goddamn well *knew* what his son was.

Again, I have to loosen my grip on Abby.

"Then one day he asked me to watch over a baby hare while he went outside to get his doctor's bag, the one he traveled with. I knew it was a test. After all, he left his cigarette *right there.*"

I don't say a word because Daniel is *right there* too. I can hear it in the drift of his voice, the aural equivalent of something floating out to sea. His psychosis strains his features like bone poking through too-thin skin.

"Do you know," Daniel says, "that they sound just like babies when they cry? Pitched high, more of a squeal than a wail—I'll show you if I get a chance—and loud. His car was in the barn, far away. Yet I saw movement and looked up."

"He came back. Because he knew."

"No." Daniel stares at me through the sliver of glass, and waits.

It's like being startled awake in that hotel room again, awareness accompanied by another instant of panicked dislocation. In instances like these, heartbeats pass and pound, and nothing makes sense until it suddenly does, and you know.

His *mother*.

Imogene had refused to enter the workroom on my first visit, and when I asked her later if she ever played pool—making polite, if stilted, conversation—disdain practically dripped from the tips of her lashes as she stared back at me. *I never enter the workroom.*

Not the billiards room that time. The *workroom*.

Daniel watches me put it together and finally nods. "There was this look on her face, disbelief, but absent of all surprise. She should have been staring at me like she'd never seen me before, but instead she came in and stood right next to me, so close she must have smelled the singe as she peered down at the rabbit's remaining eye."

Daniel smiles when I shudder.

"I know. I thought she was going to yell too, but instead she just drew the cigarette from my hand and took this long, hard drag. I can still hear the sizzle."

I don't want to ask. I don't want to know what happened next, but Daniel's gaze has fallen some, and I'm afraid he's viewing Abby through the mirrored square. "And then what?"

"Then she exhaled the smoke in my face." He pushes out his lips in imitation before his expression falls flat. "And then she turned the ember on me."

I see it too. Imogene floating to his side, same as the smoke, her knowing gaze filtering through him as well, reaching down and wrapping itself around his lungs.

"Do you know it's the only time I remember her touching me?"

What did you do, Imogene? I think, as he goes stony and silent. What exactly did she make him feel all those years ago? What the hell has landed me in chains with a drugged child as we're both lifted into the wilderness of the Inland Empire?

"I thought you loved your mother," I try, my voice a loud whisper.

"Oh, I do." Daniel never looks from the road. "I love her to death."

30

I'll only get one shot at him.

We arrive at Lake Arrowhead just past noon, veering from our thoroughfare onto a two-way road that snakes along the lake's north rim, bypassing the main village altogether. The shadows from ponderosas dapple the asphalt, snipping away at the sunlight so that I feel more trapped than ever hunched over in my bunk, curled around my daughter.

There's only one four-way stop on the way to the estate, and I can see the drivers in their minivans and midsize cars staring up at the semi's stunted cab, wondering what we're doing here, though they're not so curious that they'll remember this moment. Not until it's too late. So I look past them too, and catch a fleeting glimpse of the village, tents and tables set up for the holiday, lots stuffed with vendor carts selling flossed clouds of pink cotton candy, sugared nuts, and popcorn with so much butter it coats the roof of your mouth.

Daniel catches the direction of my gaze and smiles. "No wind.

217

It's good luck. They'll be able to dock the fireworks in the middle of the lake."

Yes. Let freedom ring.

We continue on, another five minutes on an upward loop, where every once in a while there's a break in the trees and I catch a flash of glinting blue. The midday sun sends fractured light out over the lake to coat the choppy waves in a radiant stain. Daniel is right. A handful of boats surround a floating dock anchored in the lake's middle. I spot the blue and red strobes of a police craft tied to one side just before the pines thicken again and a green curtain closes on the scene.

The road forks after that, crawling up over two more blinds on the zigzag slope, causing Abby to twitch and shift in my arms. I cradle her tightly until she stops whimpering and when I look up again, the black iron gates of the Hawthorne family estate are swinging into view.

The first time I watched Daniel punch in the gate code, I'd wondered at the family crest centered in wrought iron, marveled at the supporting marble columns, and realized that it wasn't just money I was seeing. My only reference to this sort of wealth was eighties nighttime soaps and magazines so glossy that nothing seemed real. There was something else here that I wouldn't ever be able to name. Like learning a foreign language, I'd always have an accent marking me as an outsider.

As we pull to a stop at the keypad this time, the squeal of the brakes reach inside me to rub at every nerve. My throat tightens, threating to cut off my breath, but it can't keep the creak of the gates from slithering inside to file at my lungs and heart. The wide slanting lawn pops up, a distracting emerald burst, before the guesthouse slides into sight. With its lakeside view and accompanying dock, I had initially mistaken it for the main house. I cringe now, remembering the way Daniel responded, his born-with laugh filled with knowledge I'd never have.

And then, of course, there was Imogene. Autocratic and stiff-lipped, wealth was her native tongue. She sussed out my trailer park pedigree and mining town roots with a single once-over. Imogene, who sat up straight and spoke through her teeth and snuck sidelong glances at me over an odd lunch of leek soup, clearly wondering why I was breathing her rarified air.

Imogene, who now waited for us somewhere inside with no idea that her son had come to kill her.

Daniel swings hard, taking the gravel path meant for service and deliveries. I wonder where the groundskeeper is. I know there's a live-in maid and Imogene employs a personal assistant too, but right now the grounds are still. As, I'm suddenly sure, they have been for two weeks straight.

I survey the smooth stone walls surrounding all three earthen sides of the twenty-acre estate and try to imagine climbing them and dropping into the wilds of the San Bernardinos with Abby clinging to my back. Then I sweep Abby's matted hair from her reddened cheeks, and the nervy scrape of reality floods back in. I am chained up with a serial killer and my unconscious daughter.

I turn my mind back to the hidden gun.

Beneath the long shadow of the massive house, Daniel aims the rig at a charmingly rustic barn. The doors gape wide like an oversize mouth, and darkness beckons us forward. I shut my eyes as we roll inside, but still feel the gloom sink in around us. I open them again when Daniel drifts to a stop in the barn's middle, and seconds later velvety silence floods the semi's cab.

In that terrible moment, Abby stirs.

"Mommy?"

No.

Daniel swivels, and I immediately shift her in my arms, blocking her body with mine. If he's going to stab her, he's going to have to go through me to do it.

Daniel's good eye glitters improbably in the dark. "Oh, excellent. You'll have some company until I get back."

He doesn't seem surprised by her waking. Perhaps he measured out that Versed precisely. Perhaps he wanted her to be conscious as soon as we arrived at the estate. Wants her fully aware of whatever he has planned next.

He knows my thoughts—of course he does—and smiles, but his pale skin has gone ashy in the depths of the barn, and it's so shadowed it doesn't even look like skin anymore. As he places his hand on the door, he says, "Sit tight. Hold your daughter. After all, these are your last remaining minutes together."

He doesn't bother studying what his words do to me. He already knows that too.

I jerk at my restraints after he climbs from the truck, timing it to coincide with the slam of the door. The entire cab rocks, but Daniel doesn't look back. There's more length in the bicycle chain than I thought he would allow, but not so much that I can reach the gun, and I don't test it again. No point in injuring myself before I try—

"Mommy?"

My attention arrows down.

"Yes, baby," I say, again thinking, *NoNoNoNoNo*. . . . I do not want her awake. Not now. "Yes, Mommy's here."

Abby's eyes open, flicker, and finally touch on my face, butterflies landing.

"Daniel took me," she croaks, and I watch the memory hit her like a wave, a tsunami that softens her butter cheeks, furrows her wide, smooth brow and sends tears crashing over her face. I lower my forehead to Abby's and close my eyes. I rub my lips along her cheeks and taste the heat and salt and moisture of her tears. Tears, even bittersweet, that I can never manage. "He hurt Maria."

As Abby continues to shake in my arms, I lift my head to catch Daniel digging through an old traveling chest pushed against the far wall. The stalls cutting through the middle of the barn are all empty, the smell of hay just a dry memory, but he's gathering tack together—stiff harnesses and halters, cracked reins. Equipment meant for large animals . . . and I already know what he does to animals.

I let my gaze drop, searching the cab for something sharp, anything with angles. Everything is plastic and leather, smooth or woven . . . everything except the syringe. It's tucked into the netting alongside the driver's seat, and if I stretch—if I do it before Daniel turns back around—I think I can reach it. I know just by eyeballing it that it holds enough Versed to put someone Abby's size to sleep.

Permanently. Peacefully.

"Is he going to hurt us too?" Abby asks, and her voice pops the bubble of my dark thoughts. I look down into eyes that lay soft and steady on my face. Her trust breaks my heart.

Do I say yes to a question that makes a lie out of all my life-long promises to protect her?

Do I do nothing until it's time to hand her over to a man who will make her scream and compare the sound to a hare's?

"Daniel is . . . not who we thought he was, sweetie," I finally manage. My voice is hoarse, stripped like bark from a tree. All my insides are exposed in those words.

"A bad guy," Abby says, hearing it.

"Yes." I don't hesitate this time. "Very bad."

"I knew it."

That jerks my attention back to her. "What?"

"I could tell."

"How could you tell?"

"It's the way he watches you." She fights a yawn, her trust in me complete. Something dies inside of me. "Quiet, but twitchy. The way Maria's cat watches birds out the window."

I can't believe it. Abby has somehow intuited what I should have seen all along. But then, she is not faulty, is she? She is not broken.

A loud clang sounds in front of me, and I look up, startled. Daniel has slammed the traveling chest shut and is bent, gathering up the chosen equipment. Inside, I begin to shriek. Outside, I reach for that syringe, accidentally pushing it away with the stretch of my fingers, with my haste. I whimper, and trace the netting until I feel the syringe and try to drag it toward me by the tip. It slips to the bottom of the wide, black netting and lodges there.

There's no time to cry about it, not that I would. Daniel is headed back, and as he nears, I shift so that Abby is behind me.

My body blocks hers now, and the confines of the small space actually help. Her young, gummy limbs can curl into improbable angles, minimizing her, and that's what I need right now. "I want you to close your eyes and pretend you're asleep, Abby. Can you do that for me?"

She doesn't say yes or no. She doesn't even bother nodding or shaking her head. She just searches my face like she's diving deep, going spelunking, exploring my soul. Then she closes her eyes.

Daniel is five feet away, reins dragging behind him.

I look up, bicycle chain clanking.

He is on the steps, rocking the semi.

I take stock of my weapons. Knees, elbows, teeth. It's not much. The rest of me—my long torso and legs—will be occupied in defense of Abby.

Daniel presses his nose against the window and shoots me that ashy smile.

I'll only get one shot at him, I think, just as the door swings open and Daniel is back.

31

It'll empty you right out.

He holds a horse collar in his left hand.

I know exactly what it is because I used to help my dad harness up, working next to him in the near-dawn silence, a dance of nimble fingers and soft tut-tuts, met by a warm muzzle or a cloud of musky breath. There was no place more peaceful than the stables on a cold morning. Later, for me, there was no place more violent.

I never spoke of this to Daniel. Yet I get the feeling that my arrival at this estate, in this barn, is no mistake.

He spreads out the lengths of leather on the passenger's seat, sorting through the tack and pretending to ignore me, but his awareness is coiled in the outline of his shoulders. He's so steady-handed that I know he's envisioned this scenario many times in his sick daydreams. I also know he has the knife on him somewhere, and that's what I watch for, anticipating the moment he breaks for Abby.

He sighs and turns . . . no blade in sight. His eyes glide over Abby, a look I feel as it passes me, the surging emptiness of a black hole. It's like he's staring at a mannequin—no, worse. A gum wrapper. Refuse to be disposed of, or not. Still, I can see he's convinced that she's asleep.

Don't move, baby. Please don't move.

But then Daniel's fingers tighten around the padded collar and I know he's the one I need to keep still.

"You never told me what happened," I blurt, deliberately vague. The only way to pull his attention away from Abby is to make him wonder. As his deep, glittering gaze wanders up to meet mine, I need him to ask . . .

"What are you talking about?"

"When your father left here," I jerk my head at the barn. I can smell the hay now that the door is open, and it brings back a memory of gunpowder too, but I push that away for the present violence. "After he returned to his workroom. After your mother caught you with the rabbit."

Daniel's brow corkscrews downward like I'm speaking in tongues, as if he's wondering how I know this. Does he even remember telling me?

I feel my windpipe go tight, and I go on before I can choke on my growing fear. "Did they discuss it? Did she tell him what you'd done?"

He rubs his thumb over the soft underside of the collar, a caress that looks anything but gentle. I can see how it might easily be wrapped around tiny limbs, how the lambswool cover will keep it from leaving a mark. I watch the circling thumb, looking for a quick clench, but he finally answers. "No. Mother had already left. But he knew she'd been there. Her perfume always lingers like a poisonous cloud."

He looks right through me, and I struggle not to shudder.

"She left me alone in that workroom, standing over that hare like I was the only one in the family who knew how to inflict pain. It made me want to find her and drag her back and make her tell him what she'd done."

Sure. What *she'd* done.

"Because he knew what you did? That you were the one who hurt the rabbit?"

"Oh, yes. He cried and cried over it too. You wouldn't understand, of course, being that you're so broken that you can't ever manage tears, but crying is very cathartic. In some cases"—he slowly shakes his head—"it'll empty you right out."

When I was a kid, back before I was old enough to get a job, I used to search Tonopah's surrounding desert for glass bottles and tin cans. I'd turn them in to the recycling center for money, nickel-and-diming my way to a meal. Using an old laundry bag as a backpack, I'd circumvent Main Street so I didn't run into kids I knew, then head out to the heaviest cluster of mine shafts dotting the sun-fractured hills.

I quickly found that as much as I loved the sweet melt of chocolate and peanuts in my mouth, I loved having bought it for myself even more. The food I purchased from bottles and blasting caps was something my mother couldn't keep from me. She couldn't use the money I hid in my socks for drugs because she was so strung out she didn't know it existed, and with each laundry bag redeemed, my satisfaction grew. My mother may have had her heroin dens, but I was addicted to independence.

Of course, I had to venture farther and farther afield to feed my habit. One day I rounded a limestone outcropping so fast I startled a rattler settled in the shade, digesting its lunch. Despite its bulging middle, it swung into an improbable coil and shook its tail, maraca-fast. Its black eyes were small, but they fastened like crosshairs on my bare, tanned legs.

No rattle echoes throughout the cab of the semi now, but the warning is there, just as with that snake. The promise of death sits at attention and I don't move a muscle. I pray to God that Abby stays still behind me.

Daniel flicks his left thumb against the metal hames. Flick and clink. Flick and clink. And again.

Finally, he says, "My father emptied himself out before me, and he kept crying long past the time he should have stopped, and the whole time all I could think was, 'Is this going to make her come back? Will *this* surprise her?'"

I'm still pretending to be a living statue, still watching for the venomous strike, so for a moment I don't understand what he's saying. I frown. "Surpr—?"

"I thought," he continues, over me, "I bet she won't just turn around and walk away this time."

I flash back again on my first visit with Imogene, the house tour that had me spotting the dark stains on the wall, an old splatter, and later Imogene's soured expression. *I never enter the workroom.*

I try to shake my head. It comes out as a spastic jerk. "Oh God. Oh my God. You . . . you *killed* your father—what? To get your mother's attention?"

He looks away. "I kill everything to get her attention."

The admission costs him. He deflates just a little, and now I can read a bit of *his* mind. He is more human in that moment. Not quite so evolved.

The flicker of uncertainty is an opening, and I lunge for it. "I understand, you know. I know what it's like to stand right in front of someone and still not be seen."

Daniel scoffs at that. "I've always been seen."

But what had he said before? "Yes, but she turned her back anyway."

Daniel's eyes regain their focus as they return to mine. "She won't turn away this time."

32

This time I don't try to finesse it.

The hame chain on the collar rattles when he lunges.

He expects me to fall back but I've been thinking ahead, and I rock forward instead, using up all the slack in my chain to greet the center of his face with the span of my forehead. It's a perfect header and he falls hard between the chairs, back nailing the console with a crack. His knees buckle while I reverse to tuck mine in tight.

Daniel needs leverage in order to right himself, and when he sits up I uncoil like a spring, whipping my thighs out once, and again, striking that forward leaning face, and then his chest. I ignore the burn of my abraded leg and revel in his hollow grunt. I kick until his hands fall slack, and his head lolls against the windshield, and he's out.

The slumbering thing inside of me beats its fucking chest.

Now I need the keys.

Daniel is slumped too far away for me to reach, so I wrap my bare feet around his pant leg and try to pull at him that way, but I can't get a grip. "Abby?"

The good girl, she doesn't even move.

"Abs, sit up. Hey! Hurry. I need your help." Immediate and swift, she does. She is chained like me, her restraints soldered to the other side of the bench, but if she stretches . . . "You can reach him. I need you to pull him to me."

She whimpers instead.

"Abby!"

Her head snaps around like I've slapped her, dazed fear clearing from her eyes like a hazy film of steam being wiped away.

"Pull his legs."

She uncoils from the bench and when I see how small and thin her little limbs look compared to his, to mine, I almost yell for her to get back, to move behind me. But goddammit I need those keys.

"They're in his front right pocket."

Right where he always puts them.

Abby tries, but Daniel's wedged oddly between the seats and beginning to stir. I kick at his left leg, but the swing misses. He's too far away.

"Brace your legs against the driver's seat and pull. Hurry."

She grips the cuff of his pant leg, her fingers whitening at the knuckles, and extends herself fully, then yanks. A jarring slide sends him crumpling to the floor and he moans.

"*Pull, Abby!*"

She keeps on and I reach down to bend his knees, and then he's prone on the ground before us.

"Now reach into his pocket."

The shake of her head is automatic as she gives a soft cry.

"I can't reach it from here, Abs. *Please*."

She's quivering so hard she could be standing naked in the Antarctic, but she does as I say and slides one hand into the gaping pocket, careful not to touch his body. I hear a jingle, and feel something glint inside of me. I lean forward as far as my chains will allow.

Abby slowly withdraws the keys.

Daniel's right hand whips out and clamps down on her wrist.

She squeals, drops the keys, and tries to back away, but his grip tightens, a boa constrictor around a mouse.

"Abby! Abby! Keys . . . your other hand!"

But she's frozen, literally scared stiff, and even her little voice comes out petrified. So I center myself on the bench, kick Daniel's knees wide, and stomp down on his crotch with my full weight.

Even half-conscious, he curls into himself. His groan spirals in a pained exhalation and that stops Abby's whimpers. I meet her gaze with my own. "Now. Give me the keys."

She throws them up to me and pushes back, trying to stand on her colt legs, but she's spasming too hard and has to lean against the bench instead. I want to comfort her, but I have to find the right key. There are two small ones and I can't tell what they are. They could be mailbox keys, and I have the flashing worry that the one to our restraints is still loose in his pocket, but I can't think about that. I'll have to try them both.

The weight of the other keys pulls at my left hand, which is both jittering and my non-dominant side. I bite my lip and hold my breath, even though I'm already taking in too little oxygen, even though something is screaming inside of me that *nothingnothingnothing* is going to help.

"Hurry, Mommy. He's waking."

I hurry and the key slips atop the lock and slides off the face. The whole set clatters to the floor. I try to bend, but the chains stop me short. I shoot a look at Abby past the lank strands of my chopped hair. "Kick him!" I tell her.

But Abby's never hurt anything in her life. Even after everything she's seen on this journey, after whatever it was that Daniel did to Maria, violence is simply not a part of her physical vocabulary.

I twist back around and grasp the set of keys roughly with the toes of my left foot. Sharp ridges burrow into me, and I lift my leg—the road burn flaring again—and grab the keys with both hands, trying to figure out which one I've already tried. Daniel stirs, just out of my sightline.

This time I don't try to finesse it. I just shove the key home like it's normal to be bleeding and locked up with a goddamn serial killer inside a semi, inside a barn, inside an estate that's bordering a private lake.

A crisp click, and then my chain goes slack with weight. I turn just as Daniel rises.

The bike chain still loops my hands, and I try to pull back—to reverse course so I can wind up and propel the linked metal into the side of his head, but he reaches out and simply plucks the newly unlocked end from the air. Then he gives a hard yank.

Abby shrieks as I topple. I try to catch myself with my legs but they tangle with Daniel's and he spins me like a top. I let him, lifting my head so I'm not knocked out when I hit the floor. He grunts as he pivots to rise to his knees and makes a false lunge at Abby, who—still bound in chains—cowers on the bench. I know it's just a feint. Daniel has bigger game in sight.

And when he wheels back around, I'm ready. I let him jerk me up by that long length of chain, and as he pulls me to him, I bury the syringe filled with Versed into his pulsing jugular. He must have forgotten it in the netting of the driver's side seat, but I did not.

Daniel tries to jerk away, but I use the confined space to close in tight and depress the needle before he can shake it free. His roar is an explosion, and the needle wobbles in his flesh seconds prior to him ripping it from his neck. It clatters against the window when he throws it, then drops harmlessly into the footwell. I almost smile.

Daniel hauls back and punches me square in the face.

The jab is tight—he doesn't have enough room to really load up, but there's enough rage behind it that color bursts behind my eyelids and I lose track of my limbs. Hands seize me, and there's a growling somewhere outside my body as I'm hurled back around. I know by Abby's cries of pain that I've partially landed on her. Another growl sounds, Daniel realizes that she's been faking unconsciousness, and something just lights up and flushes through my skull. It brings me back around.

Daniel is hunched in the confined space with a look so dark it could be a storm. There is spittle smeared across his face, and my kick has dislodged the bandage over his eyebrow so that his right eye is again obscured. The wound above it gapes, and the scoop of flesh that he carved from himself is bleeding again.

"I'm . . . going to kill you," he slurs.

"I'm going to kill you back," someone inside my body says.

He spins fast, going for the knife, knowing his time is short. I whip out with the strongest part of my body again and kick him in the side, and the air in his lungs heaves out over the dashboard. I reach up, fingers steady now, and by the time he recovers, Crystal's gun is pointed directly at his face.

I shift to the side of the hidden compartment, which now hangs open above me, and which Daniel finally sees. "Shut your eyes, Abby."

I don't want her to see it when I blow his other eye out of its socket.

Daniel doesn't even blink away the dare in his look. It glows steadily in him like an electric burner . . . all the way up until his eyelids droop a degree. I can actually see the Versed progressing through his bloodstream.

And I now find myself cooling, thinking, *Maybe I don't have to kill him. Maybe I can wait him out.*

Stupid mistake. I might as well have spoken the words aloud.

Daniel's eye flares with realization and he gives one powerful shake of his head. It's both a negation of my thought—I will *not* be allowed to just wait for him to faint—and a personal chest thump, a call to arms. He howls in rage and everything I wondered about him, all the murderous evil and the lies that were left unspoken and unanswered, is in that elongated cry. Eye bulging, veins popping in his throat, strained, Daniel roars until his lungs are empty of air, and on the next gasp, he comes for me.

I don't even flinch. I just pull the trigger.

Click.

Daniel slams into me so hard I feel his rage bungee into my core. Still howling, he rams his forearm across mine, and I drop the gun into his open palm. Then he flips it with practiced ease, and the butt crashes into my skull.

He's weakening, so it takes a half dozen strikes for him to pistol-whip me into submission. Abby wails the entire time, the sound wet, drowning in tears.

I feel Daniel's strength failing, but it doesn't matter. My ears buzz with rushing blood, bringing a flood of darkness along with it. I hear Daniel fall as I go limp, and Abby still cries above me, but I am spinning *downdowndown*.

I'm headed back to the desert. In my mind, at least, I'm dropping into the mines. The Coal Man's voice reaches up, cinches around my thoughts, then grows taut and pulls.

Krist-i-ine . . . are you ready? Cause I'm going to show you how long a night can really be.

And, just like the first time, there is nothing I can do to stop it.

33

Time stops when you're underground.

Josie Scott was holding court on Main Street, Tonopah, licking a Firecracker Popsicle and preening in the desert sun like she was another one of its brilliant rays. I caught her laugh first, this high-pitch bray that was some weird fusion of delight and disdain, and immediately tried to reverse direction without being seen. Josie and I were both sixteen, but that's where our likeness ended. She was, instead, my polar opposite; light-haired where I was dark, ebullient where I was sullen, monied where I was not. It was said she had roots in Tonopah that went back as far as the first Silver Rush, and that's why she wore silver jewelry on her fingers and wrists and circling her neck. Her hair was her only gold.

Josie was also my greatest tormentor. She ridiculed my hand-me-downs, my need for a part-time job at Seven Leagues antiques shop, and most especially, my mother. I put up with it because Josie had numbers on her side. She was *that* girl—the cheerleader, the football captain's girlfriend, the student-body president. I told myself it didn't matter. That I was gonna be leaving this small-minded, shithole town soon enough, and I was never looking back.

Hey, Kristine, Josie would yell across the school, the parking lot, the town. My world. *Saw your momma walking into the drugstore today. Blasting powder falls from between her legs every time she takes a step.*

And there was nothing I could say. My mother really did live like a mole by then, surfacing from the Lumbago mine only when Waylon allowed it. Prostitution was legal in Tonopah, of course, and plenty of the town's children had mothers who worked the skin trade, so there was no shame in that. Yet I was the only ninth grader whose mother had a pimp instead of being gainfully self-employed in one of the legal brothels. That was what shamed me most. She discounted her own body.

"Hey, Kristine," Josie called out that day, spotting me just before I could duck from sight. She sashayed across the dusty road, licking that Popsicle, four boys and one other girlfriend trailing along at her back. They were in arrowhead formation, pointed at me, Josie the tip. "Where the hell did you get those white Daisy Dukes? They almost look new."

I sighed and looked down. They *were* new. I'd bought them, and the blouse I was wearing to celebrate the end of the school year—the end of seeing this scornful, blond, little bully every day—and the start of summer. One year closer to graduation and freedom.

Stay away, Josie, I thought, turning back around. Don't you dare come near me and ridicule the only new thing I've had in two damn years.

"Oops." The sound came right before I felt the wetness roll down my shirt. I jerked forward, a preventative leap, but when I looked down I saw red and blue colored ice puddling around the Popsicle stick on the heated ground. It painted the back of my shorts like a sticky Rorschach test. It made all the boys tilt their heads and look.

"You useless little bitch," I said, my mother's words rolling off my tongue with automatic efficiency, finding a new target in Josie's shocked blue gaze. "What the fuck have you ever done? I don't see you working. I don't see your name at the top of the dean's list. All I see is you getting lots of practice with the football team until you're old enough to join your mother at the Buckeye."

There was enough truth to my words that they struck as intended, right at the unsure center of Josie's piece-of-shit sixteen-year-old heart. The boy nearest to her snorted, but withered again under her pointed look. The other three just shuffled their feet. Verbal battle was a girl's fight, and these boys were defenseless. The other girl gaped, though, her glossed mouth opening and closing in sharp little gasps.

But Josie wasn't run down with taunts, not like me. Sunlight bounced hard off her bright hair, and she leaned in close to blaze in my face. "And who the fuck are *you*? You aren't even waiting that long, are you? You're probably already servicing the Coal Man. Tell us, Kristine, when you pull back to swallow, are your lips rimmed in black?"

My face burned as uncomfortable laughter rose to fill the empty, dusty street, along with Josie's wild, confident brays. *The Coal Man.*

It was the nickname for Waylon Rhodes, the first person we'd met in Tonopah, all those years back. The adults called him that because he still worked the drifts, even though there was no silver left in Tonopah to mine. As soon as he had the papers on the Lumbago, he'd reinforced the mine—though not in search of silver. Instead, he'd retrofitted the opium den, its walls still stained with hundred-year-old smoke, and committed himself to disappearing inside of it for days.

He took my mother with him.

The town kids, on the other hand, called him the Coal Man due to the large chunk of fossilized glassy rock he wore around his neck. They said it was Waylon's power, like Samson and his hair. I didn't know if I believed that—there was nothing supernatural about the way he skirted the law in town with a subversive shrug and an oiled grin. There was certainly nothing out of this world about his stench, a pungent sampling of Beech Nut and body odor that lingered in a room long after he'd left.

Yet I thought of him as the Coal Man too.

He was like the mines in this town, dark and black and bored right through the middle. I might not have had the words for it when I was a kid, but six years after first meeting him under the awning of the Mizpah gas station, I knew exactly what I'd seen in his face that day, his eyes black and hard, his laugh flinty as shale. He was a man made to dig and destroy, and like the desert spreading out around us, he was everywhere.

"Ye-ah," Josie licked her lips, on a roll. "The Coal Man owns you too, doesn't he? Like property."

I felt myself go hot and knew my cheeks had flushed red. "Fuck you, Josie."

The world's weakest response.

Josie stepped forward. "That's why you're never leaving this town, Kristine. No matter how many Fodor's or Lonely Planet guides you read in that dusty, old Seven Leagues, your step-daddy already has a place for you cut out in the bowels of the Lumbago."

Stepfather. What a joke . . . and not just because there was nothing fatherly about the Coal Man. Waylon Rhodes would never marry my mother. Yet she'd yoked herself to him like a cow, just so she had the illusion of a man at her side . . . which was Josie's point.

"Yeah, I see it, clear as the sky above. Don't you see it, guys?" Josie said, whirling left and right. The girl was the only one who nodded. Josie didn't seem to care. "He's got a power over you just like he does your mother."

I should have just left. Josie Scott was a stupid bitch townie who would be here long after I was gone, and eventually this shitty desert town would sandblast the brightness out of that hair and carve lines like dry riverbeds on each side of that self-satisfied smile.

But even as I told myself this, I hesitated. My mind felt infected, like a virus. I was feverish under the combined heat of these young eyes and the old sun. I tried to blink away my anger, but all I could see were solar flashes of the years that lay before me, all the taunts and indignities yet to come.

"The Coal Man is a druggie and a drunk and ain't got any power over me," I said, voice breathless, like a steam valve releasing all that heat.

"Prove it."

"Prove what?"

"That he has no power. That you have any." She flipped her hair with one hand, silver tangling with gold. "Go into the Lumbago right now and take the Coal Man's power away. Go down and rip that charm from around his neck while he's laid out on meth and dust and your momma."

"Stupid," I said, and for a moment the word sat up. I didn't even know who I was talking about—Josie, my mother. Me.

"Totally stupid," said Phillip Jensen, earning a pointed glare from Josie. He shrugged under the withering look. "Everyone knows time stops when you're underground."

That was one urban legend I *did* believe. It was the first thing mining town parents told their kids as they begin to toddle. Don't venture too close to the mineshafts, the ghosts will reach up and just suck you down. You knew they were only trying to keep them out of danger, but the briny updraft of a century-old mine smelled *just* like a specter's breath.

"If you do it," Josie said, turning back to me, "you'll have his power and you can go wherever you want."

Now a new future flashed before me, all stemming from an action I could take if only because no one else dared. Do this now, I saw through my angry solar flares, and I could shut Josie Scott up for good.

Seeing me actually considering it, Josie moved her Keds through the bright puddle where her Popsicle had melted. Red and blue flecked the clean canvas of her shoes. She flicked her toes my way.

The boy next to her shook his head. "Don't do it, man."

"Shut up, Paulie," Josie snapped.

"If I get that necklace," I said, also ignoring Paulie, "I'll come back up here and shove it down your throat."

Fronting for the boys. A game Josie could appreciate. She brayed: "You won't get shit."

And so we drove to Mount Rushton in Phillip Jensen's pickup. Green and orange lichen covered the hillside's north face like a patched beard, though Waylon's mine straddled the clean-faced south. The pit had long been stripped of its head frame, but the others clustered in the shade of an old ore bin, murmuring to each other while I prepared to climb down into the darkness.

"Go on," Josie said, ambling so close her whisper stirred my hair. "Ore whore."

"Down your fucking throat," I told her, with a matching smirk. "So tell Phillip to keep it clear."

I lowered myself onto the first brace and was about eight rungs down when I felt the sun pull away. When I looked up, all I could see was Josie's face, bright as a wick, peering down. We locked gazes for one moment before her laughter trumpeted over me. She kicked at the mine's mouth, so that I had to hunch over, pebbles raining onto my shoulders.

No more. No more ambushes on Main Street, and no more running away. Today I would seize some power for myself.

Coughing in the dust that Josie had stirred, I continued down.

34

Never say never.

I come to in the present with a roll of my head, my neck aching sharply from its long-forward slant. I make a sluggish attempt at bleary-eyed focus, but it's at least a minute before shapes make sense.

A bed rises out of the mental mist, and on the end of it, watching me, is a blurry Daniel. He leans forward. For a moment I feel only a sense of loss as I look at him, a grief as deep as anything I'd once felt in the dark heart of the Lumbago mine, and I don't know why. Then I spot Crystal's gun dangling between the fingers of his clasped hands, and fear floods my body.

I rear back instinctively, causing pain to hiss and throb in my many injuries, but I'm restrained in a chair, each limb spread and fastened to its matching wooden arm or leg. I have to blink another handful of times before my eyes finally stick in my sockets, but when they do, I see Daniel smiling as I test the restraints.

"Nothing fancy, just duct tape wrapped around old towels.

247

And one very good Chippendale, of course." He shifts so he can tap the leg of the chair for emphasis, but misses and kicks my shin instead. "I was trying very hard to avoid any evidence of restraint, which is why you were tied so loosely in the truck. That was a mistake. Now you've put me behind schedule."

I turn my head to look out the window and have to squint at even the small amount of late afternoon sun. When my vision evens out, I see that his family's estate home looms in front of me, atop the long and sloping lawn. It stands erect, a guard with eyes that grow more luminous in the nearing advent of dusk. "—re's Abby?"

Where's Abby.

Daniel purses his lips at my dry croak, then rises and disappears into a room behind me, obviously a bathroom. The sink runs for a moment before he returns with a water glass. Looming, he tilts it to my lips. The barrel of the gun caresses my shoulder.

I jerk my head despite my thirst and the pounding in my skull, causing the water to spill down my chin. "Where the fuck is she?"

He places the water on a coaster atop the nightstand, then looks at me solemnly. "I'm afraid she's all tied up at the moment."

Tucking the pistol into his waistband, Daniel moves behind me and begins scooting my chair across the floor. He swivels it side to side, rocking me forward until I'm situated in front of the antique vanity and the room is reflected behind me: a four-poster bed and bureau in matching mahogany, a quaint stone fireplace, lake-facing windows framed in damask. Daniel bends and stares through the mirror as if positioning me just so, though I've no idea why. All I see is the window across the room, and the adjacent console holding a flat-screen TV. Finally satisfied with whatever he sees that I don't, Daniel straightens and then crosses his arms.

"Do you know where you are?"

I've never been in this particular room before, but the private dock is reflected behind me, and the bow of a vintage skiff bobs next to it. Daniel once mentioned it, wistfully, as belonging to his father, the man he murdered. "The guesthouse."

He inclines his head, giving the slightest of nods and flicking at my chopped hair. Gaze dropping to my chapped mouth, he stares at it for a long time before he finally blinks and sighs. "I gotta admit, I don't know what I ever saw in you."

Digging into his pockets, Daniel pulls out the keys that Abby and I took from him in the semi. I jolt as they clatter on the vanity in front of me, which makes him smile. He tosses his phone on the bed behind us, then withdraws the gun from his waistband. I stiffen, though I don't think he's going to shoot. Instead, he's setting the scene, like we're on a movie set. It's a killing tableau.

He tilts his head as he jerks the gun's slide, releasing the magazine but leaving one round chambered. Watching for my reaction from the corner of his good eye, he says, "Don't worry, it's not for Abby. Mother needs it."

"She knows we're here." It's not a question. After all, Daniel disappeared for *three days*, panicking after he impulsively killed a man in the OR. Yet that was two long weeks ago. "This is where you came when you disappeared."

"I blacked out," Daniel confirms, then screws up his mouth

in distaste. "I hate it when people say that, an excuse to absolve them of their actions. I don't want to be absolved. I don't need to be. Yet one minute I was leaving the hospital wondering if I was going to be caught, caught by *you*, and the next minute I'm home, at the gates." He blinks, as if still unable to believe it. "Then at her bedroom door."

I don't say anything.

"Then, suddenly, over her bed."

I frown. "But she called."

She wouldn't stop calling—at the rest stop, on the way to Baker. Again, while I approached a bloody ambulance in the abandoned water park.

"No, that was Crystal. That was her role, you see? She needed to know where you were, what you were wearing, in order to time the stops and pick you up. She had to be able to recognize you when you stumbled out of the water park."

"But I spoke with—"

"Crystal."

Crystal. That's why I'd heard traffic in the background when speaking to "Imogene" in Baker. It's why she'd sounded so falsely cheerful and affected when she'd heard my voice—when she'd been *prompted* to call—all the way back at the rest stop. And it was why Crystal had stared off into the distance, imagining as far as she could down two very different paths, before allowing me into her truck.

"Crystal did a fair job of imitating my mother too. I made her practice. Then again, she had incentive."

She'd had a family.

The disgust on my face has Daniel shooting me his poster-boy smile. It's not as handsome draped across this psychosis.

"Is Imogene still alive?" I ask.

"Of course. In fact, she's away on a spa weekend with her soon-to-be daughter-in-law. So thoughtful of you to arrange it. All her friends know she can't be reached. You two are *bonding*."

Imogene Hawthorne bonding with me. A laughable thought . . . were it not for the circumstances.

"So, what's the plan? I kill my daughter and your mother, thereby eliminating any threat for your affection, but when you're not, I don't know, *thankful* enough, I lose my mind and try to kill you too, before offing myself in . . . what? A classic murder/suicide?"

"I am shot and lose a lot of blood," Daniel confirms, then meets his own gaze in the mirror. "I barely escape with my life."

He tries on a look of wonder, rearranging his features into an amalgam of shock, disbelief, awe. It looks beautiful on him. I would believe it. I *did* believe it for so long.

Then he glares at me and the lovely veneer falls away. "Do you want to hear how I'll make my escape afterwards? So you don't worry, I mean?"

I'm silent, but he jerks his head over his shoulder anyway. "I'll be leaving by boat, which was fortunately gassed up for the night's celebration. I'll have tried to save poor, dear Abby from you, but in the end, there was just nothing I could do against the crazy woman with a terrible past who went on a murderous desert rampage. It will all be very dramatic."

He is making a speech. Performing for a crowd. I watch his reflection and envision him practicing these words in the bathroom mirror at home. I half expect him to thank the Academy.

Dramatics aside, it's clear to see that he's found a way to get rid of both the woman he believed would someday identify him as a killer, and the other, who had made him into one.

I peek back at the main house, its windows glowing like eyes with fractured, leaded knowledge. *Two weeks ago*, I think, and whisper, "What did you do to Imogene?"

"It was a very trying visit," he replies after a moment. "As you know, she can be difficult."

Light dances in his eyes, and I realize that I'm the only one he can share this side of himself with. I'll probably be the only person outside of Imogene who will ever know what he really is, and looking at him, I can see that he was right before. He is not just hot. He is *molten*.

"For all its grandeur," Daniel whispers, "there are very few mirrors in my mother's house. Have you noticed?"

He mistakes my silence for interest.

"It's because my mother cannot stand looking at things she knows are faulty. She wants her life to be perfect, but it isn't and she knows it, and so she hides from herself. She even covered up her husband's death just to maintain the illusion of perfection."

"You mean she didn't tell anyone that you murdered your own father," I correct.

"I mean that she helped me clean up."

He lets that sink in while he eases around my left side and places the gun on the vanity before me, tantalizingly close. "You're exactly like her in that way, you know. You hide from your past and from yourself and what you really are. Yet you're nothing like your own druggie whore mother. I mean, *that's* what you were really fleeing when you escaped that shitty little desert town, right? The idea that you might be just like her."

He pauses for my response, but I don't even blink. I've had these same thoughts myself, hundreds of times, and he knows it.

"No, you're not like her at all." A sly look overcomes his face, and Daniel practically drawls, "No, instead, you're just like your father."

"You don't know anything about my father."

"I know he bought a horse ranch in northern Nevada when you were born. I know he tried to improve his breeding stock by putting all his money into a papered thoroughbred. I know that horse was diseased." He waits for me to contradict him. I can't. "The Internet is such a godsend."

I know. My own Google search taught me that the papers had called it the "dry-land strangles," because it was a disease that spiked in arid weather. Yet it was the infection's nickname that'd stuck most profoundly in my mind: pigeon fever, because of the abscesses that grew to the size of basketballs in both the animals' chests and guts.

"It must have been awful for him," Daniel says. "Having to put a bullet through the head of every single animal."

His wistful smile tells me he's wishing he'd been there to see it.

I close my eyes, and the next thing I know, Daniel's breath is caressing my ear, stirring the short, hacked hair so that it tickles my cheekbones. "And what happened after it was all done, Kristine? Wait . . . don't tell me. Daddy left the barn and stood in a midnight field with the blood of all those dead horses scenting the air, and pointed that smoking shotgun up at his chin. Even though his only daughter, who'd been drawn from the house by the shots ringing through the night, begged him not to."

Even though I lunged as my father pulled the trigger, the hot mist of blood spraying me as I watched his face disappear.

Even though I was standing right there.

I try to fight off the memory he's just conjured, but for a moment I can't help it. I scent cordite and blood in a midnight field. Daniel reads it all in my face.

"Did you try to save him, Kristine?" Daniel asks not unkindly. "Or is that when you started?"

Startled, my eyes find his again.

"You know . . . standing by, watching, while all the things you love just die."

"I don't," I manage through clenched teeth, and for a moment I think, *I'd slaughter him right now if I could.*

"Your dad."

"No." I jerk at my restraints, the tape squeaking but not giving an inch.

"Your mom." When I say nothing, he smiles. "Others."

"No," I say, but it's a whisper now.

"A sickness lives inside of you," Daniel says loudly, leaning on the back of my chair. "It's why you always fall short of your biggest dreams."

Becoming a doctor. Having the perfect family. The ring, the picket fence.

"You fight and flail . . . but we both know you'll never be quite good enough. Just like him."

"No," I jerk my head, even though I have had all these thoughts. Yet that was before Abby . . . mostly. I glare at Daniel through the distance of the mirror. "No, I've never wanted to kill myself."

Unlike either of my parents, the sight of my daughter makes me want to *live*.

"Oh, Kristine."

And straightening behind me, Daniel reaches again into his pocket.

"Never say never."

35

Here's how it's going to happen.

Daniel's hand is in his pocket as he hovers over my chair, and I can feel his body heat spreading around me like a stain. He grows in dimension without moving at all, just swallows my space like a negative force, like I'm nothing. I lean away from him, a knee-jerk reaction to his nearness, but my gentle restraints are rigid. He isn't going to make the same mistake twice.

Reaching down, Daniel presses his cold fingertips to my chin, finding the hollow beneath the bone and my head tilts back almost of its own accord. He keeps pressing until all I can see are the whites of his eyes above me, because *his* gaze remains straight ahead. He watches us through the mirror, his index and middle fingers caressing the hollow of my trachea.

The cold barrel of a gun alights to kiss my right temple.

It sends a shock of activity through my mind. Ears buzzing, thoughts scattering like buckshot, I manage to grab onto one thought: *it can't be the gun.* That's on the vanity, and he already said it wasn't meant for me. Another zipping thought then, and this one hooks my breath with it: *maybe there are two guns.*

"Too bad I can't touch you physically, not for another hour and a half yet," Daniel says, and finally removes his fingers. I lower my head and swallow hard, despite my mouth being completely dry. Daniel lifts the object in his hand high so I can see it through the mirror. It's black and rectangular and has too many buttons to be a gun. I blink. "But that doesn't mean I can't still reach into your chest and carve out your heart."

He points the remote behind us without turning, confident, a magician waving a wand, and we both watch through the mirror as the flat-screen television snaps to life. He is right. He can rip my heart directly from my chest without ever moving at all.

Her head is tilted forward, her hair still tangled and obscuring her face. Her shoulders are shaking, and every so often they give a wild jerk like a heart monitor recording a cardiac jolt. The room around her is covered in burlap and tarps, but there is a window. The last of the day's light glows on her from one side, and an artificial glint assails her from above. I can't identify it, but wherever she is, my daughter has been crying for a long time.

There is no sound, yet somehow I can still hear Abby's cries in my mind as clearly as if she's in the next room. It's a superpower of mine, of all mothers. Dozens of children can be screaming or laughing on the playground, but there's one that has you snapping to attention like a hunting dog, stiff and on-point. This is how I sit as I stare at Abby, not breathing, my thighs tense, my biceps curled.

"That was a crappy stunt you two pulled back in the truck."

Daniel shifts so that he's in front of me, blocking my view of the screen. He props himself on the corner of the vanity, one foot swinging out to knock against my bare shin as he forces me to stare at him full-on. I feel the old anger well up inside of me, a flash flood of roiling heat, and for a moment I don't stop it. Instead of fighting the situation—the man in front of me and my helplessness and my anger at both—I let myself feel it, fury so primal it burns everything from existence. I can live in this white space without pain. I can hate everything with a completeness that flattens meaning into dust, and I know I'll be safe. I've lived here before.

Then Daniel points the remote at the television again, there's a click, and I hear, "Mommy . . ."

Says the one person worth every ounce of felt pain.

"Mommy . . ."

I sway at the crack in her voice. It sounds like her mind is switching directions midstream, from hope to none. Where is she . . . where could she be . . . where does he . . .

"Momm—"

He flicks a button, cutting the sound again, and I instinctively reach for her, fingers flaring against the arms of the chair.

"I know. It's not very high-tech. Anyone can do it with a camera and a wireless network. But. It can be disassembled quickly, and I think it still does the job, right?"

I barely hear him. I am entertaining a fantasy of pressing water to my baby's lips, cupping her head and neck as I do it, of washing her feet, and drying them with what's left of my hair. Anything. God, anything.

He clicks again. Her soft whimper sails to me, crisp and clear on the wireless connection. Yup, it does the job all right.

"Abby."

Victory lights Daniel's eyes, a flipped switch. For a second I don't understand it, but then Abby's voice goes crazy behind me, and I realize that she can now hear me too. "Mommymommy-mommy help. Mommy, help me—"

Sobbing and wild-eyed, Abby writhes against restraints as soft and inflexible as mine, head whipping up and side to side as she searches for me. I want to help her, but I can't—

Daniel mutes the sound, though I can still see Abby calling to me through the mirror. "Tell her that mommy has been very bad."

He presses the remote and the sound returns. Daniel tilts his head at me and I somehow find my voice. Of course I do. Anything to keep that look away from Abby. "Abby. M-mommy has been very bad."

"No, Mommy! You're a good mommy. Please, come get me. I'm—"

Daniel mutes her once more. "Tell her Mommy is going to have to be punished."

Abby is still talking when he turns the sound back on, a rush of words that flow over me, slaking my heat. I begin to shake.

"Mommy is going to have to be punished," I say, then rush on, "but I love you, baby. I love you and—"

"Tell her," Daniel interrupts in that same even voice, clicking the button, "that when the fireworks begin to shoot out over the lake, she is going to die."

He pressed the button again, allowing Abby's soft crying to fill the room, and I open my mouth. Nothing comes out. I work my jaw, but finally I just whisper, "Please . . ."

Daniel's lip twists in disgust, and he shakes his head before muting the two-way speaker and throwing the remote down. It clatters across the vanity as he moves behind me, where he picks up a rucksack that's been propped against the door. He unzips it.

The knife he withdraws is serrated, nothing at all like the precision tools he uses in the OR.

I shake harder.

"Here's how it's going to happen," he says quietly, moving back behind me and gently tucking the lank strands of my hair behind my ears. It's too short, and they immediately slide back into my face. "I'm going to ask you a series of questions. I'll expect you to answer within ten seconds. That's the only rule, and it's non-negotiable. None of this stuttering or begging." He curls his hands into himself as if begging. The tip of the serrated blade pokes me in the skull. "P-p-puh-lease."

He pulls me back, resettling me in place, his touch firm but gentle. "Let's practice once before I allow Abby to hear you again. We'll start with something easy."

"I don't—"

He lifts the knife. "Right earlobe or left?"

He's going to cut me up?

He's going to make my daughter listen?

Daniel sighs. "Right earlobe or left, Kristine. If you don't answer in five seconds, I'm going to assume the answer is both."

No time to make a proper decision . . . not that there is one.

"Left," I blurt, as he's reaching for my right ear. He detours smoothly, without hesitation, and pulling the lobe down low, begins sawing. It only takes seconds, just long enough for my surprised squeal to swerve into a throaty scream, but the fire that shoots through me burns long after he throws the flap of skin down into my lap. It's not the full ear. I can see through the tears that he's left most of the cartilage intact, but none of his surgical skills were on display as he sawed at the soft flesh, and so each breath escapes me in a guttural moan.

Daniel waits. Eventually, I straighten from my forward slump. I am breathing like an animal, chest heaving, something large hibernating inside my throat.

"Okay. Not bad for a first try." He saunters around until he's in front of me again. The throbbing burn of my lost earlobe is turning cold, but the blood hitting my shoulder is steady and hot. "The phalanges are next. I'll let you choose between distal and medial. We'll build slowly to appendages and joints, though I'll be certain to pay careful attention to key muscles."

Demonstrating, he leans forward and angles the blade into my mouth. I pull back my lips but he's not cutting or thrusting or hacking. He's just pointing at my tongue. The tip of the blade scrapes it and I taste blood. Withdrawing it, he then taps my nose. "And cartilage. And sockets."

He moves the blade to the corner of my eye, and digs a bit until the skin pops. He leans back then, and heaves a great sigh, satisfied to watch me shake. "I wouldn't move too much if I were you."

But I can't help it. For someone tied up and completely immobile, I am awfully busy, quaking and bleeding and gasping for air as I try to reassemble the thoughts in my scattered mind. Daniel drinks in the sight as if sipping a fine wine.

"I really shouldn't have gotten so angry at you for running, for fighting." He tilts his head like we're engaged in an actual conversation, like my teeth aren't clattering in my skull. "I have to say that I learned so many things along this journey that I never would have if you'd simply gone along with the plan. You forced me to improvise and exercise patience and restraint. All of those things put me in an even better place than originally intended.

"I'm still going to kill you, of course, because extinction of the faulty and the weak is a vital and necessary part of the natural evolutionary process. . . ."

And I was defective. Because I hadn't seen him. Because I could not be made better or fixed. Because the last thing the world needs is *two* Mrs. Hawthornes.

"But I guess what I'm saying is . . . you've helped to accelerate my *own* evolution. If I believed in such things, I'd say that this moment, you and me here, was fated from the start. I feel . . ." he searches out the word. "*Appreciative*. So, thank you."

He drops a kiss atop my sweaty forehead, careful to avoid my dripping ear, and then gets up and puts the knife back in the knapsack. He catches my frown through the mirror just as he opens the door, and snaps his fingers, the sound almost cheery. "Oh, wait—that's right."

Returning one final time to the dresser, Daniel points the remote at the television, and allows Abby's pleas, now kitten soft, to fill the room. "Almost forgot—you're going to need to be able to hear the questions."

36

He's going to make it hurt.

There is a long moment of pure stupidity, where my mind simply blocks out Daniel's words. I'm so dumbstruck that my ear doesn't even hurt. Then, when his meaning finally crashes over me—when I realize that it's not Abby who has to listen to someone she loves being tortured, but *me*; that it's not my body parts I have to decide are to be removed, but *hers*—I do something that surprises us both. I roar like a match has been set to my insides, and the sound is so oily and raw and feral that Daniel actually backs up three whole steps. It's a sound I thought I'd left buried deep inside a mineshaft eleven long years ago.

I pour my guts out into the cry, spots blooming behind my eyes, my earlobe and head throbbing with the sound, but my goddamn stubborn broken heart keeps on beating, despite how much I hate the world right now, how much I think I've always hated it. I suck in a breath so deep and jagged that it hacks right through my middle.

A sob bursts up and out of me so fast that it lifts me from the seat. Daniel draws back even more, tilting his head, not quite trusting his own ears. Then he blurs into an indistinct outline as tears fill my eyes and I wail for the first time since my father blew himself away in front of me.

The ability to cry hasn't been cauterized from me after all.

Daniel takes a tentative step back my way, like he doesn't want to spook me. Abby is crying out to me too, but my sorrow smothers even that, because I know what's coming for her. I drown her out with gulping howls that quake the entire world. My tears, inaccessible before, are unstoppable now.

I don't remember Daniel moving in front of me, but his eyes suddenly search my face. He studies me up close, as if he's never seen me before. My shoulders shake and my throat is seared, but the sound keeps rolling out, etched from my vocal cords to emerge raw and scabbed.

And oh, how he loves my pain. *Loves* it. I can see it when he straddles my chair and bends close to capture my release for all time, and it's with total horror that I realize he has never, ever looked at me with such love before.

Gently, almost primly, Daniel settles himself onto my lap. He inches nearer, ignoring the hot, low sounds still escaping my throat. I think he's going to kiss me again, but instead, he places one hand on each side of my chair and gently, ravenously, licks the tears from my right cheek. His hot tongue slides from my jaw to my inner eyelid, where a new tear threatens to spring.

I tilt my head up so that it's almost touching his, same as we used to do in bed. My breathing steadies slightly. We are so close that our eyes threaten to cross, and for a moment, it almost seems like there's that old magic between us. We share a look, both intimate and uninhibited. A drop of blood falls from my ear. Finally, I give a small, capitulating nod: *I see you. I see who you really are.*

And then I bite down on his fucking nose until my teeth meet on the other side.

Daniel howls, jerking back, but I hold tight and he has to strike my face with the flat of his palm to jar me loose. Wheeling away, he cups a hand to his injured nose, and even through my newly rent tears, I can see he comes away with blood. Good. I snarl when he looks at me and spit his own blood back in his face.

He is back on me in an instant, and this time the gun is in his hand. The barrel doesn't quite fit into my left nostril, but not for lack of trying. His nose is still attached, but also not for lack of trying.

My voice emerges as if caught in a bubble. "Do it, you pansy little mama's boy."

That almost gets him. His index finger twitches. "I should. I'd love to see your brains splattered against hand-painted chinoiserie."

"Let me guess? Mommy picked it out herself?"

His chest heaves against mine as he fights to control his breathing, and he finally uses my face to push up and away, though he yanks his palm back quickly when I angle in for another bite. He smacks me upside the head again, causing new pain to bloom in my shorn earlobe and my battered temples. Then he jostles my chair as he goes to check the damage to his face in the powder room behind me. I think the fucker is actually pouting.

Yet even as my eyes are returning to Abby, Daniel changes

his mind. Instead, he stops short of the bathroom and wheels back toward the front door, the duffel, and the house on the hilltop. I realize he's fleeing. He doesn't trust himself in the same room with me. He is heaving from the effort not to flatten me.

Daniel opens the door, turning only to cast me one last bloody, murderous look.

"I think," he says, through clenched teeth, "That I'll go visit your daughter now."

And even though he leaves, he flattens me all the same.

////////////

The sun is sinking from view as Daniel strolls back to the main house, leaving only shadows to yawn over the yard and the lake and the killer. I moan as he disappears from view, then catch myself as I glance at the television, and at Abby curled into the corner of that unidentifiable room. I don't want to scare her with any more cries, but my whole body hurts. Head, ear, leg, feet—I am a constellation of slim bones linked together by bright spots of pain. I am an asterism of agony.

Yet Daniel is going to appear on that screen soon. I know and dread it, but can do nothing to stop it.

When the fireworks begin to shoot out over the lake, she is going to die.

Bile rises to my throat and I have to choke it down. There's no way I can remain stoic or strong through this. He is going to take that blade to my child, my baby, and knowing I'm watching, that I understand how it feels, he's going to make it hurt.

Stand by, watching, while all the things you love just die . . .

"Oh God . . . oh God . . ." I whisper it through yet more tears.

They've been building up for years, and it seems they aren't going to stop now that they've been given rein to fall. They well fat and round in my eyes while saliva pools in my bloodied mouth. My armpits sweat. My earlobe bleeds. My whole body weeps.

"God, please . . ." I haven't prayed since my father died either.

You mean since he killed himself.

The thought is just suddenly there, uncharacteristically bitter and accusing, and it stills me for a moment. I wouldn't be here now if my father had chosen to live. *Everything* would be different if instead of fleeing his problems on that star-slammed night he'd have just bent down and taken my hand. Maybe he and my mother could have fought for our family and home together. Then she wouldn't have needed to prostitute herself in the deep, dry opium dens of a busted mining town.

And maybe I wouldn't have felt it was my responsibility to single-handedly save every damn thing I saw: my father, my mother, my patients . . . even Daniel, when I thought he was being dragged through the desert by a madman.

And Abby wouldn't be tied up in a home that spawned a psycho. She wouldn't be terrified, with an ineffectual mother who could do nothing to stop her pain. A broken mother, I think, and another tear silently falls.

Because that's what Daniel has gotten wrong. In this way, I am *exactly* like my mother. The screaming horses and my father's moonlit death isn't what I hide in the darkest corners of my mind. I'd been angry at him for that, but I'd still pined for him for years.

Yet my mother wore down my love in increments. She was a pumice stone applied to an open wound—she kept rubbing at me with every relentlessly bad decision, every unwarranted criticism, and each moment of neglect until I was finally so numb that I felt nothing for her at all. Sure, I eventually ran away, escaping to Vegas, but it was only because my mother had abandoned me first.

I lower my head, exhausted from the pain clustered in my body, by everything I've seen in the last twenty-four hours, by my newfound tears, and by knowing that, even after being alone for so long—after swearing I wouldn't repeat my mother's mistakes when it came to men—I didn't just choose wrong. I picked the worst possible man to bring into my daughter's life.

The knowledge is a blade in my body, it is the greatest injury. It wedges next to one final memory that I have wadded into a tight ball, and just like the tears, it comes roaring up from the dark. I turn to it as it rushes me and finally face it head on.

37

The surface was up there somewhere.

I'd been in the mines before, but I'd never gone deep and never alone. They were wormholes to a different world, underground museums untouched by anything more probing than rattlers for most of a century. The weak-sloped hillsides surrounding Tonopah were studded with these plank-topped holes, all chipped by Chinese laborers back when the West was still wild.

At least I knew to watch for rotting timber and duck the low backs. After leaving Josie Scott braying on the bright surface above me, I continued down into the Lumbago, sniffing for pockets of methane gas and watching for the dark rims of hanging slabs. Waylon and his customers had cut such a clear path in the drift that I didn't have to worry about where I was going. He even had old carbide lamps burning throughout the tunnels, splashing enough light on the walls to catch my own shadow snapping in and out of shape. Another ghost, I thought, the pebble-stone pop of blasting caps snapping beneath my feet as decades-old graffiti guided me deeper.

I hurried past a cache of old dynamite crates stored in an alcove blasted a half-century before, surprised that the wood hadn't been stripped for reuse before I realized how difficult it would be to drag it back up to the surface . . . and starting an open fire down here would be suicide.

Seventy feet down—I was counting—and I finally began to move horizontally. The pressure from the earth all around me was like a vise slipped around my skull. I kept my mind forward-focused, eyes searching out the next hanging slab, if only to keep it from swerving to the thought of ghosts. At some point, I stopped wondering how much deeper I had to go and wondered only what exact depth was required for time to stop.

The sound of my feet scrabbling over cut sericite was what alerted Waylon to my presence.

He was naked, lying on a platform bed with industrial wheels, an old mine cart refitted and repurposed and centered in the middle of the room. The packed floors were covered in Orientals, the wall niches painstakingly fitted with candles and colored glass. The air was filled with a sickly sweet scent, I knew it was some kind of drug, and it made my lungs constrict in defense. Grocery bags were stacked in the far corner, half-hidden by a silk curtain with a garish and frayed pom-pom fringe.

Waylon was facing the entrance, reclined on his side like a king, and when he saw me hovering in the doorway of cut rock, he pushed up to one elbow and bent a knee invitingly. "Well, lookie who finally deigned to join us."

I didn't answer. Instead I stared at the form lying next to

him, trying to reconcile the tumble of flesh with my mother. This woman's limbs were splayed wide on the matted furs of other once-living things, greasy hair spilled atop a pillow of yellowed lace. She, too, was naked, but her body was a constellation of bruises and marks. Waylon had been beating her, but I don't think she felt it. Even now, she only writhed beneath him, toward him, her arms bound above her in chains.

A spittoon sat next to a second bed in the corner, where Gilbert Anderson—a man I knew from the recycling center—was struggling into a sitting position. At least he had the decency to try and cover himself. Incense burned on a ledge above him, but did nothing to mask the smells of body odor and drugs and sex.

I took in all of the decayed decadence and thought of emperors and Rome. I thought of the way it all burned.

And, suddenly, I knew why I'd really come.

I stepped into the room, gaze firmly on Waylon's face. "I want my mother back, Waylon."

I didn't recognize my voice in the heavy stillness of the mine. The quartz ledges cut it in two, making it half of what it should have been.

Waylon glanced down at my mother with a surprised look, as if to say, why? But I did want her. I knew that now. I wanted it to be like it used to be between us, before we wheeled into this tumbleweed town six years earlier. The way it was when I was a kid and she still wanted to feed me, to nourish me. To keep me alive.

I remembered the way she used to look at my father too, with a smile that made even Josie Scott's brightness pale in comparison. That woman was somewhere inside that sunken chest, buried beneath those fevered eyes.

I wanted her back.

"I'm taking her out of the mine and this life. Now."

I could see it too. Us, rising from the Lumbago together, walking down the clean south face of Mount Rushton hand-in-hand and getting in that old Chevy and leaving Tonopah and the greater Mojave far behind to become a real family again. I suddenly wanted this more than anything.

Waylon ran a lazy hand over his hairy chest, then let it fall to toy with the tip of one of my mother's breasts. "But your momma wants to stay with me and ol' Gilbert here. Ain't that right, Janie Mae?"

He gave her nipple a hard twist, and my mother jerked beneath him, chains rattling.

"Say yes, baby, and I'll give you another hit." Waylon reached down and emerged again with a glass pipe. He dangled it above my mother's face, just out of reach.

She looked at it like it was both Jesus and the Second Coming. "Momma. Don't."

Her head bobbed, then swung my way as if on a hinge. I could have sworn a creaking sound accompanied the movement. Eyes going in and out of focus, she eventually gave up and just dropped her head back onto the stained pillow.

"And what's a smug little prude like you gonna do about it?" she finally croaked.

I told myself it was only the drugs talking. I wasn't smug; I was brave. I wasn't a prude; I was the girl who was going to save the only person left to me in this world. I'd get us both out of this mine. Because I damn well wasn't going to stand by and watch one of my parents die again.

"A trade," I told Waylon. "If you accept, my mother leaves this mine now. And she never comes down here again."

Waylon eyed me lazily and licked his fat bottom lip. "Even if she wants to?"

"She won't. Not if you stay away from her."

"And in return?"

There was only one thing Waylon would want in return.

"I stay. One night." I said. "That's all."

"That's *all*?" Waylon hooted. The earth dampened the sound, eating his laughter whole. "That's more than enough."

My heart thumped at that, but I was resolute. I wanted my mother back. "You have to promise never to come near her again."

"You got yourself a deal," Waylon said, too fast. His teeth flashed, and in that moment they were the brightest spot in the entire mine. "But Krist-i-ine . . . are you ready? Cause I'm going to show you how long a night can really be."

//////////

Gilbert took my mother away. Even guided, she stumbled across the carpets, a yelp tipping into crazy laughter as she righted herself and disappeared into the drift.

"Lie down."

I didn't move. I just thought, oh my God. She didn't turn around. I didn't know if my mother knew what I was doing, what I was giving up for her, but unlike me, I think with a start, she never once looked back.

The realization came too late. She was gone, and now I was here with Waylon.

275

"Willingly," he reminded me, "or else it's not a fair trade."

Waylon smiled as I swayed forward to sit where he was pointing. The silk threaded blankets were still warm from my mother's body. I realized it was the closest I'd been to her in months. *She didn't even look back.*

Waylon reached for the restraints, but I stopped him with the softest touch on his forearms. My fingertips were ice, but his skin blazed, and I knew then that *I* was right. It wasn't the chunk of black, petrified stone around his neck. It wasn't even the fact that he still worked the drifts. Waylon Rhodes was the Coal Man simply because he burned from the inside.

"Willingly," I said. "And then you disappear from our lives forever."

Waylon dropped the chain and climbed over me. His balls sagged and so did his gut. The coal around his neck swung like a metronome. I fastened my eyes on that. "Okay, but I'm going to work you. You don't know who you are, Krissy-Girl. Not until you been pushed to the edge."

And that's when time finally stopped.

The surface was up there somewhere. I had to keep reminding myself of that over the long hours of sweating and grunting. Somewhere up there, light was shining off of Josie Scott's head. Somewhere else my mother was sleeping off her bender. Yet as Waylon continued to pound and hammer and chisel precious things away at my core, the pull of the surface lessened for me. Like the dynamite crates and abandoned carts, I was now a part of this underground museum. I, too, was suddenly old and dusty and blasted inside.

Hours passed like days, and at some point in that artificial week, Waylon made me do a hit before trying to take me one last time. The coal on his necklace felt like a block of ice as it struck my heated cheek, and suddenly he just collapsed. His snores were rumbling over my body before I realized he was asleep. I also realized suddenly that I needed water.

I, too, now burned.

Sliding from beneath him, I fell to the floor, crashing awkwardly on my hip, though that was the least of my bruises. I'd seen Gilbert drinking from a jug in the corner and I zigzagged in that direction, my head stuffy, my stomach sensitive to my fingertips. I was reaching for the dirtied jug when I spotted my new pair of shorts. My eyesight swooped as I blinked and wove my way over to them, and I almost knocked back into Waylon, but steadied myself by planting my legs. I tottered, but didn't fall.

The pristine white denim was ruined. Holding it eye level, I wondered at the red and blue stains before I remembered Josie's Popsicle stick. I flipped them over, but didn't have to wonder about the other stain, Waylon's, at all. I remembered feeling pretty putting those shorts on that day. I'd felt hopeful about the start of summer. I pulled them on again, trying to recapture that, but all I felt this time was sore.

And so very hot.

Pivoting, I found myself studying Waylon as he slumbered. He'd face-planted, arms hanging over each side of the modified mine cart, the hair on his flat buttocks matted with sweat. My gaze swung around again, and finally fastened on the prettiest object in the den, a jewel-toned lantern more delicate and decorative than the others. Time swooped sideways in the drift, tricking me again, and suddenly I was next to it.

I opened the front cage of the lantern, then lifted it to let the light play on the onyx bead of a dry silk tassel. When the fabric touched the wick, spreading the warmth, I felt a smile rise with it. I felt a kinship with the flame.

Half of the room was engulfed in flames before Waylon felt my heat and clamored to life. The drugs he'd fed me had caused my mind to unhinge every few seconds, so I was just standing at what felt like a safe distance, watching him get wrapped up in the soiled silk sheets as he staggered from the cart. I felt someone laugh when he fell over backward, further into the den. The laugh rumbled deeper inside of me before swerving into a feral roar. Then I felt flames licking the hair on my arms, and I turned and ran.

Smoke chased me, along with Waylon's furied, frantic bellows, as I pinwheeled past boxes marked EXPLOSIVES and crevices large enough to hide in. Hard quartz corners cut at my arms and coiling pockets of methane gas followed my progress with round silence, but I kept running until I finally reached the ramp.

I was less careful climbing up the shaft than I'd been going down. Wobbling, my foot broke through a rung of rotted wood, and when the one below it splintered beneath my weight, I heard a pained grunt. Fingertips scrabbling at my ankles. I climbed faster.

I was clearing the shaft collar when I felt the ghostly swirl of the upcast. They would say later that air was blowing into the Lumbago from another connecting mine, but I knew it was really the ghosts of trapped miners. The spirits shuddered through the tunnels, awakened by the fire. Their windy, upward howls ferried with the warning scent of burning wood. Time was moving, sprinting, once again.

Open sky streamed above me, and tendrils of my long, thick hair rose, hot air ribboning it high above me.

"Wait!" Waylon called. "Take my hand!"

I paused . . . and I looked back.

Waylon had broken two more rungs above him and fallen farther into the shaft. He was too heavy and too far off to lunge for the rung beneath my bare feet. I turned away.

"Kristine, please!"

It was the first time he'd ever said my given name without turning it into a taunt. I frowned at that, looked up at the vast, hot sky above, and blinked. When I turned back to Waylon, he looked nothing like he had while he violated me in the bowels of the mine. I wondered for a moment if I looked different too, haloed by the light above me, hair snaking around my head on the breath of ghosts.

Bending, making sure each of my limbs was carefully balanced on a rung, I let go with my right hand, reached down to Waylon, and touched his heated skin. Before he realized what I was really after—before he could snag my wrist and reverse-grip—I wrapped my hand around his necklace and gave the icy coal around his neck a hard yank. His eyes widened on a strangled yelp, but I just turned and climbed the rest of the way to the surface. Waylon's shouts battered my back, but I felt nothing. His power was in my fist.

I took it slow, stumbling down Mount Rushton on bare feet, though I never fell. I had just touched flat ground when the explosion roared behind me. Pebbles shook beneath my feet but I kept walking. Coal in my fist, I did not look back.

38

Hold on, baby.

Do no harm.

I didn't adopt the oath because I wanted to be a doctor, a healer. I swore myself to it because of what I already was—a killer. My mother claimed no memory of leaving the mine with Gilbert that day, and in a belated fit of self-preservation, he actually agreed with me when I told the police I'd exited along with them. Relief almost swept the deputy's face blank, and even if I did still have the grit of the mines between my toes, I knew that as far as the authorities were concerned, Waylon had died alone in that mine, a victim of his own searing vice.

Yet every so often I'd catch my mother looking at me, and not with annoyance or disgust. Not like before. Instead, she regarded me with the same wariness once reserved solely for Waylon, and every time I caught her at it, it felt like she was looking right through that missing space. I took no satisfaction in it, because I knew that blasted out part of me had gotten stuck down there with him. With all those floating, furious ghosts.

I'd like to say I felt remorse for what I did. I'd lie to myself about it sometimes, telling myself in the darkest nights that I had no choice, that there's no way I could have saved us both. Then I'd feel something chortle deep inside of me, and I'd bury myself beneath the sheets and cover my ears with coal-stained fists.

I didn't bother looking for Josie Scott. She was nothing to me now, less than a fly to be swatted at, and after the explosion she didn't dare seek me out either. Yet I did catch her stutter-step as she paused in front of the window of the Seven Leagues a week later. She was fixed on a calcified chunk of rock swaying lightly from a nail head on a worn leather cord. It hung right between the porcelain figurines and a collection of bottles bleached amethyst by the sun.

I felt a happy fury rise to my throat watching Josie trying to gaze upon it without appearing to look, and when she finally lowered her eyes and walked away? I swear I tasted smoke in the back of my throat.

That's when I knew the truth. If given the chance? The only thing I'd change about that night would be to blow up that mine-shaft sooner.

And then my belly began to grow, tight and round, pulsing with life. With every movement, anger bloomed. I didn't care. The rage, at least, drove out the pain. It kept the other kids from meeting my eyes in school. It kept the whispers I knew were flying behind cupped palms from ever reaching my ears. By fall, I was brittle and chipping apart. By winter, I was dead to it all.

And then it was spring and it was time and I was ready to hate her.

I walked to the town's sole hospital by myself that day, braced against the world and almost welcoming the rolling pain. Bright and familiar, it was the only thing I'd felt in months. Dead silent, dead-eyed, dead to the life inside and around me, I pushed and pushed and waited for coal to emerge from my womb.

The lusty, cutting wail almost stopped my heart.

Borne in the depths of the mines, carved into me before being carved out of me, this girl-child raged. Stunned, I watched her rail against the unfairness of being born with sounds and emotions that I no longer had in me. Astonished, I just stared when the nurse placed a squalling, red-faced being in my arms, and then stared some more when the thing actually paused to pin me in place with murky, knowing eyes. Then she blinked.

"What?" I said almost defiantly.

The center of her hairless eyebrows pulled together in a frown. She blinked again. Still warm from my body, she just lay there all pink and solid, looking at me like I was the one newly born. It was a spotlight stare, and something never before seen bloomed inside of me to fill up that empty, blasted space. I stared back, unblinking, as it took root, and after a moment, I shifted her closer. The little brows relaxed, and something inside of me recalibrated.

We went on like that, in a call-and-response pattern, one unknown need meeting another. She pushed out her pink tongue, or flailed, or slept—and I responded—nursed, swaddled . . . kept watch. At some point, the nurses left the room, but I was too busy blossoming inside to notice. For the first time in nine months, I felt full and round, entranced with the sight of this tiny fury.

My mother came the next morning, but only because they'd told her I'd changed my mind.

"So, that's it?" For the first time since Waylon's death, her smirk was back. "One night, and you think you're fit for this?"

"Oh, Momma," I sighed, though I was calmer than I'd ever felt in my life. I had someone else to be furious for me now. "You know."

She stared hard in challenge, thinking I meant how it felt to be a mother. "Know what?"

"You know," I said, and I pinned her back with that see-right-through-you stare. "Just how long one night can be."

///////////

Back in the present, I'm crying again. My sobs jerk the breath from my lungs, convulsions causing my stomach to spasm as I choke on my own snot.

"Damn it." I squeeze my eyes shut until light burns behind my eyelids.

And what's a smug little prude like you gonna do about it?

An unexpected growl erupts from my cramping belly. I can no more stop it than I can the tears—it escapes me like a living thing, swift and wild and hovering on the periphery of my blurred vision, waiting to see what I'm going to do. I avert my eyes, staring back out the window, but instead of the lawn, the estate, or Daniel, this time I catch my own reflection. Despite the hacked hair and shorn ear and red-rimmed eyes, despite the tears, I recognize the woman I see there. I saw her once before, in Waylon's upturned face.

Krist-i-ine . . .

I jerk at the tape binding my wrists.

You don't know who you are . . . not until you been pushed to the edge.

I growl again and realize the sound matches the reflected image, matches the heat that has kept flaring up inside of me as I've been forced on this sick road trip. It's as combustive as the fire that roared as I rose to the surface of the Lumbago, icy coal curled in my fist.

What's a smug little—

"Same as last time," the reflected woman interrupts, snarling, bleeding. "I'm gonna bury that motherfucker."

And I look around for a weapon.

Daniel has thoughtlessly left no sharp objects lying nearby. The bedside tables echo the chinoiserie motif and are thickly lacquered, without hard edges or drawers. The desk before the lake-facing window is a surprisingly simple Parsons design, no more than three sides of a rectangle topped with a cluster of faux roses and two shining gold pens. Even if I could get over there, I can't see myself severing duct tape with a Mont Blanc.

Bed aside, the only other furniture in the room is the console holding the television, but I can't reach it while bound to the chair, and Daniel was overly occupied with that area anyway. I doubt he'd have forgotten to clear it of anything that might help me.

I need to fashion a weapon for myself, but as I glance around at all the ninety-degree angles in the room, all these walls and doors and blocks of furniture, there's not one sharp corner to be found.

"Mommy . . ."

The cry is tiny and desolate, the mewling of lost prey, and my throat tightens as I glance back at the television, though Daniel has not yet appeared. "Hold on, baby," I say, because he can't hear me, because he's not with her. Yet.

I lean forward to test the chair. The intricate scrollwork on the seat and arms is delicate, but it might as well be a concrete slab at my back. I try again for my feet, but the chair's weight forces my head down, and I see nothing but blood dripping from my ear to the carpet below me. I push to the balls of my feet and manage to scoot forward a few inches, but I'll never be able to right myself if I topple forward, so I settle all four chair legs back on the floor, and blow the sticky, jagged lengths of hair from my face.

I can't break the chair, so maybe a window? If I can create a shard of glass, rub it against the tape . . .

But there's nothing to swing at it, save my head, and I've taken enough blows there already. I could rub up against a bedpost or a desk corner until it gives . . . no, that'll take hours, and the sun is already slipping away. Fireworks will soon light the sky.

I have no leverage, no range of motion, no mobility.

I look back at Abby and feel my face crumple, but push back the tears this time and try to focus on the room I'm in. I need to cast it in the light of that ornate lantern in the mining den. I need to start thinking like Daniel, like Waylon, and forget for a bit all about *do no harm*.

That's when, through the mirror, I note something I passed right over before. I have to blink a few times to wrap my brain around it because it's not a proper weapon like a knife or a gun. Smaller than my palm, it's propped against a virgin cream candle on the nearest side table. It's made mostly of paper, but like me, it only needs a little spark to find its strength.

All I have to do now is scoot over, grab hold of the book of matches . . . and set myself on fire.

I stare at the gold matchbook—a detail that's as prettily staged as the rest of the room—and my mind flashes on all the burn patients I've seen come through the OR. It's one of the worst types of injuries. Skin insulates and protects everything inside of us, it regulates temperature and sensation. It's a living organ in itself. Burn victims are stripped of all those things.

Plus, most victims of home fires are overcome in minutes. I've heard it dozens of times, and I've even asked the EMTs, *Why didn't they just leave the house?*

Modern homes burn faster, came the answer. *The building, the furniture—it's all more combustible. Used to be you had thirty minutes to escape. Now it's three, and if they're sleeping . . .*

But this isn't a modern home. Everything in here is antique. And Daniel has succeeded in one thing, at least: I am now wide-fucking-awake.

I begin rocking, edging my way toward the table. I totter in my haste and topple forward, gut tipping first, but the chair arms smack the side table and send a rumble up my forearms. Still, it stops my tumble. Unfortunately, I'm now unable to close the distance between me and the matches. I shift my weight back to my toes, but momentum flings me forward and I turn my head just before I face-plant on the table. The lamp crashes atop me— God, I'm so sick of being hit in the head—and when I open my eyes and my vision finally settles, I see the book of matches has fallen flat. "Shit."

"Mommy . . ."

I jerk my head and send the lamp crashing to the floor. Good thing Daniel isn't with Abby yet, because he'd hear my attempts at escape. Then again, maybe that's exactly what he wants to hear.

I'm stuck in this forward tilt, thighs burning as I strain to remain upright because the table is threatening to topple under my weight too. The tendons in my neck strain as I stretch my chin forward as far as I can, but the matches remain millimeters from reach. Exhaling hard, I let the chair's weight swing me back again.

Sweating, I glare at the book of matches for a moment, then launch myself forward without thought. My forehead strikes the glossy top with a resounding crack and pain shoots through my temple and left cheek and destroyed ear. The world tilts. The chair slides away, the table remains standing, but I manage to snag one lacquered leg as I tumble and the table tips and finally falls. I bite my tongue when I land, and pain blooms red in my mouth.

Ignoring it, and Abby's cries somewhere above me, I search the thick, pale carpeting for the gold matchbook. There. Half-hidden under the bed, the heads of the red-tipped matches stand out like runway flares beneath the ruffled bed skirt. I have to shift to my left side in order to extend my hands before me, and this sets the road burn there roaring to life while catapulting me farther away from the bed. Eyes squeezed shut, I take a deep breath and use my core to scoot forward, trying to use the pain to keep me focused, though I can't keep from crying out as I stretch for the cardboard book.

The chair smacks against the bed frame, jarring, and stopping me short. I extend my shaking fingers and for a second I feel my middle finger scrape the matchbook's cover before I push it farther away, under the bed. "Shit."

Arching back, I swing around, grimacing again from the inflammation searing my left side. This time I ram up against the bed with the chair legs, but that's okay. I just need to point my toes, give another scoot with my core—burn some more, *GodGod-God*—and then the top of my left foot scoops the matches up like the bumper on a pinball machine.

My left side goes numb as I swing back around, and I'm sweating as I stretch my fingers high, feeling the burn in the tendons of my wrists and fingers. Giving one final push, I drop my left hand down, directly onto the matches.

But I'm right-handed.

I fight anyway to work a match from the book one-handed, suddenly aware that Abby is too quiet. I don't know why. I can't see the television, but something tells me to move faster.

There's this bar trick I saw once, a way to fold the matchbook cover over and apply the strike zone to the extended match. It's possible to do one-handed, but if done properly, the whole book of matches will light at once. That means that even if I'm successful, I'll only get one shot.

I fumble both the first and second attempts, my hand cramping with the impossible position. And then a third.

Closing my eyes, I stop breathing for a moment before trying again. Keeping my fingers stiff and tight, I angle my wrist painfully high while gripping the matchbook between my middle and ring fingers. I snap them just as I hear, "Mommy."

The heat pounces, and I react like anyone would to fire lapping at their fingertips. I jerk away, but catch myself right before I drop the book, and flip it so that the remaining matches burst into flame. Then I lift the orange bloom to the filmy bed skirt, and force myself to stop thinking. The skirt catches fast and I jerk my body toward the upward licking fire. It's going to quickly turn to ashes—it's literally out of my hands now—and if I don't get free, I'll be trapped on the floor, still taped to this chair as the blaze grows. Making fists, I squeeze my eyes shut and tilt my wrists to the spreading flame.

It's like plunging my flesh in scalding water and holding it there. Gritting my teeth and battling a scream, I fight to keep the tape over the flame. The towels Daniel placed between it and my wrists to keep from leaving marks shields me somewhat, but the aluminum in the duct tape amplifies the heat, and I wail as the hair on my forearms singes. Hearing me, Abby calls out. It's the only thing that keeps me from jerking away from the fire.

My body finally rebels for me. I strain against the tape, even as I try to keep my wrists thrust forward, and my voice lifts free of my chest and floats somewhere on the other side of the room. I bear it for one more moment and I know it's the last, I'm not strong enough to take this agony any longer, yet when I finally yank back, the tape abruptly gives.

My left hand no longer bound, I push from the burning bed with a cry, dragging the top swath of the bed skirt with me so that I have to move away from that too. The filmy lace curls orange, lashing close to my face, and I thank God for my shorn hair. Somewhere above me, Abby is calling to me.

Left arm or right. Tongue or ears. Eyes or nose . . .

Using singed fingertips and my teeth, I rip the strips of tape from my other arm, then claw at my legs, coughing from the newborn smoke, all the while thinking, *hold on, baby. Hold on.*

Then I'm crawling for the door, tiny flames climbing up to bounce atop the white coverlet as I fling it open. The flames crackle as oxygen kisses fire, and I break hard right and gasp into the cool mountain air, ignoring every burning part of me as my feet find purchase and I sprint up the sprawling green hillside. Thirty minutes. That's the most time I have until this place is engulfed, and I'm going to need every second to find Abby. Because I have a vow to break, and it isn't going to be the one I swore to her—to keep her safe—in the cab.

Do no harm.

As I stumble toward the enormous house, Abby's cries still cupped in the shells of my ears, I think, *No. Do* serious *harm.*

Do whatever it takes.

39

There's no place to hide.

Daniel has locked every window and door. At first I'm tentative as I turn knobs and push at screens and claw at leaded French doors, but then I realize that he isn't trying to keep me, or anyone else, out. He's setting the scene. Everything in the house, from the placement of priceless ceramics, to the dishes and the utensils, and the beds that are made and those that are not—all need to tell the same tale of a crazed PA from Las Vegas who concluded her murderous rampage on this lakeside, hilltop estate.

So I trample azaleas as I yank at the frames of three sets of bay windows. I claw at the ground, searching for a cellar entrance, and scour the area for a ladder leading to the second floor. The music echoing from the hotel across the lake masks my futile scraping, my labored breaths, but it won't hide the shatter of glass if I try to break in, and stealth is still the only weapon I have.

I finally back away to look at the entire home, risking exposure, but Daniel isn't staring back at me from one of the leaded windows, and all I see when I look at the grand house is a giant, vaulted tomb sinking into shadows. Then my gaze latches onto the marble banister on the second floor and traces the wide lake-facing patio. The entire lake—and, thus, the fireworks show—is visible from that patio. So is the guesthouse.

Looking more closely, I see that the patio doors are also flung wide, and I think back to the video of Abby. Daniel took care to mask the room where he's hiding her, but the way the natural light struck Abby's face spoke to a west-facing orientation. I'd also caught the glint of fractured light, likely a chandelier, and those don't hang in boathouses or barns. She's somewhere in that ornate tomb, and she's in . . .

"The workroom," I mutter, and break into a sprint for the back of the house. The servant's entrance has a slim staircase that leads directly to that landing, and I know from my last visit that the old workroom sits to the right of that. It makes sense that Daniel would want to end this in the room where he killed his father, exactly where it all began.

I barely feel the gravel cutting my bare feet as I wheel around the corner to the back of the house. The stumpy concrete stairs of the back entrance don't even look like they belong to the same home, a clear sign that the people entering here don't either. *I'll fit right in*, I think, and am already leaping to the top stair, an easy vault from the ground when the wooden door is flung open and nearly hits me square. Even barefooted, I skid against the gravel and know instinctively that the sound has given me away.

Or it would, except for the tinkling of piano keys inside the house. Daniel loves to listen to his jazz while he works.

I tuck in tight to the concrete wall, ignoring the spiderweb crackling against my thigh as I duck my head low. All Daniel has to do is look over the side to see me squatted there, but the heavy door is blocking me, and I risk an upward glance to find him skipping down the steps, headed back to the barn, an old doctor's bag in tow. He is still setting the scene.

He is whistling under his breath, and the door is closing automatically behind him, though the hinge spring keeps it from shutting too quickly. I am reaching forward to stop it with my hand when Daniel suddenly stops whistling and curses loudly. I duck again, but I can't be sure he hasn't seen me. For a moment, there is only silence, with a veil of oblivious chirping coming from the copse to our left.

He's returning, his footsteps crunching in an even march on the pebbled ground. He yanks the door back open, and I'm wondering what he's forgotten when I hear four uneven beeps sound through the closed door, followed by a longer fifth. He's setting the alarm behind him, not taking any chances.

So I only have this one shot.

He flings the door open again, and this time I anticipate it and snag its bottom edge with my left hand, timing it for the apex of the swing. The burn along my wrist blazes, but I don't make a sound. He'll still see my fingers if he pauses, but no . . . he's impatient now, and just sets off again toward the barn. The music and his own sharp steps conceal the slight shift of stones beneath my feet as I slip onto the concrete block and slink inside. The door shuts behind me. The alarm stays silent.

I'm standing in the gloom of a black-and-white tiled vestibule, and I automatically reach for the string on the bald bulb above me before I catch myself. Moving forward in the dark, I jam my foot on the staircase, then do it again when I misjudge the depth. Between that and the way the old stairs groan beneath my weight, I'm lucky Daniel is outside. Finding my bearings, I rush upward and am rewarded with the sight of a wide landing. The floor put on a white marble face, and though no lights burn, an ambient glow enters from the opposing terrace. I was right. The French doors have been flung wide to the lake and the night. The guesthouse is settled in the foreground, and I think I see a flicker of something bright bouncing around the windowsills, but mostly it's dark from the smoke and toxins roiling around inside. It'll stay that way until it flashes over.

I have to find Abby first.

"Abby?!" I risk the yell because Daniel can't be back yet, and it'll be worth it if my daughter hears me and calls back in reply.

Nothing.

I veer right, because the workroom door is ajar, jazz horns and light spilling around the doorframe. Even though I know he's outside, for some reason I expect Daniel to suddenly be there, jerking the door open, gun or knife or both raised high. Forcing myself to move quickly, I'm already inside the room before I register that the sound I'm hearing is not the beat of my own thudding heart.

Maybe familiarity keeps me from recognizing it at first, but I blink at the vitals monitor as if seeing one for the first time. I also expect the room to resemble the billiards parlor from the last time I was here, but instead I'm shocked with the sight of a makeshift OR. Daniel has pulled out all of his father's equipment, it seems, for old time's sake.

An antique chemist chest is propped open on the wet bar, rubber hoses trailing from it, part of some kind of intravenous or enema kit. The fluids are attached to an antique stand and held in a glass container, not a bag. Old, rusted forceps sit atop a tarnished silver tray, and a gold-plated syringe gun lies next to an open decanter of whiskey. The only nod to twenty-first century electronics is a flat-screen television showing the same image of Abby, now motionless and staring glassy-eyed into some unknown distance. That's the source of the jazz music.

In this room, however, is Imogene Hawthorne.

She is bound to the massive oak billiards table, her wrists and ankles ringed in red and tied to the outer pockets with rope. Naked but for a diaper, goose bumps rise from her emaciated flesh. She has bruises, many that have gone green and mottled, but there are newer ones too. It might just be my eyes, but they seem to bloom, even as I stare. There are no puncture marks on her body, but the sweet-and-sour stench of unwashed hair and skin mingle with the more pronounced scent of human waste. The sagging diaper holds a sweeter decay too.

I track the feeding tube to an inflamed, red incision in Imogene's stomach, though the bag system near Imogene's head is empty. How long has she been without food or water?

Crystal did a fair job of imitating my mother too. I made her practice. Jesus.

"Imogene?" I whisper. She doesn't respond, and I know I can't help her now. I need to get to Abby. Yet as I'm turning, I spot a glint of steel at her other side. The gun Daniel flashed in the guesthouse.

Don't worry, it's not for Abby. Mother needs it.

Relief washes through me as I skirt the table. It's good to have a weapon, even if it holds only one bullet.

"I'm coming, Abby," I mutter, reaching for it.

Imogene's eyelids spring at the sound of my voice.

I fumble the gun beneath that soggy stare, my heart hammering as I slide it back onto the edge of the pool table and quickly move to Imogene's face. Her lips are chapped and her tongue is swollen from dehydration, but her watery blue gaze tracks me with full awareness. "Com—com . . . ing."

God. She's alive.

"I know." And I break into action, same as in the OR, sacrificing gentleness for speed as I work to free her wrists. She'll be immobile, but I can lift her. At the very least, I can hide her while I search for Abby. Who knows, if Daniel returns to find the focus of his psychotic obsession missing, he might even forget about Abby and me long enough for us to escape. But I can't just leave her here.

"I'm going to get you out of here, okay?" One wrist is free. I move to the other. "Just hold—"

"Hello, sweetheart."

I whirl to the doorway, hands already held out in defense, but the room is empty except for Imogene and me. I blink before chills wash up my spine, and then I swing the other way. I catch, from the corner of my eye, the exact moment Abby lifts her head.

"No . . ."

Daniel steps into view, into the same room as my daughter. A scalpel gleams in his right hand as he shifts to stare directly into the camera. He knows I'm watching, and despite the part of his face that he's carved away—despite the injury I've caused to his red, crooked nose—his face blooms with an enormous smile.

////////////

I kill everything to get her attention.

Daniel claimed that he used to bring his father the small animals and wild game that the elder Dr. Hawthorne toiled to heal and revive, but he was lying.

He brought those poor creatures into this house all those years ago for the same reason Abby and I are here today. They were for Imogene. So that she could *see*. And he has set her up now so that this time she can't possibly walk away.

I am in front of the television, palms bracing the screen, unaware of even having moved. Daniel's pixelated form saunters to the room's center, obscuring my view of Abby, and my eyes wildly search the remaining space. Where the hell are they? It could be a large space or small. As he said, the setup is not elaborate. He needs to dispose of it easily.

I turn to face Imogene. "Where is my daughter, you bitch?"

Imogene's head lolls to the side. "Com—ing . . ."

"Where is she?!" I shout it, but don't expect her to answer and turn back to the screen, getting in so close that I threaten to go cross-eyed. Daniel has left nothing uncovered, no way to identify Abby's room, and even if I run now, even if I guess right, I'm already too late. He's about to start asking questions.

Left arm or right. Tongue or ears. Eyes or nose . . .

And the guesthouse is burning inside. And I am not there to answer.

"First question," Daniel begins.

I howl at the screen, as if I can will myself through it. My ears roar with blood and the nonsensical cry, and the whole world narrows into a pinprick the size of that screen. Daniel jerks up-right and stares back at the camera, and I realize that he's heard me. Right before the gunshot roars.

Ducking automatically, I reel around as Daniel's voice reaches into the room.

"Mother . . . Mother."

Imogene's lower jaw is missing. The right side of her skull has been blown away and sits on the table's railing in a jagged flap. Her ear is perched atop her head, and the gun lies next to her shoulder on the table, still smoking.

"Oh my God." Nearly hyperventilating, I glance back just in time to catch Daniel slipping from the screen. I can't blame Imo-gene for killing herself once she finally got the chance, but *fuck*.

Com—ing.

I bolt for the door, then pull up, realizing my mistake. He's coming that way, and he's hurrying too. A thump sounds some-where in the core of the cavernous home, and I think about lock-ing the door against him, but he'll either break it down or return to Abby . . . and he'll know exactly where I am. He'll also know full well that I can see my daughter from here.

There's no place to hide. He'll look everywhere until he finds me. And as crazy as it sounds, even as every cell in my body urges me to flee, I know the best way to find my daughter is to stay close to the only person who knows where she is. I have to let him come.

As the pounding of feet hitting the marble staircase reaches me, I imagine Imogene's raw croak again. *Com—ing*.

I know . . . and I've just climbed into place when the door to the billiards room swings wide.

40

What is left to do?

I know the exact moment Daniel crosses the threshold. The air in the room depresses like a syringe, the weight of his presence squeezing out the oxygen and filling it with something noxious instead. His breath is ragged from running and, I imagine, from the damage I inflicted when I bit down on his nose in the guesthouse.

I grit my teeth together as he says, "Hello, Mother. Don't get up."

I am stemming like a rock climber beneath the pool table, spread-eagle and tense, completely motionless just thirty-six inches above the Persian rug. My limbs are tucked into heavy, squat ledges beneath the giant table, which form pockets to hide me, though the position forces me to stare directly down if I'm to keep my back pressed against the table's underside. It was the only place I could think to hide where he might not look, and one I think doubly safe, as his attention will likely be focused on what's atop the pool table, not under it.

"You can't see it from where you are, but the sun has already set." His voice floats over like a memory, and I know he's looking out the window facing the lake. He can't view the guesthouse from there, this room faces the east lake and the hotel, yet dusk has arrived and if there's light . . .

I shift my eyes enough to make out Daniel's shadow sliding across the floor like a specter. Even his silhouette looks capable of murder.

"The police vessels are already positioned in the center of the lake, and it looks like the fire marshal is double-checking the fireworks on the floating dock. We wouldn't want anyone to get hurt, you know." The chuckle in his voice tells me that despite Imogene's death—or maybe even because of it—all is still well in Crazyland. Daniel does not yet know of things that burn. "Some of our neighbors have already started gathering in the middle of the lake. Do you remember when we used to do that? Every Fourth of July, pile on the blankets? Pack a basket into the Pace-ship, motor onto the lake with cheese and bread and wine. A day of celebration. Of independence."

Chills ratchet my spine as his voice shifts in the room. He's looking over his shoulder, speaking directly to his dead mother. I push the back of my head against the heavy mahogany at my back and reinforce the pressure on my palms and flats of my feet. The burns at my wrists throb and flare, but I don't cry out as I use leverage to keep my legs from buckling. The pressure builds in my head, and I pray my ear is no longer dripping blood.

"The hotel is at full capacity, of course, and the DJ is on the lawn, spinning pop music for the kids. I know, you'd prefer a full string orchestra, but all those little redundancies seem to be enjoying themselves. They've set up a buffet line for the cookout too." He pauses. "I know. So gauche."

His footsteps shush-shush over the carpet, and I try to look up, but that causes my right arm and leg to shake and I quickly still and close my eyes. Daniel hacked off my long hair in order to both frame and terrorize me, but now I'm thankful. Were it still long, even plaited, it would be hanging down like a curtain, calling attention to my presence. Instead, wisps of the shorn bob float around my head and cause a different worry by tickling my nose.

But by then Daniel is too close to see beneath the pool table. He is looming over Imogene's body, likely studying her with that clinical gaze, the wheezing of his breath rattling with all those things that are broken inside of him. *I am molten.*

"You've done a hell of a job on your dental work, Mother."

His fingertips trail the table railing, scratching as if he's grown claws. I catch him pausing at the short end and imagine him fondling her cold, chapped toes, scratching at those too. He moves along my right side and abruptly stops.

"But what's this?" And he is bending, reaching for the rope that'd bound Imogene's right wrist, the one I carelessly let drop to the Oriental rug. I force my breath to stop in my chest, but I'm certain he can still hear the pounding of my heart. If I were still bleeding from the ear, I bet he could scent it.

Daniel picks up the rope, fondling it with his talented, deadly fingers, and then straightens, knees popping. "Two weeks without moving an inch, and now all of a sudden you break free?"

He doesn't know it was me. It's unbelievable, but then he

hasn't seen the guesthouse's windows winking with flame, so why would he? He probably can't even imagine a world in which things don't evolve as he wishes. My gaze shifts right as he steps away. He is in front of the old French armoire, the one holding the television and the black-and-white image of my daughter.

"Is *this* what gave you the will to fight?" His voice gleams. "A little girl? Another redundancy? Or do you simply want to make sure I don't make a mess of your bathroom floor?"

Imogene's bathroom. Upstairs. South wing. A gilt-and-marble bathroom with a fireplace and two chandeliers.

I have to fight every instinct not to release my body weight and drop to the floor. I have been chased through the desert, thrown from a motorcycle, cut, and burned. Even healthy, I cannot outrun Daniel. But now I know where Abby is, and the lusty cries from the day she was born bloom raw in my mind.

In front of the armoire, the rope falls to the floor.

"I have to admit, I'm a little put out by all of this." I imagine him waving his hand in the air, dismissing his mother's corpse. "I mean, I had so much more to ask you. For so many years you simply refused to talk, and I tried to respect that, I did, but now that I've come for answers, you can't. You can see why this might leave me a little . . . upset."

I don't know what he does then. I can't imagine what sort of act he's performing above me, but all I know is that the ragged breathing suddenly quickens, and there's a gurgling that pitches high, even as he finishes speaking. *Upset.* The clipped word bookends the other sound, a pained noise I don't understand.

Until I do.

His mother is still alive. Somehow, she's still *alive*.

"So I guess I'm going to have to do all the talking." His words hide my gasp, but accentuate her hiss, a sound that I'm somehow sure is supposed to be a wail. I squeeze my eyes shut. I can't imagine what he's doing. What is left to do?

"See, I've always wondered what you were thinking that night, as we scrubbed this room clean." He pauses, just a moment. "No, *you* made me wrap him in hay sacks."

Oh God. He's talking to her.

"No, no, that's not the point. The point is you just watched me carry him away. I mean, thirty-two years of marriage, and then . . . what? After you told me to row to the center of the lake, then what?"

He chuckles lightly at her unspoken reply, and I blink hard against it, a sound I used to love. "Sure, I'm happy to tell you what I thought. Once I'd rowed to the middle of the lake, I thought, the house looks so perfect from here. Just the way she likes it."

I kill everything to get her attention.

"I sat out there for a good hour, but you were right. He never regained consciousness. It wasn't until after I loaded him down with the salt bricks, in his underwear, in his shoes, that I realized . . . I felt alone. Probably the way you've been feeling, huh?"

It was like hearing half of a phone conversation. Imogene might not be listening, but Daniel was determined to have his say.

"It was just so dark out there. No other boats on the lake, no light. I couldn't even watch him sink. But then, I looked up, and you were at the window. Remember?"

A gurgle, but I don't think Imogene was remembering.

"Yes, you were. I saw the curtain move. You were silhouetted between damask. For a moment I even felt the light reach me. But then you disappeared and you took the light with you."

She never looked at me again.

Daniel pauses, and this time the silence takes me by surprise. I have become lost in his narrative despite myself. I haven't forgotten the danger to me, though, and it reasserts itself as Daniel places his hands on his knees and leans forward. Those talented, killing hands . . . only inches from my face.

"Not one word. Not to the police after they dragged the lake. Not at the funeral, where his old college buddies waxed on about accidental drownings. Not even to me, as if I didn't know what I'd done. All through the service, the burial, the reception . . . never once did you look my way."

Imogene's breath rattles, the sound moving like a choppy wave through her bony chest. I close my eyes and imagine him facing her, his broken nose tip-to-tip with her displaced one. He whispers, "I had intended to give you one last thing to watch tonight, Mother. I brought you the child just like I used to bring you the birds, the hares. I wondered, will she look this time? Will she see me now?"

Air wheezes from Imogene without ever touching her lips. The sound is desolate, like the wind back on the flats of the high desert where Daniel crucified a man just because he could. Yet Daniel sucks in a deep breath at the same time, and I imagine the scent of tin-fresh blood and smoky gunpowder infiltrating his lungs. I can almost see his chest expanding, his eyes closing as he sucks in all the tension and toxins in the room, all the violence and pain of the world, into his sinew and muscle. I don't

41

I brace and wait for the burn.

All I have to do is follow the music.

Yet it's not solely the horns of the twenties jazz that draws me up the third-floor staircase in search of my daughter. Instead, I follow Daniel's voice. He's humming, feeling good, though he is not done yet. Not by a long shot.

It's why I carry the rope. It's why, despite exhausting myself beneath that pool table, I do not stop. My head throbs where I've been hit, first at the rest stop by the swinging steel door, and later by the butt of Crystal's gun. I am dehydrated in a way I never thought possible, and my wrists have gone numb where they've been seared. My earlobe is gone. The road burn along my abraded left side has stiffened like old jerky. I am all cried out.

Yet I, too, am feeling molten.

Maybe that's why I don't bother to hide myself as I climb the center of the sprawling marble staircase, silent on bare feet.

It's past dusk, nearer to full dark than not, and I can almost sense the gathering on the other side of the lake. Tourists and residents will be leaning against wooden balconies, palming icy glasses of wine, eyes already turned up to the velvety sky. Maybe someone has noticed the smoke from the guesthouse as it plumes and rises into a darkening sky, but they're too far off yet to smell it. More likely they just dismiss the strange flickering all the way across the lake. They're not looking for mere light; they want an explosion. They are ready for fireworks.

I think of Abby and realize—so am I.

The stairs curve right to offer up a pretty but useless sitting area with chairs I'm sure have never seen a backside and books with uncracked spines. The most inviting thing about the area is the moonlight that filters through a leaded dormer window. It allows a clear view down the long, dark hallway and of the shadow just moving through the double doors beyond.

The master suite doors are flung wide, and I walk through like I'm invited. Another lightly used sitting area languishes beneath a pale moonbeam while a solid four-poster bed lies in total darkness. I picture Daniel standing over it, above his sleeping mother, before I blink and slip further into the spacious room. The carpeting deadens my footsteps, but I'm no longer worried about sound. Jazz streams from around the corner, amplified by space and marble.

I need to do something before Daniel's questioning voice joins the scatting and the horns, but I'm afraid of the mirrors. I don't know what he'll do if Abby is within reach and I appear suddenly, reflected behind him.

So I double back, fall to my hands and knees, and wriggle beneath the giant bed until I am facing directly into the cavernous master bath. There's a full foot of space over my head, but my image does not, in fact, reflect back at me. Burlap and tarp are layered in mounds, no doubt dragged in from the barn in order to catch and soak up the blood Daniel anticipates spilling in this room.

Blood, like that which covers Daniel as he stands halfway through the long, elegant bathroom, dead still and back to me as he studies my daughter. She is propped in the corner, just as I saw on the TV sets, except the sun no longer reaches in through the leaded windows. Yet he has strengthened the lighting, and the room's two antique chandeliers cut sharp angles across her body. The small video camera is directly across from her, balanced on the vanity, and it also gazes at her with a steady red eye. Daniel has positioned himself just out of view of the lens, head tilted to one side.

He finally gives a short nod and steps in front of the camera.

I take the opportunity to roll from under the bed and slip to the threshold of that long, cavernous room, rope clenched in my hand.

By the time I press my eye to the crack of the hinged door, Daniel has already folded himself cross-legged before Abby. My daughter lifts her head, sees him speckled red, and immediately begins to cry, curling tighter into herself. Daniel seems content to wait for her to calm and just turns—back still to me—and shoots a grin directly at the camera beside him. I step from behind the door, finger already pressed to my lips. Abby's gaze immediately darts my way, and she whimpers, "Mommy?"

"Yes," Daniel says, shifting back, and her eyes swerve back to his. "Your mommy is watching."

Goddamn straight.

I slip into the tarp-covered room, light as a ghost and moving to music from another era.

"You know, I've always wondered why people have children," he says, half to Abby, half to the camera. "I mean, I've *heard* all the reasons given, but the idea that it provides you with some sort of legacy after you're gone, that it somehow marks you as having been here and makes your life somehow significant . . . why, that's just selfish. And it's a fallacy. As for unconditional love . . . why not just love yourself unconditionally?"

Abby stares, her face a mixture of fear and confusion, but there's a focus to it too. She is working actively to keep her eyes averted from me . . . yet Daniel senses the change in her too. He tilts his head at her and makes a low sound in the back of his throat. "You look just like *her*."

Then he edges closer to Abby, almost in a pout. I force myself to keep inching forward slowly. There's still too much space between us for me to rush him, as evidenced by how quickly he reaches over and pulls his father's old medical bag to his side. He doesn't even hurry, yet I've only gained one more step.

"My fault," he says, and he almost sounds friendly, normal. "I meant to cut your hair before."

He slips a pair of long, black shears from the bag. He is prepping her, I realize, same as he would a patient in the OR, reducing her to her most essential parts. Angling himself so that the camera catches the action, he grabs a fistful of her long hair, and begins to snip. Abby's gasp covers any sound I might make as I tiptoe across burlap.

Abby tries not to move as her hair drops in piles atop the

tarp and scatters over her knees, but she's shaking uncontrolla-
bly now, which makes me want to dart to her. Yet there's still a
Jacuzzi tub to navigate, and then another ten feet beyond that.
If Daniel turns and sees me now, those shears in his hand can
instantly shift, from cutting to stabbing.

"Now, I don't want you to worry," he goes on, raising his
voice over her whimpers. He thinks I am tied in the guesthouse,
helpless to do anything but watch. This bathroom floor is his
makeshift pulpit. He is speaking to me. "Death is just another
life event. Do you understand what I'm saying, Abby? Your life
means nothing. And neither will your death. You are, just like
most people, totally inconsequential."

Finished, Daniel leans back on his palms, a clump of hair in
his left hand, scissors in the right. My daughter looks plucked,
like a bird with no feathers. Daniel sighs and throws her hair
aside, then reaches out to steady her shaking chin with his fingertips. I freeze too.

"Some final advice, Abby . . . don't hang on to life like a dog
with a bone. That's inelegant. Instead, let death come for you.
You can feel it, I'll make sure you feel it," the smile is in his voice
as he raises the scissors, "but then you have to let it go."

"You first, asshole."

Daniel must think that Abby is the one who has spoken because his eyes remain fixed on her as I loop the rope over his
head and give a hard, satisfying jerk. I'm okay with that. I want
hers to be the last face he ever sees.

His hands claw at his throat and he begins to thrash beneath
me. I have leverage on my side, but he has strength, and he has
not spent the last twenty-four hours being physically and emo-

tionally abused. His fingertips find my burned wrists and dig there, scoring my flesh as he twists and flings me down, fighting for purchase.

All I need to do is keep to his back, directly behind him. He reaches to grab for my face, so I cross my wrists and pull harder. Daniel was right. All of my yoga classes and weight training and running on a treadmill were futile. I was going nowhere, running and lifting and fighting for nothing . . . until now.

I push against the cabinets with my heels, dislodging the tarps and exposing all that hard marble as I backpedal, trying to pull Daniel away from my daughter. Abby's wails accompany the jazz horns, and in the exposed marble of the bathroom she sounds both near and far away. I realize I am distancing her from me as well as Daniel. I need to be alone for what comes next, back with the ghosts that sweep along on deadly, billowing upcasts in the mines.

Daniel growls so loudly that the sound knocks backward into my chest. His flailing gains new purpose, and while his right elbow misses me, it tells him where I am. He immediately arrows back his left, and it lands home in the center of my rib cage. A pained explosion of breath sends the back of his hair up in a puff, and my grip loosens. He follows up with a headbutt that has me tasting tin, but we're too close for it to knock me out, and I'm too hot to care. He kicks out, and Abby yelps. The sound boomerangs back to pulse through me, and I thrust my hips forward behind Daniel and knuckle that rope.

Daniel gurgles, and his face goes purple beneath me. His eyes are beginning to close. He's no longer scrabbling at me, but is instead slapping the floor with open palms, probably wondering which way is up. I'm about to flip him to his stomach and show him, when I hear the scrape of metal across marble. I only realize that he's holding the scissors after he thrusts his body to the side, leaving my long body exposed to the shears.

His arm lifts, and silver flashes in the pretty, fractured light. I shut my eyes and tell myself, no matter what, to hang on to that rope. His shoulder rotates and his arm pistons down. I brace and wait for the burn.

Jazz scats and skitters along my limbs. Goose bumps rise. Daniel jerks beneath me.

I open my eyes to find Abby bent forward, Daniel's wrist pinned beneath her chained hands and knees. It may be surprise more than weakness that has his fingers falling open. I look into Abby's face as the scissors clatter to the floor, and I'm surprised too. For a moment she seems so far away. Then I blink, and she snaps back, and the jazz roars, and I flip Daniel to his stomach.

"Not so inconsequential after all," I hiss in his ear, and outside of his beloved jazz, it's the last thing he ever hears.

42

I give a laugh that sounds like a cry.

I don't pull much longer. I, too, have learned in the last twenty-four hours that there is strength in letting go.

"Mommy?"

Abby's been saying my name for a while. Sprawled over the bathroom floor, I have been staring down at Daniel's back, and at the rough rope cutting into his neck. I am trying to feel something, but I don't. So I blink and return to Abby, return from that far off place where I needed to go in order to set her free.

"Baby." My voice wheezes as if the rope had been wrapped around my neck. I hold out my arms, but for a moment it looks like Abby won't come. The hands that so ably kept those scissors from ripping at me remained clutched to her chest, worrying and threading each other like tatting lace.

Then I realize she's tied up; she can't move any farther away from the cabinet. I'm the one who has to come all the way back.

It shifts something inside of me, and suddenly I'm throwing

317

myself at my daughter, and then we're both sobbing as I take a mother's inventory, only pulling away after I have accounted for all limbs. My fingertips are sore, my wrists burned, my earlobe shorn, leg scraped from thigh to ankle, and I'm pretty sure I have a concussion, but I pull and tug and finally use the scissors to cut her bindings loose. I don't look inside the doctor's bag. I don't want to know what Daniel planned to do.

"Mommy . . ."

I nod, but keep working, and I don't look up until I feel Abby shift.

"Don't look at him, baby," I say, and gently tilt her head back my way. "Just look at me."

When I free her, I can't help it. I check for injury once more, find only rope burns at her wrists and ankles, and then yank her into another smothering hug that has us both rocking back and forth.

"He cut my hair." Muffled by my shoulder, her voice trembles. I force a smile as I pull back, cupping her cheeks between my palms.

"Yeah, now you're just like me." Dropping my hands to hers, I pull her to her feet. We both wobble. "Wanna know what else makes you like me?"

Teary eyed, Abby nods.

"You're strong." We are both so incredibly strong.

"Come on." I guide Abby out of the bathroom, careful to block Daniel's body from view. Duke Ellington's voice swells as I shut the master bedroom door behind us.

My first instinct is to call for help, but by the time I reach the second floor landing, it's clear that Daniel has relieved the grand

home of telephones. He probably removed them before returning to Las Vegas two weeks ago, just in case his mother managed
to get free.

We curl down to the ground floor with its wall of window,
each bearing witness to the black lake. It's full dark now, but
dozens of boats have settled in for the fireworks show, and the
bobbing lights dot the smooth surface like giant fireflies.

However, a larger glow in the foreground has begun to eclipse
those dainty lights. It hasn't flashed over, the guesthouse windows have yet to blow, and the lawn remains silent and dark, but
I catch a whiff of smoke at the same instant I realize I left Daniel's
phone on the bed inside. That's okay. The fire marshal and police
are on the lake. We can wait for them to notice the fire.

"Fuck that," I mutter, and wheel Abby to the front door.
"Come on, baby. Back to the barn. We're getting out of here."

I hate the idea of climbing back in the vehicle that'd been our
prison, and Abby stiffens at the sight of the truck too, but the
sheriff's station is just downhill, and this is the fastest way off the
property. I'm leaving now.

"Not long," I tell Abby, but as I climb to the driver's seat, I
know I am reassuring myself as well.

The keys aren't there. I stare for a moment, but think, *Of
course*. Daniel took them with him. They're in his pocket, in the
house. I don't want to go back in there, and I already know Abby
will buck at the thought. It's a horror-film move anyway. Nobody
who goes back in the house ever lives.

I climb back down and meet Abby's hopeful gaze with a too-
bright look. It twists wrongly and I drop it. "Not even a horse to
ride out on," I joke, but neither of us smiles.

I take Abby's hand in my own and head back to the front of the barn. The estate walls are insurmountable, and the foliage of the encroaching forest is thick beyond that. We can leave the way we came in, walk down the winding lane that led up to the estate from the village below, but there aren't any lights or sidewalks on that swerving road. I didn't just fight to the death for us to be taken out by some unsuspecting driver and a tight bend.

A shot rings through the night just as we clear the barn. Abby yelps and I jerk and the sky rips open with silver sparkles. Light scissors overhead, and while the sight is thunderous and sensational and beautiful, it is also impossibly ordinary. It's the first normal thing I've seen in over twenty-four hours, and it feels like a dream. I can't help it. I give a laugh that sounds like a cry.

Dozens of boats stud the lake, but the firework dock at its center glows red and blue. *That's* where I want to go. I want to get off this estate before the guesthouse burns to the ground. I want to skip out of here in the boat on which Daniel intended to flee. I want to use the lake where he drowned his father to extinguish the heat inside of me once and for all. I want to reach those police boats and safety on my own terms. And I want to do it before the last bright bloom falls from the sky.

"Let's go," I tell Abby, and hand in hand, we run down the great, sloping lawn.

43

I stretch for it with my burned wrists.

Of course, the key to the old Paceship is back with Daniel, tucked in his pocket too. Damn it. Disappointment washes over me, but then I spot the neighbor's open skiff tied to the other side of the dock and almost laugh. I'm exhausted and injured, but you know what? I'm alive. I can damn well row to the police at this point.

I tell Abby to grab two life jackets from the antique vessel while I untie the rowboat. It bobs in stop-motion on the fractured water, each overhead burst ricocheting off the waves like cannons. I can feel the heat and smell the smoke of the guesthouse burning behind me—but I wait to look at it until after I've unmoored the skiff and pushed away with my paddles. Until Abby is safely tucked into the fore and the shoreline is receding behind me.

I turn just as the windows explode and the rooftop becomes engulfed in flames. It blazes so suddenly—so hot and bright and loud—that it surprises me. Like it's a real accident. But after a moment, I think, *No, the home is just burning. Burning and free.*

321

Like me, says the person inside of me who fought Daniel.

Shhhh, I tell her. *Go back to the mines.*

The mines. That's what got me out of that house. I wasn't just thinking about climbing out of the Lumbago and leaving Waylon behind. I was leaving *all* of it behind. The misguided conviction that I had the power to save my mother, who didn't want to be saved. The sense that I was inferior to the Josie Scotts of the world. The yearning for someone I loved, my father, to have seen me standing before him and simply chosen instead to stay. Even Daniel,who'd never really existed as I'd wanted him to . . . though I damn well wasn't going to blame myself for that one.

Yet my mother's voice, which has always haunted me, has been completely silent for the length of this journey, and I think I know why. I think it's because I'm facing all of it squarely now, and I can clearly see it wasn't my fault that one violent night led to another and then another still.

I'm about to turn my face to the blistering sky, turn my mind to what happens next, when something takes shape on the wide sweep of lawn. I think it's only shadows at first, maybe drifting smoke, but then it flashes in front of the burning guesthouse and stills. The dance of flames liquefy the solid silhouette at the edges.

Then he roars.

He rages without sound. He rages because he has been choked to death and still lives. He rages because he is molten.

I begin rowing as fast as I can.

"Abby!" I shriek over the sound of whistling rockets, but I don't know what else to say after that. Even over the deafening concussion of fireworks above, I can still hear the outboard motor rumble to life.

I glance over my shoulder as I row. We're at least a hundred yards away from the periphery of vessels clustered in the lake's center, and while the sky continues to explode brilliantly, the attention of all those closest to the Hawthorne estate is pinned there. Their eyes spark in the flames from the hillside as tiny bombs shake the sky overhead, yet they're blind to what's right in front of them: Abby white-knuckling the bench in the fore of the tiny skiff, and me, paddling furiously. So I'm the only one who sees the fear climb back into my daughter's face, and as her mouth twists into a silent O, the taste of freedom sours in my mouth.

Should I tell her to lie down in the bottom of the boat? The nose of Daniel's boat is pointed directly at us now. We'll splinter to pieces if he doesn't slow, and I already know he's never going to do that.

Should she jump? Should we both? No, he'll see it if we do, and he'll just angle his motor's blades to chop over our bobbing heads.

"See that?" I yell at her, and point at the red-and-blue beams of the police vessels bobbing in the lake. Silver and gold spirals rise in the air, illuminating her way. "You have to swim there."

"No—"

"You're safer in the water!" You're safer away from me.

"No! Mommy, no—!"

But she is. Same way I'd have been safer far, far away from my mother . . . though she'd never cared enough to say so.

I do care . . . which is why I have to remind myself that Abby is a great swimmer before I tilt the skiff and bump her shoulder at the same time. I dump my daughter into the churning lake, and by the time she surfaces I'm well out of reach. I have to tell myself I am not turning my back on her. I am, instead, pushing her toward the light.

I've angled a hard right to draw Daniel's speeding boat away from Abby, but I'm afraid it's not enough . . . and equally afraid that I'll give in to impulse and reach back and grab her just to hold her close one last time. So I reverse instead . . . and head back to the estate.

Daniel doesn't realize it. The bow of his boat is riding high, and while the water reflects the colored whorls trimming the night sky, the landscape goes inky in between blasts. I square up and stop rowing, breath caught in a time lapse between my mouth and chest as Daniel bears down on me. He's crouched over the captain's chair, holding fast to the mahogany steering wheel. The boat is old, yes, but it's solid birch and huge compared to the skiff I've stolen. We are like a bull and matador out here, though I don't have or need a cape. Daniel only sees red when he looks at me.

The force of the crash reverberates through the waves.

I try to time my jump, but it's nothing like in the movies. I am exhausted, and the fact that I gain any air at all is due to the force with which Daniel slams into the rowboat's hull. My spine jars along with the resounding crack of wood, and for a moment, as I sail, I think I see him too, a backlit starfish suspended in the night air. Then I disappear into the black lake.

I try to stay down. I need the weight of water between me and the flying debris, but my life jacket's tug is insistent, and sure enough, the blunt slap of something large cannonballs off my thigh. The force pushes me lower, and I swallow water going down.

There is no silence or reprieve beneath the waves. Light and explosives drum overhead in a climactic finale—it's so loud now I can't even be sure anyone noted the crash—and I breach a surface choppy with waves, gasping beneath a sparking sky.

My wooden dinghy is gone. Bits of it float and bump me, but I push them away and look for bigger shadows. I find them in the ripped hull of Daniel's vintage boat. It seems to be in two large pieces now, both tilted on end like swizzle sticks, and each taking on water fast.

Treading water and spinning about myself, I scan for movement. The lake is night-numbed and cold from the mountains, the frigidness magnified deeper by my feet. The rocking waves are oiled with spilled gasoline. It sits sharp in my nose, and I spit and hope the police vessels, or anyone, will take notice and head our way. At least Abby was far away at impact. I imagine her swimming for the nearest boat or dock, and pray—please God—that she's already there.

Glancing down, I consider removing my life jacket, but the bright orange color and reflective strips are all that make me visible to approaching crafts, and once the fireworks stop, the lake will go dark. Meanwhile, there's an island a few hundred yards away. Kicking hard, I stretch for it with my burned wrists. Despite my body's aching protest, my heart gives an approving thump. *I am still alive*, I think, just as the fingers close around my left ankle.

Daniel rips at me with his bare hands. He doesn't let go when I kick or when he's forced to surface, closer than I think. He pops up during a series of overhead flashes, and his image burns like a negative against the throbbing sky. Then he's gone, back under again and dragging me with him.

Something strikes me in the back of the head, and I flail for it, for anything to keep me above the bouncing waves. Yet Daniel coils about me, determined, and I feel a sharp pain in my right thigh, and realize, he's fucking biting me.

I go under, forced down by his weight as he climbs me like a vine. He's still biting me, this time in my ass . . . though I can't figure how he can bite me there when his face is at my chest. Then it registers, what's really going on, and I flail harder. I hear myself yelp as I kick, but I'm pinned as much in place by the life jacket as I am by Daniel's ceaseless grip. His head bobs up again and he gasps, wild-eyed, right in my face.

"Isn't it amazing," he says, breathing heavy, "how closely celebration and destruction resemble one another?"

And then he stabs me with the scissors again in the side.

Fireworks explode behind my eyes as I ram my forehead into his battered brow. I push away, strokes wild. I have lost my way. I don't know where I am in the water, I only know where I am in relation to Daniel, and he's a shark. He's following my blood. He's going to slice me open before anyone sees us and then leave me in this oily lake the same way he left his father.

The thought panics me so much that I don't even realize what I've backed into until I touch it again. I spin, sense Daniel behind me, and flail at his wrecked boat with a desperate gasp. The damaged vessel tilts, threatening to flip, so I duck beneath the cleaved hull—still fighting the damn jacket—to try to board it from the other side.

He's waiting when I surface, smiling at me through broken teeth. The frenzied sky builds to a crescendo above us as I push away. Too late. His hand is already raised and the scissors spark in the celebratory light.

They rip through the left side of the life vest, right above my heart. I flail for the boat beside me, find purchase on the lip and feel the hull tilt my way. I jerk, and everything inside of it shifts and tumbles as it flips upside down. Daniel has to release me and duck beneath the waves just to keep from being hit.

Trapped in the hollow of the capsized boat, I feel steel strike my padded shoulder, and my instinct is to dodge it too, but then I reach out and grab instead. Daniel will be back any moment, and I need a weapon.

It's too heavy, though. It's already slipped beneath the waves, bubbling past my thighs, and the attached rope skitters through my fingers, sailing down. I finally twist it around my battered right wrist, then drop my head back on my orange life vest and play dead.

His dark head pops up a moment later. He looks like a slick seal as he closes in, but I can't see his expression, so I know he can't see mine either. My wrist is torqued in an unnatural angle beneath the wave, and the weight at the end of the rope tilts me to one side, but my life jacket keeps me bobbing, so Daniel suspects nothing until I whip out my left hand and begin looping the slack around his shoulders.

I lift my head only after his arm is secured to his side, and that brings him to life, but by then I've already made him a necklace. I wrap my legs around his as he begins to thrash. I draw him in close, circling him until the entire length is used up, before tying off with a vertical weave. Then I let the anchor fall.

He doesn't even blink as he disappears beneath the surface. His eyes are pinned on me, and his head even tilts upward as his dark hair fans around his pale face. I'd wanted Abby's face to be the last he ever saw, but as I watch him disappear, as one final deep-throated pulse rocks the sky above us, I decide that this works just fine too.

When he's gone, I push out from beneath the shattered hull.

I lay atop the waves for hours. Maybe minutes. Either way, it's long enough to know that I'm bleeding out, though I'm too numb to feel it. I cry as I wait to die, but after a bit I begin to laugh too. At some point, I hear Daniel coming after me again with the scissors.

But he doesn't appear. Instead, as firework ash falls from the stunned sky to lay another dark coat across the black lake, I float on my back and watch the stars wink back into focus above me. They throb for a bit in time to the beating of my heart, but disappear again right before I close my eyes, washed away in a thrumming whirl of red-and-blue light.

44

It's nearly nightfall, but there's a bit of time yet before the fireworks begin. The air is still, filled only with the hum of adult conversation along the deck of Lake Arrowhead's grand hotel, and the lawn teems with children bopping to tunes they all seem to know but that I've never heard. They dance in front of the DJ booth, as if thanking him for spinning, and the tween girls squeal in groups, their plastic glow-stick necklaces and bracelets zigzagging in neon against the deepening night.

The sounds lap at me as I lean over the edge of the patio, a full glass of white wine beading in my hand. I had this idea of Abby standing next to me, united as we face down the holiday on the lake where it all almost ended one year ago. Independence Day. I envisioned her looking up at me and marveling at the way I stare out over that cold water without flinching, maybe saying she can't believe how strong I am, so that I can be motherly and wise and remind her that the same strength lives inside of her.

But it never works out the way you think, does it? Abby is preoccupied with barbecue and sticky lemonade, and a girl she just met is whispering in her ear like they've been friends for the whole of their lives. They're likely discussing their favorite apps or clothing stores or school subjects . . . or something far too important to be interrupted by a lecture on the merits of being strong in the face of adversity and evil. So I just mark her position on the soft, cool lawn, cataloging everyone around her too, and then turn back to face the lake alone.

I am not sure what I expected by coming back here.

Now that I'm on speaking terms with all of my emotions, I'm often surprised at what pops up. I regularly startle myself and others by bursting into tears in the strangest, even benign, moments. Abby's parent-teacher conference had me blubbering like a rejected reality-show contestant. Commercials for fast food and insurance send me lunging for the tissue box. Sometimes the tears fall down my face and I don't even know it until I find myself rubbing the scar that still stretches red along my left leg. Or unconsciously covering my reconstructed earlobe with hair from my new shoulder-length bob. I am told it suits me.

The therapist says the wildly swinging emotions are normal, that it's my mind continuing to recalibrate. She also warned that it was probably too soon to face Daniel's ghost alone, but I know what happens when you don't give closure to unresolved business, and as I look at the gaping black hole directly across the lake—everything shadowed and dark but for the turrets spaced along the sharp roofline—I feel another tie that binds me to my dusty past loosen its stays and fall away.

"It's beautiful, isn't it?"

The question comes from a man leaning against the other end of the railing. He smiles and lifts his wine glass my way, and I smile back while searching his face for signs of recognition. My own face was splayed across newspapers countrywide in the weeks after Daniel's rampage, and the hospital administrator finally called me into his office and suggested that it might be best for me to take some time off. I didn't blame him. The tabloid reporters loved their headlines and hounded me with loaded questions, following me all the way into the hospital in efforts to bait me, trying to get photos of all my wounds.

As expected, they found a more receptive subject in Lacy, who was quoted as saying that she had sensed I was under duress in the roadside diner. That as soon as I ordered cherry pie, she'd just known there was something off about the map and my treasure hunt and my boyfriend.

Wish *I'd* known.

However, this man doesn't give off the sharklike air of a reporter. His face remains politely open, and he keeps a comfortable distance between us, which is fine with me. My therapist is working on that too.

You're still so young, she'd said, as if that matters more than experience.

And you're still so hopeful, I'd replied, because, even though she is twice my age, she's never witnessed a man flattened in a casino parking lot, or seen one crucified on a hillside, or encountered a woman—and a dog—buried in a closet.

Clearly, the man at the other end of the railing never has either, because he seems hopeful too.

I decide not to hold it against him and politely answer his questions.

Do you live around here?

No. I've recently moved to Los Angeles.

What do you do there?

I'm studying to become a doctor.

So you're a healer?

I pull the sleeves of my sweater down to hide my scarred wrists and nod. It means another round of med school and residency, a six-year commitment at the least, but I figure as long as I'm starting over, I might as well go all the way.

"Mom?" Abby, I realize, has been saying my name.

"Yeah, baby," I blink as if coming to, the man immediately forgotten.

"Can I go down to the docks to watch the fireworks from there? Some of the other kids are going."

My fingers tighten around my wineglass. "I'd rather you stay in sight."

I'd rather you stay tucked by my side, in my pocket. I'd rather you climb back inside of me, where my heart is supposed to live.

Abby looks as though she's going to argue for a minute, then surprises me with a smile. Reaching up, she runs her thumb across my forehead, one side to the other, and smoothes the frown from my brow. It's a habit she picked up at some point in the last year when we started sleeping together in the same bed. I'll wait until I hear her breathing ease out before I go to sleep, but sometimes I'll wake in the middle of the night to find her caressing me this way, totally still and silent, but wide awake as if memorizing my features. That's how she's looking at me now.

"Okay," she finally says, and skips lightly away.

I watch her go, and I feel so alive.

That's what I'm thinking as I turn away, smiling, and catch sight of *him*.

It's not much to go on, just the flash of a dark head and a pair of wide shoulders disappearing around a myrtle hedge, but it's enough to make me startle. That's nothing new; my breath regularly catches in my throat. I have to relearn how to breathe dozens of times in any given twenty-four hours. So I don't trust the bump in my chest, but given the environment—given that they never found Daniel's body—I am following the man before I know it, cutting through the buffet line on the lawn, chasing a ghost down the zigzag path I've just forbidden Abby to traverse. All the while I'm thinking, *it can't be.*

I push past a couple strolling hand in hand, my throat tight with the leaden ball of real panic. The stone-walled path forks into two directions near the lake's edge, and I have a decision to make: head up to the pool, where guests are lounging with their faces turned to the sky, or down into the darkness of the water and docks. I make my choice, dodging children that glow with green and yellow and orange neon, and skirt a couple engaged in a hard embrace next to one final hedge. I round the corner and stumble when I come eye level with the boats glowing on the lake.

The flashback hits me square, a sprint toward a dock just opposite this one, a frenzied row before a crash. A blade in the lake. I suddenly feel watched as I stumble toward the hotel's lone dock. The gate is shuttered on it, and a sign hanging on a chain marks it as off limits, but it isn't secured. In fact, it's ajar half an inch, though there's no one and nothing moving on the long, flat dock.

Leaves flutter in uneasy whispers, and something small and brown skitters in the brush behind me. I look back up at the deck where I stood minutes earlier and see its outline losing its contours, everything going hazy with nightfall. I think I see the man who smiled at me leaning over slightly, like he's caught sight of me as well, but his features are indistinguishable in the deepening gloom.

Inconsequential, comes the whisper from across the lake.

I step onto the dock. It creaks beneath my weight, a groaning metronome keeping time to my footsteps as I scan the surrounding water. There's nothing. I lift my gaze to the small island in the lake's middle, then the mountains across from me, but everything is dark. I am alone.

The lake's center is identical to the way it was the year before; cool water and light waves rocking stilled boats, a centered dock with hot fireworks and police strobes. Pockets of black sit up along the opposite shoreline, perfect for burying secrets. Yet try as I might, I can't sense Daniel here. He's gone, and I think I should go too, back up to the balcony to watch the rest of this show with Abby and everyone else who has come here to celebrate.

I don't move, though, and I'm not sure why until the first firework sears the air with a piercing whistle. It breaks into an explosion that colors the lake in violent red. Awe-filled sighs float down from the hotel patio but I don't look up like everyone else. Instead, I keep my gaze trained on the onyx pocket directly across from me, where a giant mausoleum lays buried in an encroaching forest.

"Are you watching me?" I ask, in between aerial concussions. At first I'm just talking to Daniel, but then I realize I'm really speaking to all of them: my father and mother both, Waylon Rhodes, all buried deep.

"I hope so," I tell them, without blinking. "Because I'm going to climb on top of all the things you people tried to do to me, and I'm gonna use them to get everything I want."

That, I think, turning back around, *is evolution*.

Then I head back up the path to the hotel under the umbrella of beautiful violence. I climb up and up, out of the darkness. I go forward, to my daughter and to my life. And this time I'm the one who doesn't look back.

ACKNOWLEDGMENTS

A mere "thanks" to my agent, Peter McGuigan, seems inadequate. He believed in this book before it was written, and exhibited kindness beyond measure and patience beyond duty throughout its creation. I remain ever grateful. To Kristen Weber, who reinforced to me that good books are not merely written, but rewritten, and who helped me repurpose my writing for the thriller market. Not a lot of people can say no to an author with nine books on the shelves, but your *no*—provided with explanation—turned this book into a big *yes*. Which brings me to Ed Schlesinger. I can't help but think that I was on the receiving end of some beautiful black magic to have you as my editor for this book. We seem to sip occasionally from the same poisoned well, so thank you for loving this (1000%!) and for your keen and passionate editorial eye.

Audrie Dugger helped with All Things EMS; Alyssa Stone, PA-C, was the first person to walk me through the training, insight, and skill required of a physician assistant; and John Notabartolo, PA-C, read through the manuscript with an eye toward veracity in that world. (LeAnne Notabartolo reads my books too, and then invites me for cocktails to discuss pretty much anything *but* my writing, and for that I am grateful too.)

337

David Blatty copyedited without pointing and laughing (at least not in the margins). Any deficiencies that might remain in the text are, sadly, my own.

Jann McKenzie always reads with a critical care, and her emoticons and personal reactions (Eww!) are received with a glad heart. Crystal Parnell and Kristine Perchetti gave me permission to appropriate their given names for my own mean purposes, and I stole Daniel J. Hale's as well. I'm not sure he knows that. Perhaps he does now.

As ever, to my husband, James, for Intangibles. You are a solid and supporting force greater than the entirety of the Mojave.

Finally, to and for the readers who've followed me over from the fantastical . . . see, guys? I told ya I'd give you another girl with grit.